MURDER
at the
ISLAND
HOTEL

BOOKS BY HELENA DIXON

HELENA DIXON

MURDER
at the
ISLAND
HOTEL

bookouture

Published by Bookouture in 2024

An imprint of Storyfire Ltd.
Carmelite House
50 Victoria Embankment
London EC4Y 0DZ

www.bookouture.com

ISBN: 978-1-83790-062-6
eBook ISBN: 978-1-83790-061-9

Murder at the Island Hotel is dedicated to my lovely Tuesday Zoomers.

PROLOGUE

TORBAY HERALD, FEBRUARY 1936

Advertisement

The stage is set for the grand opening of the brand new, magnificent and exclusive Bird Hotel situated on Bird Island. The hotel is due to be opened at Easter with an exclusive performance by the noted opera singer, Miss Marie Monbiere. The hotel, formerly the private residence of Colonel Montpelier, has been completely refurbished into a stylish and modern hotel for the discerning holidaymaker. With luxurious marble bathrooms, fine dining, unrivalled sea views and all comforts. Advance bookings are now being taken and a brochure is available from Sir Norman Whittier, proprietor of the Bird Hotel, Bird Island, Torbay, Devon. Telephone enquiries Torquay 362.

Dear Mrs Bryant,

I regret that I am unable to accompany you on the planned assessment visit to the Bird Hotel this week. Unfortunately, I am suffering from a case of shingles and must rest at home on my doctor's advice. I am most sorry to inconvenience the hoteliers' association at this late stage as I know Sir Norman was very anxious to become a member before the hotel opens its doors to the general public.

I do hope you can find someone else with the relevant hotel experience to accompany you.

Yours sincerely,

Vera Ampleton-Finch

CHAPTER ONE

The electric light above the dining table was on. Outside, the weather was grey and dull with rain beating on the French doors. Kitty Bryant was just finishing an early breakfast with her husband, Matt. Bertie, their roan cocker spaniel, lay stretched out at her feet.

Kitty sighed as she reread Vera's note.

'Is there something wrong, darling?' Matt looked up from where he was perusing his own post.

'It seems so. You know that I had agreed to assist Grams with screening the applicants who wished to join the Torbay Hoteliers' Association? Vera Ampleton-Finch from the Somerton Hotel was supposed to accompany me to the hotel I'm due to inspect this week, the Bird Hotel, but it seems she has shingles.' Kitty set the note down and helped herself to the last triangle of toast from the smart chrome toast rack.

Kitty and her beloved Grams were the proprietors of the Dolphin Hotel in Dartmouth and Kitty was very experienced in hotel management. Since Kitty's marriage, just over a year ago, they had appointed someone who took care of the day-to-day running of the hotel. Her grandmother had retired, and Kitty only helped out when needed. Most of her time these days was spent assisting Matt with their private investigative service.

However, her grandmother had become a little bored in the last few months and had accepted a post as head of the Torbay Hoteliers' Association. One of the remits of the association was that any new applicants for membership must have their premises inspected by a committee member, or someone appointed by the committee, before being permitted to join.

Kitty had agreed to assist the association by undertaking the inspections of prospective new members' premises ahead of the start of the main holiday season. Mrs Ampleton-Finch had been set to accompany her on an overnight stay at the Bird Hotel, a new and exclusive property set on remote Bird Island, just off the Torbay coast.

'Oh dear, what happens now then? Isn't this the hotel that's been in all the papers? The one on the island?' Matt asked.

'Yes, that's the one. Sir Norman Whittier bought the place from Colonel Montpelier about two years ago. It used to be a terribly run-down, gothic-style house; the colonel was known as a bit of a hermit. Since then, Sir Norman has knocked the old house down and built this rather lovely-looking white villa, all curves and sea views. Bird Island is not really much of a place, mostly rocks and some grazing, as far as I know. I think there is just the hotel, a few cottages and a lighthouse there. Oh, and lots of birds, of course,' Kitty said before crunching her toast.

'Can't you find someone else to go with you? It doesn't have to be another committee member, does it?' Matt set aside his own pile of letters.

Kitty picked up her linen napkin and dabbed the crumbs from the corners of her mouth. 'No, it simply has to be someone who is knowledgeable about the hotel trade. I would still have to write the report and recommend the hotelier for membership, or not, as the case might be.'

Matt smiled. 'I would happily volunteer to come with you

for a night away in the lap of luxury but, sadly, I don't think I have the kind of knowledge you need.'

Kitty smiled back at him. 'No, and there is the small matter of your court case. Speaking of which, you had better get a move on. Chief Inspector Greville is depending on you if he is to secure a conviction for that fraudster. You have worked so hard on this case that I am sure he relies on you far more than on his new inspector.'

Matt was in the middle of a complicated trial and was due to present his evidence to the judge over the next few days.

'You're right. Don't fret, darling, I'm sure you'll think of something.' Matt rose from his seat and kissed the top of her head before hurrying out of the room to set off for Torquay.

Kitty sighed and dropped her napkin back down on the table. Bertie lifted his head to give her a reproachful look as she prepared to clear the breakfast things.

'Sorry, Bertie.' Kitty collected up the used crockery and piled it onto a small wooden tray. As she did so her gaze fell on the fading bouquet of dark-red roses which stood shedding their petals on the mantelpiece.

The flowers had been a Valentine's gift from Matt the week before and were now sadly past their best. Alice would have gathered up the petals to make rose water by now if Kitty was still living at the Dolphin.

'Of course! Alice!' Kitty wondered that she hadn't thought of her right away.

Alice was a chambermaid at the Dolphin and Kitty's dearest friend. What she didn't know about the hotel trade wasn't worth knowing. There was also the matter of how sad her friend had seemed since Valentine's Day.

Alice had been walking out for quite some time now with Robert Potter, the son of their local taxi driver and a business owner in his own right. Just lately though Kitty thought the shine had worn off their relationship. Alice no longer seemed to be collecting items for her bottom drawer and Robert had not given Alice a gift on Valentine's Day itself. Instead, he had arrived the day after clutching a box of chocolates and some rather tired-looking flowers.

A stay in a grand hotel as a guest might be just the ticket to lift Alice's spirits and put the spring back in her step.

'That sea looks a bit choppy.' Alice gave the small, blue-painted boat tethered at the quayside a dubious glance as the breeze lifted a few stray auburn curls from under the brim of her navy felt hat.

The sky was a dull gunmetal-grey and the damp sea air clung to Kitty's face and the wool of her winter coat. They were waiting for the last of the passengers to arrive, ready to be transported across to Bird Island. It seemed that Sir Norman had invited a small group of people to test out his hotel before opening the doors to the paying public.

'It is a little, but it's a short crossing,' Kitty reassured her friend and looked around with interest at their fellow guests. She was pleased Alice had agreed to accompany her to the island. The other two gentlemen present had nodded to Kitty and Alice but, apart from Miss Marie Monbiere, had not introduced themselves, something which amused Kitty.

Marie Monbiere was a noted opera singer and it appeared she had been informed of their visit by her fiancé, Sir Norman. Marie had performed recently at the Pavilion Theatre in Torquay, which Kitty and Matt had attended with her grandmother and Mrs Craven, her grandmother's friend.

Miss Monbiere, having made their acquaintance, was currently complaining to one of the men, a tall, thin, older man with silver hair and moustache, about the delay in boarding the boat.

'Honestly, this is so typical of Paul to be late. I cannot think why Lambert has insisted on giving him this opportunity.' Miss Monbiere huffed and lifted the collar of her fur coat more closely about her neck as she glared at the other gentleman accompanying them.

'Because I feel, my dear, that Paul still has a certain cachet at the box office,' the other man said, overhearing her complaints.

Kitty assumed from this that he must be Lambert. He was another tall man, younger than the first, with dark hair and a slightly seedy air.

'Well, it's not good enough. I see Selena and Alec are not here yet either,' Marie announced with a sniff.

Alice exchanged a glance with Kitty. It looked as if their fellow guests were going to be an interesting group.

A large blue motor car pulled up nearby and a young, pretty girl with short, dark curls climbed out and hurried towards them. She was followed by a good-looking man of around the same age who carried all their luggage over to the quay for the captain of the boat to place on board.

'Oh, I say, are we late? I'm frightfully sorry. I simply couldn't find my compact. I spent ages looking and it was in my handbag all the time,' the girl explained breathlessly as she greeted the rest of the group with kisses on their cheeks. She gave a curious glance at Kitty and Alice.

'We are still waiting for Paul, so I suppose we can overlook your tardiness for once, Selena,' Marie said.

'We had best be on our way, miss, else we shall miss the tide. Is there anyone else in your party still to come?' the captain asked.

'Just one gentleman, but if he misses the boat then he will have to come across later.' Marie accepted assistance from Lambert and the captain to board the boat.

'He might not get across to the island if'n he in't here in a minute or two. There is storms forecast and we won't be able to get over,' the captain warned as the rest of the party stepped onto the boat.

Kitty and Alice followed Marie and Selina and settled themselves in a sheltered spot.

'I said as this sea looked rough. I'm glad as I didn't wear my best hat, this spray would have soon put paid to it,' Alice muttered as she huddled up next to Kitty.

'We'll be there soon, and your hat looks perfectly darling.' Kitty hoped that her friend was a good sailor. The waves had white caps and she could see the wind had risen slightly while they had been at the quay.

'Wait for me!' An older man carrying a large brown leather valise came rushing towards the boat just as the captain was about to cast off.

The other men hauled him on board in the nick of time as the engine started. The captain steered the boat away from the quay and out of the harbour towards the distant dark outline of Bird Island.

The crossing was mercifully short and several of the passengers looked quite green around the gills by the time the small vessel tied up alongside the wooden jetty on the island.

'Oh, thank heavens that's over,' Selena remarked as she was assisted ashore by her male companion.

Alice and Kitty were helped off the boat by Lambert and the other older gentleman, while the latecomer tussled with the captain about carrying his own bag.

Overhead, the seabirds, which had given the island its name, wheeled and screamed on the rising wind. The captain deposited the rest of their bags on the jetty and immediately set off back for the mainland. The approaching storm making a rapid departure necessary.

Kitty looked around her with interest. She had never visited the island before but had viewed it from the deck of one of the pleasure boats which offered short cruises around the bay.

The Bird Hotel was situated a short distance away on top of a steep rise. The curved and gleaming white walls a stark contrast to the darkening grey of the sky and the red soil and green grass surrounding it. One path led towards the hotel and another curved away in the direction of the lighthouse. Kitty could see it sitting short and squat on top of an outcrop about half a mile from the jetty.

A middle-aged man in a cap leading a small donkey cart approached them from the direction of the hotel.

'I see Albert is here to take our luggage. Anyone not wishing to walk may also take a ride to the hotel,' Miss Monbiere announced as the donkey came to a stop.

The man touched the brim of his cap to her. 'Morning, Miss Monbiere. Sir Norman is waiting for you all in the drawing room if you'd like to go on.' He started loading the bags onto the cart.

Kitty tried to place his accent. He wasn't a local man she was sure of that. The group promptly set off walking up the path following Miss Monbiere, who naturally appeared to know both the island and its staff quite well.

The man and the cart followed behind them with their luggage with the exception of Paul who had insisted on carrying his leather valise himself. Kitty wondered what could be inside that he was so unwilling to entrust it to the donkey cart driver.

'Blimey, this is all a bit different to the Dolphin, isn't it?' Alice said as she fell into step beside Kitty. 'Think your gran might like to get a donkey?'

CHAPTER TWO

After a short, steep climb the path levelled off and took them around to the front entrance of the hotel. Kitty vaguely remembered the house that had stood there before as a crumbling red-brick mansion with gothic towers and turrets. They entered the grounds through a gap in a low stone wall.

The new hotel was a gleaming white two-storey villa with curved walls and a flat roof. The large windows had black metal frames and Kitty guessed they offered panoramic views of the sea. The entrance doors were painted navy and planters stood on either side. Yellow daffodils were bending forlornly in the wind which was now gusting in strongly from the sea. A haze had already started to form around them during the short walk from the jetty.

The man and the donkey cart continued on around the corner of the hotel, presumably to unload their bags elsewhere. Alice and Kitty followed Miss Monbiere and her party through the front doors of the hotel. The reception area was spacious with a pale-grey marble floor. Black leather armchairs were grouped companionably around a couple of low chrome and glass tables. Vases containing white lilies and pink roses adorned the discreet reception area in the corner of the room. Everything appeared sleek, modern and expensive.

As they stood waiting in the reception area an older woman appeared wearing a smart black and white maid's uniform and a slightly sour expression. Their coats were taken and hung in a cloakroom near the reception desk. The woman then offered around a silver tray containing filled champagne glasses.

Alice followed Kitty's lead and accepted a glass from the tray, her eyes wide with astonishment as she did so. A flight of stairs in chrome and glass led up from the far end of the reception area and coming towards them down the stairs was a tall, debonair older man in a well-cut grey suit.

'Welcome, welcome to you all,' he called out over the gentle hubbub of conversation which had commenced with the arrival of the champagne.

Kitty assumed this must be their host, Sir Norman Whittier, hotelier and famous restauranteur. His distinguished features were familiar from the newspaper accounts of famous guests who dined and danced at his various establishments.

'Norman dearest!' Marie Monbiere rushed forward to greet him.

'My darling, Marie, how was the crossing? Not too rough, I hope? A storm has been forecast but we shall be safe and snug here, my love.' He bowed over her hand before kissing her cheeks. Kitty noticed the large diamond on the singer's engagement finger sparkling in the light.

Alice rolled her eyes at Kitty at this display.

'I am delighted to welcome all of you to the Bird Hotel. A wonderful space for you to rehearse what is my darling Marie's first foray into playwriting. No doubt you will find it much improved since your last visit here.' He chuckled as he spoke to the group. 'You are all also assisting Marie and I to ensure that the services we offer our future guests will be exceptional, creating a memorable and unique experience.' Sir Norman waved his hand over Miss Monbiere's party. 'And a special welcome to Mrs Bryant and Miss Miller who are joining us from the Torbay Hoteliers' Association, here to assess our wonderful new hotel.' He bowed and cast a beaming smile at Kitty and Alice.

The other guests immediately turned their attention towards Kitty and Alice.

'Thank you, Sir Norman,' Kitty said as Alice shifted uncomfortably at being the focus of attention.

'Now, dear friends, my darling Marie will show you around the public rooms while your luggage is placed in your bedrooms.' Sir Norman's dark brows knitted together when he noticed that Paul still had a tight hold on his leather valise. 'Paul, would you care to hand your case to my staff while you look around?'

With the attention of the group now switched on Paul, he reluctantly gave his case over to the maid who had carried in the champagne.

'Follow me, my loves,' Marie called in a clarion voice as she set down her empty glass on the silver salver and prepared to lead the way towards the other rooms.

Alice and Kitty tagged once more onto the rear of the group as Marie took them through a set of ornate polished wood and chrome doors into a charming and comfortable lounge. More stylish leather furniture and small tables were set in groups, while large windows offered a view towards the sea. A small but well-stocked bar was situated in the corner of the room.

Kitty guessed that in better weather the outlook from the room would be quite spectacular. Now though the mist had closed in even further and the grounds outside were barely visible through the white blanket of fog. A sharp spatter of rain sounded against the glass as Marie extolled the virtues of the space and showed the group the black grand piano at the far end.

'What do you think of it so far?' Kitty asked Alice in a low tone while the others were busy admiring the room.

'He's not stinted on the costs, has he? This lot hasn't come cheap,' Alice murmured as she ran her fingers across the back of one of the leather armchairs.

Marie moved the group on into a smaller lounge, again affording what would probably be a delightful view when the weather improved. This room was cosier with a large fireplace, generously stocked bookshelves and Turkish carpets.

A billiards room followed and then finally a rather beautiful dining room with an ornate glass-domed ceiling and tables set in the windows so diners could enjoy the view. The tour concluded and everyone started to wander back towards the lounges.

'Well, Mrs Bryant, Miss Miller, I do hope you approve of the style and comfort of our public rooms?' Sir Norman had appeared at Kitty's elbow.

'Oh yes, they do look most delightful,' Kitty agreed politely.

'Of course, I personally approved the choices in the soft furnishings and décor.' Marie Monbiere slipped her hand onto the crook of Sir Norman's arm. 'Everything is in the latest fashion.'

'My fiancée has excellent taste in such matters,' Sir Norman said as he smiled at the singer.

'It all looks very nice,' Alice agreed.

'Come through to the reception area and I will ensure Ethel gives you your keys. I'm sure you both wish to freshen up before lunch,' Sir Norman said.

Kitty and Alice dutifully accompanied their host and his fiancée back into the hall. The older woman who had served the champagne was now behind the desk. Sir Norman clicked his fingers at her, and she presented them both with keys attached to polished wood and chrome tags.

'Mrs Bryant, you are in Guillemot and, Miss Miller, you are

in Shearling. The rooms are interconnected should you so choose and are just at the top of the stairs.'

Sir Norman consulted his gold fob watch. 'Luncheon is at one in the dining room.'

Kitty and Alice thanked him and made their escape up the stairs. The top of the staircase opened out into a wide landing that followed the curve of the building. Kitty's door was first with the room name engraved on a chrome plate above the door. Alice's room was a little further along the corridor.

On entering her room Kitty discovered that her carpet bag had been placed on the luggage rack next to the rosewood wardrobe and her things had been hung up and put away for her. The rain was pounding now against the glass of her bedroom window, and she could hear the wind gusting around the walls outside.

The room itself was spacious and luxuriously appointed with a small sitting area with armchairs and a low table. Kitty perched on the edge of the bed and bounced tentatively on the mattress. It certainly appeared comfortable, and the pale-pink coverlet matched the rose-patterned curtains. The wallpaper behind the bed also depicted abstract flowers to match with the soft furnishings.

Kitty wondered what Alice's impressions were of the place and the people. On the surface everything seemed delightful. Even so, there was something a little strange. An air of tension throughout the hotel. It could be emanating from the thespians, perhaps some kind of rivalry over parts. She hoped it wasn't because of the inspection she and Alice were about to make of the premises.

Two doors led from the room. One opened into a well-appointed marble bathroom with dark-green and gold tiled walls. The other, Kitty presumed, must be the connecting door to Alice's room.

There was the sound of a cautious knock on the connecting door before it opened a crack and Alice peeped in.

'My room is ever so grand.' Alice stepped into Kitty's room and gazed around.

'This one is too,' Kitty said. 'May I take a look at yours?' As a hotelier she was fascinated by the amount of money that Sir Norman appeared to have lavished on his hotel.

Alice's room was identical to Kitty's except that it was decorated in shades of blue with forget-me-nots as the floral motif. Kitty rejoined her friend.

'They seem a rum lot who came over on the boat with us,' Alice remarked as she took a seat on one of the rose-pink velvet armchairs in Kitty's room.

'I agree. It looks as if Sir Norman and his fiancée are using the cast of Miss Monbiere's play to road test the hotel while they rehearse. It should be an interesting visit.' Kitty took the chair opposite her friend.

'That storm is picking up outside as well now, the sea mist has proper come down. The easterlies are always bad this time of year. I hope as it's all cleared away for when we have to go back on the boat.' Alice frowned at the water racing down the outside of the metal-framed windowpane.

'Yes, I did think we may end up having to stay for an extra day if the boat is unable to return tomorrow,' Kitty agreed.

'Good thing as we packed a few extra things,' Alice said.

Both Alice and Kitty were well versed with the winter gales that would blow in from the east causing rough seas and damage to property in exposed places around the coast. Kitty hoped that Matt would be safe riding his Sunbeam motorcycle through the narrow Devon lanes back and forth to the courthouse.

Alice picked up a small, folded pamphlet which had been left on the table. 'It looks as if this is to tell the guests all about the island and the hotel.'

'What does it say?' Kitty was curious to know if it gave

much background about the hotel's proprietor. She couldn't imagine there would be much to say about the island itself.

Alice gave an unladylike snort as she read the leaflet. 'It sounds a bit fanciful if you ask me. It says as the island was used by pirates back in the day before the late colonel owned it. Sir Norman Whittier, the renowned restauranteur, intends the island to retain its status as a bird sanctuary while providing guests with a uniquely luxurious escape from the world. Pirates, I ask you. There's never been any pirates on Bird Island. It was used for grazing sheep.' Alice dropped the pamphlet back down on the table.

Kitty grinned. 'You can't blame him for trying to make it sound a tad more thrilling. Pirates will beat sheep any day of the week.'

'Well, I think it's all a gimmick.' Alice tossed her auburn curls. 'The Dolphin has real smugglers' tunnels behind it, but we don't go shouting about it.'

Kitty's smile widened at her friend's loyalty. 'Very true. Come on, let's walk down to the dining room and try out the food. It's almost one o'clock and I must admit I'm quite hungry.'

When they arrived downstairs they found that the tables in the dining room had been reset so that everyone was seated together at one long table. Sir Norman was at the head, with Miss Monbiere on his right-hand side.

'Mrs Bryant, Miss Miller, do take a seat. We thought this would be friendlier, give us all the opportunity to become acquainted.' Sir Norman waved his hand expansively in the direction of their fellow guests who were busily taking their places at the table. Kitty could see the arrangement made sense given that they were the only guests at present.

Alice and Kitty took their seats near the end. Kitty was beside the young man who had accompanied Selena.

'Alec Standish, how do you do?' He offered his hand to her as she sat down. He had a pleasant American accent.

'Kitty Bryant.' Kitty shook his hand.

Alice was beside one of the older men who had been conversing with Marie at the quayside in Torquay. 'Colin Frobisher, delighted to make your acquaintance.'

'Alice Miller, pleasure I'm sure.'

Further introductions to all the party followed and Kitty discovered that Colin Frobisher was Sir Norman's friend and a financier. Lambert Pike, seated beside Miss Monbiere, was a theatrical agent, and Alec Standish was to be the leading actor in Miss Monbiere's play.

'Selena is the romantic lead, of course,' Alec confided, 'and Paul Browning is to play her father.' He nodded towards the man who had insisted on carrying his own case to the hotel.

'It all sounds very exciting,' Kitty agreed. She could see that Alice was listening with rapt attention to Lambert Pike's tales of stars he had worked with. Kitty knew Alice would love this, as her friend adored going to the picture house and bought all the magazines with stories about the stars inside.

The first course was placed before them; cream of leek soup, in delicate white china bowls. Kitty sniffed appreciatively. So far, the hotel certainly appeared to be reaching the standards required by the hoteliers' association. She could see that guests would certainly appreciate the luxurious setting and exclusivity promised in the advertisements.

Along with the soup, white wine had also been provided. Kitty couldn't help noticing that Paul Browning was already on his third glass before the empty dishes had been collected.

'Miss Monbiere said that she was responsible for the interior design of the hotel,' Kitty remarked as a plate of lamb cutlets was placed in front of her.

'Yes, from what Marie has said she is a full partner in Sir Norman's venture. She has excellent taste and Sir Norman takes dreadful advantage of her. if you ask me.' Alec added more gravy to his meal from a china sauce boat. 'I get the impression that fitting this place out has taken most of her savings.' He lowered his voice as he spoke. 'It's caused a few arguments between them, I believe.'

'Everything does appear to have been quite beautifully done,' Kitty said. She supposed that must be why Sir Norman had been pushing to join the association if his fiancée had invested so heavily in his project.

Out of the corner of her eye she noticed that the bottles of wine had been discreetly removed from the table after everyone, except Paul Browning's glass, had been refilled.

'Sir Norman said you and your friend were here to inspect the place?' Alec asked affably.

'Yes, he has applied to join the Torbay Hoteliers' Association. Alice and I are here on behalf of the committee to see if the criteria for membership are being met. If they are then the hotel is given a badge and a rating which they may use to attract guests. It can make quite a difference to a business's success or failure,' Kitty explained.

'You! I say, you there!' Paul Browning had raised his arm in the air and was clicking his fingers in the direction of the middle-aged man who had been serving their meal.

Conversation around the table died as the waiter turned to see what Paul wanted. Kitty realised the waiter was the same man who had collected their luggage with the donkey cart.

'Sir?' the man asked.

'Where's the wine? I need another glass.' Paul brought his hand down forcefully on the tabletop, making the cutlery jump and the water in the glasses slosh slightly from side to side.

'I'm very sorry, sir, but the wine has been finished. If you would care for more water, I can refill the jugs.' The man glanced in the direction of Sir Norman and Miss Monbiere and Kitty assumed they had requested the wine be removed.

Paul threw a malevolent look towards the head of the table

but thankfully subsided in his seat and permitted the man to continue about his duties.

Once the conversational hum had been resumed Kitty asked in a low tone, 'I take it that Mr Browning has something of a problem with alcohol?'

Alec grinned. 'Oh yes, that's why his work has been so scarce lately. He's unreliable you see. A marvellous talent when he's sober, but of late that's seldom the case. I was surprised when Lambert suggested he join the company. Still, I suppose like the rest of us he has come cheap.'

A dessert of apple pie and custard followed while the conversation switched to Miss Monbiere's play and the rehearsal schedule. This, it seemed, was to commence with a read-through immediately after lunch in the main lounge.

Kitty had already determined that she and Alice would inspect the kitchen and storage areas in the afternoon. The rain had grown heavier while they had been dining and the view from the windows was now completely obscured. The table lamps had all been turned on, creating small islands of soft yellow light throughout the downstairs areas.

The company went off to rehearse, while Colin Frobisher and Sir Norman left through a polished wooden door behind the reception desk, which Kitty assumed must be Sir Norman's private office. This was a similar arrangement to the Dolphin.

'We should give the staff time to clear the kitchen up a little before we take a look.' Kitty linked arms with Alice. 'Shall we go and enjoy the smaller lounge for a while first and allow our lunch to digest?'

'Yes, and I can tell you some of the stories that Lambert was telling me. You won't believe your ears at some of them,' Alice agreed happily.

CHAPTER THREE

'Missus is away for a couple of days then?' Chief Inspector Greville remarked to Matt as they retired from the courtroom for lunch at a nearby tea room.

'Kitty and Alice are inspecting the new hotel over on Bird Island. I hope they made it safely across the bay before this storm started.' Matt frowned at the rain cascading down the outside window of the tea room.

'It's not far so I expect they got there all right. This weather is set to get worse though, so she may have to stay an extra day or so before it calms enough to return.' The chief inspector helped himself to the last slice of bread and butter which had accompanied their fish and chips. 'I wouldn't mind if Mrs Greville was to go away for a few days,' he muttered mournfully.

'How are the family?' Matt asked politely. He was familiar with the chief inspector's mild grumblings about his wife, his mother-in-law and his sons.

'Not too bad, thank you. The boys are growing up, you know. Eldest will go to the grammar school in September.' The chief inspector gave a wry smile. 'And a pretty penny that will cost too with all the uniform and sports equipment.'

Matt took a sip of his tea. 'Still, I suppose it will all be worth it. I'm sure you're very proud of him.'

The chief inspector dabbed at the corners of his moustache with his linen napkin. 'Oh yes, of course. I daresay when you and Mrs Bryant hear the patter of tiny feet then you'll find just the same things.'

Matt swallowed his tea the wrong way and broke into a cough. He and Kitty had briefly discussed the possibility of children before they had married. However, since he had lost his first child during the last war, becoming a father again had not been a high priority for their marriage. Little Betty's death had been one of the most painful experiences of his life.

'Steady on, old chap.' The chief inspector helpfully slapped him between his shoulder blades.

'Sorry, choked on a crumb.' Matt finished coughing and settled back in his seat to catch his breath. The chief inspector's remark had taken him by surprise.

The chief inspector looked at his watch. 'Ten more minutes until the court rises again.'

'It's a good job we only have to cross the street.' Matt called for the bill as he eyed the heavy rain outside.

'I think my turn on the stand should finish today,' said Chief Inspector Greville. 'Inspector Lewis is being called to give evidence tomorrow.' He appeared slightly concerned by this, a frown puckering his forehead. 'Slippery customer, the accused. I really hope we get a conviction.'

Matt could understand his worry about the case. Inspector Lewis was not a favourite with either himself or Kitty. They had worked with the man on a few cases now and he had been obstinate, intransigent and obstructive every time. He had made it very clear that he disliked private investigators. And, in Kitty's case, he especially disliked female private investigators.

'I'm sure the inspector will be well prepared, sir,' Matt reassured his friend as they rose to put on their overcoats.

'He had better be,' Chief Inspector Greville replied ominously as they prepared to dash across the rain-drenched street into the welcome dryness of the courthouse.

* * *

Kitty and Alice spent a pleasant half an hour in the quiet of the smaller lounge. Occasionally they heard voices coming from the rehearsal but nothing to disturb their peace. The doors in the hotel seemed to be of good quality and muffled the sound well. Kitty was pleased to see that her friend appeared more cheerful and less stressed than she had been since Valentine's Day. She longed to broach the topic of Alice's friendship with Robert Potter but hoped that Alice might be first to bring the subject up.

'We had best go and take a look around at the kitchen and the stores then. They should have cleared most of the washing-up by now.' Alice looked at the sleek chrome clock on the mantelpiece.

'We should indeed,' Kitty agreed, rising somewhat reluctantly to her feet. She had been quite comfortable in her chair.

They made their way out of the lounge – luckily there was another door which opened onto the corridor so they could avoid disturbing the rehearsal. The kitchen naturally lay beyond the dining room and Sir Norman had informed the staff that Kitty and Alice would need to visit the staff areas.

'Hello!' Alice opened the door to the kitchen and peered inside. 'May we come in?'

The kitchen was a large square space and Kitty was pleased to see that the same care that had gone into the front of house furnishings had also been spent on the working areas.

'Please to come in, miss. Sir Norman said as you would be

wanting to look around.' The man who had been serving at the table was now swathed in a large apron as he dried up the last of the huge pots and pans that had been utilised for lunch preparations.

'Gosh, this all seems to be very well equipped.' Alice looked around approvingly.

'No expense spared, miss.'

Kitty thought she detected a slightly sour note in the man's reply. Ethel, the lady who had been on reception and who had served the champagne, appeared to be busily engaged in chopping more vegetables ready for dinner.

'Are there just the two of you working here?' Alice asked.

'At the moment, miss. There is supposed to be a girl coming from the orphanage on Friday whom we're to train for the housekeeping,' the man explained.

'It's a lot of work for two people even with someone else coming soon to give assistance.' Kitty's brows raised slightly. 'You must both be very experienced?'

'Yes, miss. Been in this trade all our working lives. Me since I were thirteen and Albert, my husband here, since he were fourteen,' Ethel said, tipping the last of the carrots into a pot and placing the lid down.

'And have you worked for Sir Norman for long?' Alice asked as she inspected the contents of a well-stocked store cupboard.

Ethel exchanged a glance with her husband. 'A bit too long, I reckon. A few years now, first in London and then at his country house in Suffolk.'

'It will be quite a change living and working here on the island,' Kitty said. 'It's quite remote at this time of year.'

Again, Ethel and Albert's gazes met. 'Aye, maybe we won't be staying too long, it depends how it all shakes down. It's a bit lonely being just us and the cottagers,' Albert said as he started to set up some trays ready for afternoon tea.

'I suppose with the Bird Hotel being a new venture it's hard to know if it will work.' Kitty sensed there was some subtext running between the couple when it came to their relationship with Sir Norman that she was not party too.

''Appen so,' Albert agreed as Ethel picked up her knife and started to prepare the parsnips.

Alice and Kitty completed their tour of the kitchen and stores and made good their escape back into the hall. They inspected the public cloakrooms and were about to return to the lounge, when the door to the office partially opened as if someone was about to come out and the sound of raised angry male voices reached them.

'It's ridiculous, Norman. It's no good trying to talk to you. You can't continue on in this vein. Have you spoken to Marie about all of this?'

Kitty recognised Colin Frobisher's voice.

She looked at Alice as Sir Norman mumbled some kind of response.

'If you don't tell her, then I will. The pot is empty. The well has run dry. I cannot express myself any more clearly. If you continue on as you have been you will face severe repercussions.' There was a thud as if Colin Frobisher had banged something down in order to make his point.

Alice caught hold of the sleeve of Kitty's dress. 'We'd better make ourselves scarce. I think Mr Frobisher is coming out.'

Kitty was forced to agree. It would have been awkward if either of the gentlemen had found them standing there. Even so, she would have dearly loved to have discovered exactly what the men were arguing about.

Kitty and Alice slipped into the smaller lounge. Alice sat herself back down with a sigh of relief. 'Goodness, are these hotel inspections all like this or is this one especially odd? I thought as the staff were being very cagey.' She looked at Kitty.

Kitty sat down in the chair opposite her friend. 'No, usually they are very straight forward. This is peculiar, isn't it? There's a very strange atmosphere here. I thought I had imagined it. Perhaps it's because the hotel isn't officially open yet and our fellow guests are not paying customers.'

'Hmm, them others are definitely an odd lot,' Alice conceded as a muffled burst of piano music sounded from the lounge next door.

'Theatrical people are very strange.' A cold shiver ran along Kitty's spine. One of their early cases had involved a theatrical family. It had not gone well. Matt had been arrested for murder and Kitty herself had almost been killed before the culprit was caught.

'I wonder what Sir Norman is charging for people to stay here?' Alice mused. 'It's only as I can't see how he intends to make it pay.'

Kitty knew what her friend meant. Running a hotel was expensive and this one would have extra costs involved with everything having to be supplied to the island by boat. The hotel was not overly large either so it would need to be full most of the time.

'I think in the prospectus that he supplied to the association there was mention of the hotel being booked out exclusively for parties of guests. A bit like a private house, and also during the summer, day visitors could attend for luncheon and high tea.'

Alice sniffed. 'They would have to be well-heeled visitors, I reckon, to make this pay.'

Kitty grinned. 'I rather think you're right. Still, that isn't our concern. We are here merely to determine if the standards meet those required for membership.'

Alice glanced around at her surroundings. 'It's all very grand. I never thought as I should see the day when I stayed somewhere like this as a guest. Perhaps work somewhere like this as a maid, maybe.' She smiled shyly at Kitty and a faint pink flush coloured her cheeks.

'You absolutely deserve to be here as a guest, and I for one am glad that Vera Ampleton-Finch was unable to come. I would much rather be here with you,' Kitty declared stoutly. She rather doubted that Mrs Ampleton-Finch, a somewhat nervous widow in her late fifties, would have enjoyed the boat ride to the island.

A flurry of raindrops smacked against the windowpane and Kitty shivered. 'I hope Matt will be all right riding his motor-cycle into Torquay and back.' The wind would be gusting on the exposed parts of the coast road and the sea would probably have come over the wall onto the road in places.

'He's an experienced rider and he won't take no risks.' Alice rose to stand by the window peering out at the gathering gloom outside. 'I expect as this place will look a lot more inviting in the summer. It's almost dark now what with the hour and this terrible weather. The wind is fair blowing outside, not as it's moving the fog much.'

'I hope your mother won't be worried about you being here during a storm,' Kitty said. Alice was the eldest of eight children. Mrs Miller was a good mother and very protective of all her brood. Alice's younger sister, Dolly, also worked at the Dolphin assisting Mr Lutterworth, the hotel manager.

'I dare say as she'll fret a bit, but she's lived in Dartmouth all her life and she knows the way of it at this time of year. The captain will have put back to Torquay safe and sound, so she'll know as we'em in the hotel.' Alice returned to her seat as the door opened and Albert appeared carrying a small silver tray set with china tea things.

'Afternoon tea, madam.' He set it down on the table in front of Kitty.

'Thank you, that's terribly kind,' Kitty thanked the man and he returned to his work.

'Ooh lovely, he must have read my mind,' Alice said and lifted the lid of the teapot to stir the leaves.

Kitty had to admit that she too was ready for a drink. Alice poured the tea into the brightly geometric-patterned painted cups and they settled back to enjoy the break.

'What did Robert say when you told him you were accompanying me here?' Kitty asked once she had swallowed her first sip of tea.

She had been trying hard not to mention Robert's name in an effort not to seem nosey, but thought Alice might think it queer if she didn't mention him at all.

Alice's lips set in a mulish line. 'I wouldn't know. I didn't tell him as I was going away.'

'Oh.' Kitty wasn't certain how to respond.

'He can find out for himself when he comes to call for me and finds as I'm not there,' Alice declared.

'Have you two fallen out?' Kitty asked as she helped herself to one of the small biscuits that had accompanied the tea.

Alice set her cup down on her saucer. 'For us to fall out I'd have to see something of him in the first place. Too comfortable that's what he is, taking me for granted. Well, I'm not having it.'

'I see.' Kitty wasn't quite sure what to say. Alice sounded as if her mind was made up on the matter.

'Christmas, I had just a box of chocolates. I spent hours making him his presents, that nice scarf I knitted him, and I bought him those new leather driving gloves. Then there was this Valentine's Day, I swear as he forgot all about it until the day after. We've been walking out together for ages now. A girl has a right to a bit of consideration.' Alice's lower lip trembled, and Kitty could see her friend was distressed.

'Oh dear, Alice, I didn't realise. Have you spoken to him about how you feel?' Kitty asked as Alice pulled a small, white cotton handkerchief from her pocket and dabbed fiercely at her eyes.

'I'm not about to beg him for his attention.' Alice tipped her chin upwards with a determined air. 'We've been walking out for long enough as he should know to treat me with a bit more consideration. I had been hoping as I'd have a ring on my finger by now. People talk, you know, when you've been seeing somebody for a long time and no ring appears.'

Kitty was well aware of how the gossip mill worked in a small town where everyone knew everyone else. Alice had been collecting items for her bottom drawer for quite some time ready to set up her home. Her expectation of a proposal was not unreasonable if the relationship was to develop.

'But do you have any idea why things may have changed between you? You always appear so well suited,' Kitty asked as she finished her tea.

She knew Robert and his father well and he didn't seem the sort of young man who would string a girl along.

'There's nobody else I don't think. Well, not as I know of. He's just always distracted and busy with that blooming business of his.' Her friend tossed her auburn curls.

Robert owned an ancient charabanc and had recently managed to acquire a newer coach which he used to take people on day trips around the local area. During December he had been operating shopping trips to Exeter and Plymouth.

'I think perhaps you need to talk to him, Alice. Tell him how you feel,' Kitty suggested.

'We'll see how he is when I gets back. If he's missed me then I'll think about it. If I get home and he hasn't even noticed as I've been gone, well, that'll be that. There's plenty more fish in the sea, as our Betty says.' Alice appeared firm so Kitty thought it best not to pursue the subject any further. She also thought it best not to mention that Betty was not best placed to give romantic advice given her own lack of success on that front.

Alice's cousin, Betty, was an older only child and had been given a lot more freedom than Alice and her siblings. She constantly moved from situation to situation in an attempt to 'better herself'. She had also stepped out with quite a few young men. Alice's mother disapproved of her niece and regarded her as 'fast', due to her fashion sense and fondness for cosmetics.

A gust of wind hit the front of the hotel shaking the glass in the metal frames. The rich-burgundy velvet curtains stirred as a draught forced its way in. There was a sudden increase in noise from the adjoining lounge, piano music and singing that combined with the sound of the wind howling outside.

'If this doesn't blow out overnight, we will definitely have to stay for longer,' Kitty said as the lamp on a nearby side table flickered.

'Do you think they have generators? The power might well go down at this rate.' Alice gave the lamp a nervous glance.

'I would imagine so. The money that has been spent on this place they must have realised that being on an exposed island would place them at the mercy of the weather.' Kitty had raised her voice to be heard over the noise from the rehearsal next door.

Alice looked reassured by Kitty's words. Fifteen minutes or so later the connecting door from the larger lounge opened and Alec Standish popped his head in.

'Ah, there you both are. Marie wanted to check that you were being looked after. Our rehearsal has finished now. I hope we didn't get too loud?'

'Thank you, yes. Tea was lovely and we were not disturbed at all. I hope the practice went well?' Kitty said.

'As well as one might expect for a first read-through,' Selina said, wandering into the room and pausing for Alec to light her cigarette. The girl's dark-green corded-velvet dress showed off her slender frame and suited her pretty features.

Marie Monbiere followed the two actors into the lounge. 'Considering Paul was half-cut you mean.' She took a seat near Alice.

'Now then, Marie, he'll clean up before the opening night,

darling, I promise you,' Lambert said, joining in the conversation.

'When and where are you opening?' Alice asked.

'We have an out of London provincial short run booked for two weeks' time. Short notice, I know, but we wanted to get it into London in time for Easter, before this place officially opens,' Lambert said, glancing around the lounge.

'It sounds terribly exciting,' Alice remarked politely.

'Terrifying, more like,' Lambert muttered.

CHAPTER FOUR

The lights in the hotel continued to flicker as Kitty dressed for dinner. Before going upstairs, she had attempted to telephone Matt to see if he was at home. She had wanted to make sure he was safe and to ask how the court case was going. The telephone had just rung out, however, and she assumed he must not have returned from Torquay yet.

She had managed a brief conversation with her grandmother to assure her that she and Alice were safe and unaffected by the storm at present. The line was crackly, and Kitty suspected it would probably be cut off before much longer with the way the wind was now howling loudly around the hotel.

Alice knocked on the connecting door when she was ready to go downstairs. Kitty had given her one of her older gowns as her friend had been concerned that she might not possess anything dressy enough for such a smart hotel. Her friend was a clever seamstress and she had soon adapted it to fit.

'You look smashing, Alice. That colour looks much better on you than it ever did on me.' Kitty admired the sapphire-blue satin evening gown which brought out her friend's trim figure and bright eyes.

'You don't look so bad yourself. Shame as Captain Bryant isn't here to admire you,' Alice returned the compliment as she helped close the side fasteners on Kitty's green silk gown.

'That's very kind.' Kitty gave her appearance one last check in the dressing table mirror. 'We had better go down. Miss Monbiere said we were to gather for cocktails in the main lounge before dinner,' Kitty said.

Alice raised her eyebrows. 'Let's hope as that Paul don't have too many before we sit at the table. I thought there was going to be fisticuffs at lunchtime over the wine.'

Kitty grinned. 'Absolutely, let's go and enjoy ourselves.'

The rest of the party were already gathered near the piano when they entered the room. Albert had changed into a white jacket and was busy working a silver cocktail shaker behind the bar.

Lambert was playing the piano, while Selina had perched herself beside him to turn the pages. Colin Frobisher was deep in conversation with Paul Browning as Marie laughed and joked with Alec Standish.

Kitty and Alice approached the boat-shaped burr walnut bar.

'Madam, miss, what can I get you?' Albert asked.

Kitty studied the array of bottles. 'A Negroni for me, please.'

Albert looked at Alice who instantly blushed. 'And for you, miss?'

'Why don't you try one too? I think you'll like it, they are supposed to be a good aperitif,' Kitty suggested, suddenly realising her friend was not too familiar with cocktails.

Alice agreed and Albert quickly mixed them their drinks before departing in the direction of the kitchen, presumably to ready things for dinner.

The lights flickered again as they made their way to one of the leather sofas. Even with the curtains drawn and Lambert's piano playing the sound of the storm could be heard as it raged about the hotel.

Kitty sipped her drink and tried to relax. She was still concerned about Matt getting home safely. Still, she supposed, if one was to worry, there were worse places to do it.

'My dear Kitty and Alice, I do wish the weather had been kinder for your visit. I take it that all went well when you inspected the kitchen this afternoon?' Marie asked.

'Yes, thank you. It was most impressive,' Alice responded. 'Is Sir Norman not joining us for drinks?'

Kitty realised her friend was right. Their host was absent from the gathering. Marie frowned and looked at the stylish clock above the bar.

'Dear me, I expect he's lost track of the time. Once he gets in that office of his there is no prising him out of it. I dare say he'll be along in a minute or two.' She flashed a bright smile at them and resumed her conversation with Alec, although Kitty thought the woman appeared slightly anxious.

'Are you enjoying your cocktail, Alice?' Kitty asked as her friend took a cautious sip of her drink.

Alice's nose wrinkled in distaste. 'I think I'd really rather have a nice cup of tea. I'm not much of a drinker.'

Kitty giggled at her friend's expression. 'Apart from the odd sip of champagne?' she teased. 'Never mind, at least you can tell Dolly you tried one.' Alice's younger sister was always encouraging her to try new things.

Albert re-entered the room and announced that dinner was ready to be served. Lambert replaced the lid over the piano keys and gallantly offered a hand to assist Selena to her feet.

'We should go and winkle Norman out of his den,' Marie declared. 'He really is hopeless at keeping track of the time.'

'I'll go and fetch him,' Colin Frobisher volunteered and left the room.

Kitty finished her drink and placed her empty glass besides Alice's almost full one on the side table.

'There's no answer from the office and the door is locked. Has he gone upstairs to dress for dinner, do you think?' Colin asked as he reappeared in the doorway.

'Shall I pop upstairs and see?' Alec Standish suggested, suiting the action to the words.

'Oh really, this is too bad of Norman. He knows Ethel is very sensitive and hates us to be late for dinner. It upsets all her timings,' Marie huffed as she draped her silk wrapper around her shoulders. They all made their way into the reception area.

Alec clattered down the stairs, a worried look on his face. 'He isn't in his room, Marie. I looked in and his dinner suit is still hanging up ready.'

'Norman!' Marie used the full amount of her considerable operatic lung power to call for her fiancé. The sound had scarcely finished reverberating off the marble surfaces when Lambert spoke.

'He must be in the hotel. He wouldn't have ventured outside in this weather, surely. Perhaps he has been taken ill in his office,' he suggested.

'I'll try the door again.' Paul rattled the handle and hammered fruitlessly on the office door. 'Locked and no answer from inside.'

'Is there another key?' Colin asked.

'Um, in the drawer of the reception desk, I think,' Marie said, starting to appear quite anxious now. Her hands fluttered helplessly as Lambert opened the drawer and rummaged through a selection of keys, all bearing small white tags attached with string.

'Got it.'

He hurried over to the door. Paul stood aside and Lambert juggled the key into the lock. The others crowded behind him as the door opened to a terrible sight.

Sir Norman was in his seat, sprawled forwards and face down on his desk. An ominous dark red pool of blood was beside his head marring the pristine polished wooden surface. His right hand rested on the desktop; his fingers curled limply around a handgun.

Marie screamed and promptly fainted into Alec's arms. Selena looked as if she were about to be sick and Paul Browning didn't look much better.

'Good Lord.' Colin Frobisher stared horrified at the scene before seeming to gather his wits. 'Ladies, please return to the lounge. Lambert, perhaps you might assist me, although I fear it is too late for Norman.'

Alec half carried, half dragged Marie away with Selena hurrying after them. Paul Browning went with them.

'May I assist you, Mr Frobisher? Alice and I have some experience in these matters,' Kitty said calmly as the older man produced a cotton handkerchief and mopped his brow.

'Forgive me, Mrs Bryant, but I really don't think that this is the place for young women such as yourselves...' Colin started to protest, halting when Kitty gave him one of the business cards from her silver evening purse.

'While we came here on behalf of the hoteliers' association, I am a full-working partner in my husband's business,' Kitty said.

Lambert's brows raised as he took the card from Colin and read the contents. 'A private investigator, eh?'

'You may take a look if you really insist, Mrs Bryant, but it appears to be a sad case of suicide,' Colin said, glancing at the prone body of his friend.

'Has Sir Norman left a note?' Kitty neatly sidestepped her way between the two men and entered the office. Alice remained pale faced at the door.

'I... I don't know.' Colin Frobisher followed her as she looked at the top of the desk, taking care not to touch anything.

A fountain pen with the cap off lay on the blotter but there was no sign of any note, or indeed any letters. Just some blank stationery.

She could see there was a large wound in Sir Norman's right temple, and she swallowed hard, determined not to look weak in front of the two men.

'There is no sign of a note, which is rather odd.' Kitty frowned. There was something about the position of the gun and Sir Norman's hand which bothered her. And why would the lid be off the pen? Had someone been in and removed something that Sir Norman had been writing?

'That is peculiar,' said Lambert. 'I would have thought that Norman would have wanted to explain his actions. He must have planned this, surely. And why do this now? With all of us here?' Lambert frowned and looked more closely at Sir Norman's position.

'We will have to inform the police, although when they'll be able to get here, I don't know. This storm sounds as if it's set to continue all night,' Kitty said.

Albert had approached silently along the corridor. He paused next to Alice and peered into the office. At the sight of Sir Norman's body his knees buckled, and he hung on to the doorframe for support.

'I came to see why no one had come down for dinner.' The man kept his eyes trained on the figure at the desk. 'We heard Miss Marie shouting.'

'As you can see Sir Norman is dead. Please tell your wife what has happened. I'm afraid no one will have much of an appetite for anything tonight,' Lambert said.

Albert nodded and hurried away to the kitchen as if relieved no one wished him to offer any other kind of assistance. Alice stepped inside the office and pulled the door shut.

Colin picked up the ivory Bakelite handset of the telephone

on the desk and tried to dial. 'The connection is down. The storm must have cut us off.' He replaced the handset.

'It was a poor connection earlier when I telephoned my grandmother,' Kitty said.

'What do we do now?' Lambert asked. 'Poor Marie, she will be inconsolable. Why would he do such a thing?'

Kitty had exactly the same question going around in her head. It made no sense. Sir Norman had been eager for their visit. He was looking forward to opening the hotel to paying guests. Even if he was suffering from some kind of depression or problem, why not wait until everyone was gone?

'I may know why but I think until I speak to Marie it's best that I keep that to myself.' Colin's expression was grim.

'Forgive me, Mr Frobisher, but does something strike you as not quite right about the position of Sir Norman's hand?' Kitty asked.

The gun was placed loosely in his grasp. She would have thought that it would have fallen from his grip when he pulled the trigger.

Lambert frowned. 'I see what you mean, Mrs Bryant. It looks wrong and forgive me, Colin, you knew Norman better than me, but didn't he have a problem with his right hand?'

Colin blinked as if just realising the implication of Lambert's question. 'Yes, he had a damaged tendon. He did voluntary firefighting during the war. He has scar tissue, so he trained himself to use his left hand instead...' His voice trailed off.

'Why would he shoot himself with his right hand then?' Alice asked.

Lambert swallowed and looked at Colin. 'He wouldn't have. His finger was most affected. He couldn't have pulled the trigger. He would have used his left hand.'

'But... you realise what that would mean?' Colin stared aghast at Sir Norman's right hand.

'It would explain the lack of a suicide note,' Alice said.

'And the odd position of the gun,' Kitty added.

'You're suggesting he was murdered, and this was staged to look as if he killed himself?' Colin shook his head in disbelief. 'Surely not, Mrs Bryant.'

'I take it the gun is Sir Norman's?' Kitty asked.

Colin nodded. 'Yes, I believe so. He kept it in his desk drawer. Although I had no idea that it was loaded.'

'I think we shall have to leave poor Sir Norman where he is for now. I suggest the room is locked and perhaps Alice or myself retain the key until the police arrive,' Kitty said.

'But that hardly seems proper,' Colin Frobisher protested.

'I know, sir, but if Sir Norman's death was not by his own hand, then we owe it to him to ensure whoever did this is brought to justice, 'tis only right,' Alice said in a calm voice.

'I rather think the ladies have a point, old bean,' said Lambert. 'We can't do anything more for Norman now. Let's do as Mrs Bryant suggests and return to the others.' He placed a hand in the middle of Colin's back and started to steer him back into the reception area.

He paused at the door to fumble in his pocket for the key to the office and gave it to Alice.

'I can't believe it. Whatever shall we tell Marie?' Colin asked.

'We tell her that the police have to come before we can do anything. I think we should keep any suggestion that things are not as they initially appeared to ourselves until then,' Lambert said as he guided Colin away.

'Bless me, have a nice little holiday, you said. Stay in a posh hotel,' Alice said, shaking her head in mock despair as she and Kitty came out of the room and closed the door behind them. 'I should have knowed better. Should have knowed that I'd end up bang up to my neck in murder.' Alice locked the door and gave the key to Kitty for safekeeping.

'Sorry, Alice. It's not as if I go looking for these things, you know. Are you all right by the way? I know we've encountered these kinds of situations before, but it's still a ghastly shock.' Kitty couldn't help feeling guilty that once again she had dragged her friend into a murder.

Alice linked her arm through Kitty's. 'It was bit of a facer, I must admit.' She shivered and glanced back at the closed door. 'I might even have to finish that horrible drink.'

CHAPTER FIVE

When they entered the lounge it seemed that everyone had been in need of a restorative drink. Paul Browning had taken charge of the bottle of brandy from the bar and was pouring a generous helping for everyone.

Marie Monbiere was lying prone on the sofa, a pile of silk cushions under her head, while Selina chafed at her hands. Alec approached her with a crystal tot of brandy, but Selina waved him away.

'In a minute, Alec, she has not come round yet.'

Colin Frobisher took the first tumbler of brandy and tossed it straight back with a grimace. Lambert sat nursing his drink between his hands, a sombre expression on his face.

Kitty and Alice both accepted a drink and took seats on the armchairs near the piano where just a moment ago everyone had been enjoying a pleasant evening. A sip of brandy helped to revive Kitty's spirits a little and she was pleased to see that Alice's complexion had been restored to a healthier colour.

'I suppose there is nothing more we can do now except wait for the storm to abate,' Alec said, taking a seat near Kitty.

'No, the telephone line is dead so we can't even inform

anyone on the mainland of what has happened yet,' Kitty said, wishing they had been able to get through.

'Lambert said you are a private investigator, Mrs Bryant. Were you here at the hotel in that capacity?' Selina asked.

Kitty was a little taken aback by the question. Had the girl thought that Sir Norman had employed them as investigators?

'No, I was here purely as an inspector for the hoteliers' association. My family have owned the Dolphin Hotel in Dartmouth for a very long time. Alice and I have a great deal of experience in the hotel business.' She wondered what Selina may have thought a private investigator would be needed for on Bird Island.

'Oh, I see, I just thought, well never mind.' Selina returned her attention to Marie who made a moaning sound as she stirred on the sofa.

'Oh, tell me it's a terrible nightmare. My poor, poor Norman.' A single tear rolled down Marie's cheek from beneath her closed eyelids. The singer's eyelashes fluttered and she opened her eyes.

'I'm so sorry, Marie,' Selina said. 'Here, do try and sit up a little and take a sip of brandy.' Selina looked to Alec, and he immediately rose to assist her.

Between them, they managed to prop the opera singer up a little more and Alec pressed the tumbler of brandy to her lips.

'Why... why would he do such a thing?' Marie wailed as soon as she had swallowed a sip. 'We were so happy. The hotel was his dream, and everything was going so well with the play and our wedding plans.' She sniffed and fished a tiny delicate lace-edged handkerchief from somewhere inside the low-cut neckline of her crimson evening gown.

'I'm so sorry, Marie,' said Lambert. 'Norman doesn't appear to have left any kind of note. You have no idea why he would have done this? He never indicated to you that he was worried or upset about anything?'

Marie dabbed her eyes delicately. 'Nothing. We were so happy. I mean, I know there were some financial concerns with the hotel. But I had supported him with the expenses and the profit forecasts were good.'

Alice caught Kitty's eye at this mention of the expected returns for the hotel.

'Colin, you were with him this afternoon,' Marie said. 'How did he seem to you? Did he mention anything that was bothering him?' She twisted her head to look at Colin Frobisher.

Colin was staring morosely into the bottom of his empty brandy glass. 'We discussed his business affairs, as usual. He argued with me, as usual. I went over the accounts with him, well the ones for this place.' He gave a slight shrug. 'There was nothing to indicate that anything like this would happen. When I left him he was grumbling and said he needed to get on with his work.'

Paul Browning proffered the rapidly emptying brandy bottle and Colin accepted another top up.

'Did anyone else see Sir Norman this afternoon?' Kitty asked. 'After Mr Frobisher left his office?'

'We were in rehearsal until teatime, although I think a few people left the room at some point,' Selina said.

'Marie, you went to see Norman, didn't you? Colin came to join us, and you slipped out to ask him something about the tour,' Paul said, pouring himself a generous helping of brandy and almost finishing the bottle.

Marie looked confused. 'Oh yes, I did during tea, but I only popped my head around the door of the office. He was on the telephone. He said we were making a racket. I didn't wish to interrupt him, so I came back in here.'

'But he seemed all right then?' Alec asked.

'Oh yes, darling, of course. A bit cross about the noise but I assumed he was having trouble getting a connection on the phone.' Marie dabbed at the corners of her eyes once more. 'Forgive me, but I think I would like to go to my room now and have some time to myself. This has been the most awful shock.' She rose, swaying slightly as she did so.

Alec immediately placed his arm around her to support her. 'Do be careful, Marie. Please allow me to assist you upstairs.'

'You are such a dear boy.' Marie gave him a rather watery smile and they left the lounge.

'Well, what a ghastly turn of events.' Selina took a cigarette from her shagreen evening purse and inserted it into a small ebony holder. Colin immediately sprang forward to proffer her a light.

'It was awful, absolutely awful. I don't think I shall ever forget the sight of him when we opened that door.' Lambert did look as if he was still in shock.

'You went to his office too, this afternoon, didn't you?' Paul asked suddenly, looking at Lambert with slightly unfocused eyes.

Lambert frowned. 'Did I?' He paused as if trying to recollect where he had been just a few hours earlier. 'Oh yes, I did. Strange, I'd forgotten, probably because it was so unimportant. I think I was there just before Marie. I wanted to ask him about the payments for the theatres for Marie's tour. He said he was busy and said he'd talk to me after dinner. I thought he looked a little unwell, and he was in a bad mood from being interrupted.'

'So, it would seem that he had no intention of taking his own life at that point then,' Kitty said.

'No, I suppose not.' Lambert shifted uncomfortably.

Kitty could understand his unease at continuing the fiction that Sir Norman had shot himself.

Alec came back into the lounge. He was accompanied by Albert who still seemed to be pale with shock.

'Mrs Jenkins wishes to know if anyone would care for anything to eat or if she should close the kitchen.' Albert looked at the guests.

'Thank you, that's very thoughtful of her. Perhaps if she could provide some cheese and crackers before she finishes her duties. I doubt any of us has the stomach for anything more substantial,' Kitty suggested, looking at Lambert and Colin for approval.

'Yes, good idea. Thank you, Jenkins,' Colin agreed as Lambert and Selina nodded.

Albert disappeared back to the kitchen.

'Marie has gone to bed. She says she has some sleeping draughts the doctor gave her at Christmas when she was unwell. I advised her to take one and try to rest.' Alec took a seat back on the armchair. 'This is all terrible, just terrible.'

Selina blew out a thin, final plume of smoke before extinguishing her cigarette in one of the large Lalique glass ashtrays that were placed around the room. 'I cannot imagine how she must feel. She was so looking forward to taking her play on tour and making her debut as a playwright, and now *this*.'

'There will be so much to sort out. Will she even wish to continue?' Colin asked.

Lambert shrugged gloomily. 'The theatres are booked, but Norman had still to pay and finalise a few of the places. Bath, Oxford and Cheltenham, I think. We have insurance, of course, but I doubt if it will cover an event such as this.'

'Was Sir Norman funding Miss Monbiere's play?' Alice asked.

'Partly, my dear. Marie was obviously using her own money but, since she had plundered her savings to support him with this hotel, he had agreed to cover some extra stops on her tour,' Lambert explained. 'I don't think she could afford to do it all on her own.'

The chinking of crockery announced Albert's arrival pushing a modern chrome two-tiered trolley. Mrs Jenkins had sent a board with three kinds of cheese, butter, pickle, fruit and crackers.

'Thank you, Mr Jenkins,' Alice said as the man placed the food beside the largest of the coffee tables.

The servant returned to the kitchen. Kitty and Alice took up plates and began to help themselves to food. Kitty guessed that the others would soon follow suit. Sure enough, Alec and Selina followed their example, before the other men also rose to join them.

The tension which had been present in the room seemed to dissipate slightly with the arrival of the food.

'It's strange, it feels so late.' Selina glanced at the clock above the bar which read just after nine o'clock.

'I think as it's the storm that's not helped. It's not been light all day really and these lamps keep flickering,' Alice said as the light nearest to her blinked into darkness and flashed back on again.

'I hope the telephones will be back tomorrow,' Kitty said. She dearly longed to talk to Matt to get his views on what they should do next. Knowing they were cut off from the mainland with a murderer in the hotel was quite a frightening thought. She couldn't help hoping that when the police did come across that they would get Chief Inspector Greville rather than Inspector Lewis.

'Yes, I'm sure they will be able to advise us even if they aren't able to make the crossing,' Colin remarked. 'This wind doesn't sound as if it's likely to blow itself out in a hurry, I'm afraid.' He lifted his head to listen to the sound of the gale whistling around the hotel.

'Surely, we should have taken Sir Norman and laid him out in a spare room or something. It doesn't seem right to just leave him where he is. I mean won't he... well, you know, set or something?' Selina asked with a delicate shudder.

'If it were a straightforward suicide then I would agree with you,' Lambert said.

Kitty and Alice exchanged glances at Lambert's slip up.

Selina, Paul and Alec looked at him. 'What do you mean? He shot himself, didn't he?' Selina said.

'There's no note that we could see and there are a few, well, anomalies,' said Kitty. 'In any unexpected death it's best if the police see the scene before anything is touched or moved.' Kitty tried to avoid arousing the suspicions of the others that all was not as it seemed.

'Anomalies?' Paul pronounced the word carefully, a cracker crumb stuck to the corner of his mouth. 'What kind of "anomalies?"'

'Just a few things that seemed a bit strange. I'm sure the police will probably sort everything out when they get here,' Kitty said. 'Speaking of strange things, does anyone here know how many keys there would be to each room?'

The others turned puzzled faces towards her.

'Only, the door to the office was locked and we had to get in with the spare key from the reception desk. The other key wasn't in the lock on the other side of the door or on the desk,' Kitty said. It was one of the other things that had bothered her about the scene when they had found Sir Norman.

Surely if he had intended to shoot himself, he would have simply locked the door and left the key in the lock. Finding the door locked with the key missing suggested that someone else could have locked the door after the shooting using the spare key from the desk.

Alec shrugged. 'Norman probably dropped it in his pocket. I think Marie said there were a couple of spares for each room. I lost my key almost straight away when we arrived. I found it afterwards, of course. I'd left it on the piano, but Mr Jenkins had to let me in my room with the spare before I found the original one.'

'You're probably right,' Kitty agreed. 'No doubt that's where the police will find it.'

'It's a rum go about there being no note though,' said Alec.

'Norman was a bit of a one for always having lots to say. I would have expected him to have made dozens of notes all sealed in special envelopes addressed to all of us. He definitely would have left one for Marie I would have thought.'

'Who knows what was going through his mind to do such a terrible thing.' Paul slid his empty plate back onto the trolley. He fiddled with his jacket cuff as if it bothered him. 'Still, "What's done cannot be undone, to bed, to bed, to bed," as the bard says.' He rose unsteadily to his feet. 'I shall bid you all a goodnight.' He staggered off towards the stairs taking the almost empty brandy bottle with him.

'On that point I agree, we can do no more for now. Thank you for your assistance this evening, Mrs Bryant. Let us hope that a boat can reach us tomorrow,' Colin said, following Paul from the room.

CHAPTER SIX

By a mutual consensus, the rest of the party also decided to have an early night. Kitty and Alice were the last to go upstairs.

Kitty was unsurprised when Alice accompanied her inside her room rather than departing to her own quarters.

'I wish these blooming lights would stop playing up,' Alice remarked as Kitty turned on the lamp only for it to promptly go out for a few seconds before springing back to life. 'The storm sounds louder up here.' She shivered as she perched herself in one of the armchairs.

'I know. It could be the flat roof, or perhaps it's a sign that it's moving across us.' Kitty hoped that was the case.

'I don't know as I can shake that picture of Sir Norman from my mind,' said Alice. 'It was pretty horrible, him just lying there across the desk, and all that blood.' Alice's face crumpled and Kitty rushed to sit beside her, placing a comforting arm around her friend's slender shoulders.

'Oh, Alice, darling, I'm so sorry. You've been frightfully brave.' As she spoke the lamp went out once more and a loud crack of thunder sounded overhead. 'Would you rather stay in my room tonight, with me? There's plenty of space,' Kitty offered.

The truth be told, Kitty too was feeling uneasy, and she missed Matt. She could understand Alice's wish for companionship. The flickering lamps and the thought of Sir Norman lying dead in his study downstairs didn't help either.

'Are you sure? I wouldn't be no bother. I don't snore or anything.' Alice's face brightened in the gloom.

'Of course. Nip and fetch your things. I think we shall both feel braver together.' Kitty gave her friend a reassuring squeeze.

Alice hopped off the chair and hurried through the connecting door. Kitty went to her vanity case and took out the flashlight she had brought with her. Since several of her previous cases with Matt had involved creeping about in the dark, she had resolved she would be better prepared in future. Now with the lights playing up and no sign yet of the generator working at least she had some light she could rely on.

Alice came back carrying her things in a bundle. Kitty switched on her torch and Alice sighed with relief. 'Oh, that was good thinking. I shan't feel half as bad knowing as you've got that.'

'I packed it when we returned from Scotland in the new year. I thought if I just left it in my vanity case then I should always have it with me,' Kitty said as she wriggled her way out of her evening gown and into her nightdress.

Alice followed suit and before long both of them were tucked up in the very large and comfortable bed. The lamp had remained off and Kitty supposed that either the generator didn't power the lamps or that a bulb or fuse had blown.

'I don't know what you can put in the report to the hoteliers' association about all this,' Alice murmured sleepily from somewhere in the darkness.

'No, our reason for being here seems pretty redundant now. I wonder who will end up owning the hotel? I would have thought it would be Miss Monbiere since it seems much of her money has gone into financing it. I suppose it may not even open after this,' Kitty said.

'That would be a shame.' Alice yawned. 'I've been thinking about the note and the key. We never looked in the desk drawers, did we? I suppose there could have been something in there.'

'True, but I really don't think this was a suicide. The man had a damaged tendon in that hand so couldn't have held the gun steady to pull the trigger on that side. His grip on the gun was not right even if he *could* have managed it with that hand. He would have dropped the gun when the shot was fired, and it would have fallen in a different way. It wouldn't have been lying there beside him with his hand curled around it.' Kitty had been giving the matter some thought now the initial shock had begun to wear off.

She was becoming more certain than ever that Sir Norman had been murdered. And the killer had to be someone else within the hotel. The island itself only supported the lighthouse, three small cottages on the far side, and the hotel. She couldn't see anyone venturing out in such wild weather to kill Sir Norman, and no boat would have been able to land.

Kitty lay awake for a while, unable to sleep. Lightning lit up the room and Alice stirred uneasily beside her.

'I'd love a nice cup of hot milk to help me sleep. Do you think as we might be able to go to the kitchen to get one? I noticed as there was a little spirit stove in there when I was inspecting the cupboards,' Alice said.

'I don't suppose under the circumstances anyone would object. We wouldn't make a mess and we can explain to Mr and Mrs Jenkins tomorrow,' Kitty said.

They got back out of bed and tugged on their dressing gowns before slipping quietly out of Kitty's room and on down the stairs. The flashlight proved useful as they made their way through the hall and into the kitchen.

A small oil lamp was on the kitchen dresser and Alice found a match and lit it, while Kitty hunted for a small milk pan and some cups. The spirit stove soon had the milk heating well and Alice tipped the hot drink into their mugs before placing the pan to soak in the large white-stone sink.

They extinguished the lamp and the stove and prepared to make their way quietly back through the hotel. Kitty had her mug in one hand and the flashlight in the other when Alice placed a warning hand on her arm.

Kitty immediately switched off her torch and listened. Together with Alice she slowly crept forward, trying to identify what they had heard. At the office door behind the reception desk the shadowy figure of a man was stealthily trying the door. He rattled the handle futilely a couple of times before muttering an oath under his breath. He then stepped away and opened the drawer of the desk containing the spare keys to the rooms.

After rummaging through the contents of the drawer and apparently failing to find the key to the office, the man closed it and headed towards the stairs. Kitty and Alice automatically flattened themselves against the wall of the corridor as he came closer. A flash of lightning briefly illuminated the reception area and Kitty's heart bumped against her rib cage.

She breathed a sigh of relief as he passed without noticing them. They waited until they heard him reach the top of the stairs. A moment later a door further down the landing above them closed. Kitty's legs trembled from their close escape, and she took a few seconds to steady herself.

'That were a near thing,' Alice breathed as Kitty switched on her torch once more to light their way. 'Did you see who it was?'

'Paul Browning,' Kitty replied quietly as they climbed the stairs.

Once safely back inside their room with the door closed, Kitty sank down on the bed with Alice beside her.

'What was he up to then, prowling about and trying to get into the office?' Alice shuddered. 'Wild horses wouldn't drag me back in there. Not until Sir Norman has been took out, bless his soul.'

Kitty moved the skin that had formed on the top of her milk carefully to the side of the cup with the tip of her finger. 'He wasn't there when you gave me the key to the office. He only heard us mention it when I asked if there was another one when we were in the lounge.' She sipped her cooling milk.

'Perhaps as he thought the spare key had been put back in the drawer,' Alice suggested.

'Maybe, but why did he want it? What did he hope to find in that room?' Kitty asked.

'Perhaps as he has thought there might be something in the desk drawer, a note or something? Or perhaps as he has something in there that he wants?' Alice said before drinking her milk.

'Or he killed Sir Norman and there is something we overlooked that could incriminate him,' Kitty said.

'Well, whatever the reason, I am not agoin' back down them stairs tonight. We can work it out in the daylight and hopefully the police can come and take it on.' Alice set her now empty cup down on the bedside table and took off her dressing gown and slippers.

'Yes, you're right.' Kitty placed her own cup down and joined her friend back beneath the covers.

Much as she wanted to take another peek around that office, like Alice she would prefer to do it in daylight and preferably once Sir Norman had been removed.

* * *

Matt had slept poorly due to the storm. The rolling of the thunder overhead always reminded him of the roar of the guns on the battlefield during the war. Consequently, he had spent much of the night in his chair downstairs. Bertie had snored at his feet while he had played some of his classical records to drown out the storm.

He wondered how Kitty and Alice were faring on the island. He had attempted to telephone the hotel when he had returned home, but the line remained out of order. He tried again after breakfast but had no luck.

The sea, as he rode his motorcycle back to Torquay to continue the court case, was still rough. Huge waves during the night had deposited drifts of seaweed and sand on the road where they had crashed over the sea wall. The water was still choppy and there were no boats visible on the sea beyond the safety of the harbour wall.

Inspector Lewis was due to present his evidence today and he was already in the waiting area when Matt arrived. His sharp eyes and smart suit made Matt feel somewhat dishevelled as he took off his long leather coat.

'Rough old night last night, eh?' the inspector greeted him cheerfully as Matt entered the room.

'Yes, they were just beginning to clean up the seafront as I came through. The meadows in front of Torre Abbey are flooded.' Matt took a seat on one of the hard-wooden benches beside the inspector.

'How do you think the case is going?' Inspector Lewis asked, inclining his head in the direction of the courtroom.

'Chief Inspector Greville gave evidence yesterday and I presented mine. I was asked to return today in case they had further questions once you had been called.' Matt gave a small shrug. 'We shall just have to hope the jury sees through the defence's rather spurious arguments.'

He hoped it would end in a conviction. The case had been particularly complex and both he and the police had spent a great many man hours on it.

Inspector Lewis was called, and Matt was left on his own in the waiting room. He knew that Inspector Lewis's evidence was only minor and wouldn't be likely to take long. His role had been mostly to corroborate what Matt and the chief inspector had already told the court.

He took from his pocket the folded newspaper that he had picked up from the newsstand at the station and began to read. By the time he had finished the main stories and the sports pages Inspector Lewis had returned looking quite pleased with himself.

'They're not calling any witnesses for the defence. Just putting old chappie boy himself on the stand,' Inspector Lewis said.

'It shouldn't be too long before they send the jury out then,' Matt remarked, preparing to fold the paper so he could look at the crossword.

A woman rattled into the room pushing a battered wooden trolley containing a small metal urn and some thick white utilitarian crockery.

'Cup of tea, gents, while you'm waiting?' she asked.

They accepted her offer with the inspector offering to pay for the tea. Once she had served them, she clattered away again.

They had scarcely had time to drink their tea when Chief Inspector Greville arrived in the waiting room.

'Inspector Lewis, Captain Bryant, I'm glad you are both still here.'

'Sir?' Inspector Lewis had risen to his feet when his superior had entered the room.

Matt could see from the chief inspector's demeanour that something was very wrong.

'I have just taken a telephone call at the station from Mrs Bryant on Bird Island. It seems there has been an unexpected death.' Chief Inspector Greville looked at Matt. 'The telephone line was extremely poor, so it was difficult to make out what she was saying. It sounded though as if Sir Norman Whittier has been shot.'

Matt leaped to his feet. 'Is Kitty all right, sir? And Alice?'

'The line dropped before I could ask many questions, but she sounded her usual competent self,' the chief inspector assured him.

'Can we get across to this island? Where is it?' Inspector Lewis said, looking confused.

'It's that lump of rock you can see from the harbour on a clear day. It's not very far but the sea was still too wild when I rode in this morning,' Matt explained. Inspector Lewis had joined them from the Yorkshire police force when Chief Inspector Greville had been promoted. Kitty and Matt believed his colleagues there must have been glad to see him leave, however his recent arrival in Devon meant the inspector was still vague about the local landscape.

'From the report your good lady provided it sounds as if we need to get over there as soon as the sea is navigable. I hope you have good sea legs?' The chief inspector turned to Inspector Lewis, who looked slightly green at the question.

'The jury has been sent out here now, sir, so I believe a verdict should be in soon. Shall I go down to the harbour and see when we are likely to get a passage to the island?' Matt offered. The sooner he could get to Kitty and Alice the better. He didn't like the sound of an unexpected death.

'Thank you, that would be most helpful. I shall return to the police station and keep trying the line to see if I can get more information. Lewis, stay here and report back with the verdict.

Captain Bryant, I suggest you meet me at the station once you know about the boat and we can plan accordingly.'

* * *

Kitty had tried the telephone line on the reception desk constantly from the moment she had woken and gone downstairs. The storm had passed but the wind was still battering the hotel. From the windows, she could see that the sea was still rough with white caps on the waves as they crashed against the jetty.

When she had finally managed to get through to the police station the line had been poor and had scarcely held for long enough to report what had happened before she was cut off. Still, at least now the police were aware of Sir Norman's demise. She reported back to the others as they gathered for breakfast in the dining room.

Marie Monbiere had remained in her room and there was no sign of Paul Browning. Lambert and Colin were both concerned initially that it was Kitty and not one of the men who had contacted the police. When she had explained that the line had been poor and luckily she had known who to ask for, they were slightly mollified.

'It is very good of you, Mrs Bryant. Lambert and I did test the line when we came downstairs, but it was still dead at that point. We are very fortunate that you and Miss Miller are here. Even so, it's not really a pleasant task for a lady.' Colin sipped his tea and peered worriedly at her and Alice over the brim of his teacup.

'At least now the police have been informed. If the telephone line is reconnected again, they may be able to give us some advice or instructions, even if they can't get a boat over just yet,' Alice said, placidly continuing to apply a thick layer of butter to her toast.

'That's very true, Miss Miller,' Lambert agreed.

Selina, who arrived in the midst of this discussion, shuddered as she took her place at the table. 'I barely slept last night with the storm and thinking about poor Sir Norman. It's all so ghastly.'

Alec helped himself to bacon and eggs from the covered dishes before sliding into his seat beside her. 'Does anyone know how Marie is this morning?' he asked.

'I saw Mrs Jenkins taking a tray of tea to her room as I came downstairs,' Selina said, wrinkling her nose at Alec's loaded plate.

'That's good. One doesn't know quite what to do or say in these situations,' Colin said, appearing to be deep in thought as he stirred his tea.

'That's very true,' Lambert agreed. 'My cousin stepped in front of a train after he returned from the war. Shell shock they said. My aunt never recovered.'

Silence fell momentarily across the breakfast table.

'What will happen with Miss Monbiere's play?' Alice asked eventually. 'Do you think she will continue?'

'The theatres are booked, and Marie is such a trooper, but, of course, this is so terrible. The poor woman is quite distraught,' Lambert said, looking at Alec and Selina.

'I feel we owe it to Marie to at least continue rehearsing. Selina can read Marie's part as well as her own for now. It will take our minds off it all and keep us busy, if nothing else,' Alec said as he wiped the remaining yolk from his plate with the crust from his toast.

'You have a point. There is nothing we can do for Norman, but we can show our support for Marie,' Lambert agreed.

'Do what for Marie? What's going on?' Paul arrived at the breakfast table and slumped down heavily onto one of the chairs. 'Do tell me there is good strong tea left in that pot, dear girl.' He waved his hand in the vague direction of the chrome teapot while looking at Selina.

The actress sighed heavily and placed the tea strainer over his cup before pouring the remnants of the tea, inky and dark, into his cup. 'Bad head, have we?' she asked sweetly as she clumped the pot back down on the table.

Paul winced. 'Banging, darling, simply banging.' He added a splash of milk to his cup and stirred it carefully.

'Mrs Bryant has managed to contact the police. With luck they may be able to telephone us back once the line is working again. They may even manage to get across today if the sea dies down,' Colin said.

Paul's complexion paled slightly, and Kitty saw his hand tremble as he picked up his cup.

'The police, eh,' Paul muttered before taking his first sip of tea.

CHAPTER SEVEN

'The telephone connection to the hotel is still dead. I've asked for it to be looked at as a matter of urgency. Doctor Carter is on standby to accompany us as soon as the boat captain tells us he can make the crossing.' Chief Inspector Greville leaned back in his battered leather office chair and looked at Matt and Inspector Lewis.

'Thank you, sir.' Matt crossed his legs and narrowly avoided toppling a pile of manilla folders which had been unceremoniously dumped on the floor to provide a spare chair. The chief inspector's office was as usual piled high with paperwork and featured an overfull, battered metal ashtray.

'What do we know about the dead man? This Sir Norman Villiers?' Inspector Lewis gazed around at the chaos of his superior's office with barely concealed irritation.

'Sir Norman purchased the island some two years ago from Colonel Montpelier,' said Chief Inspector Greville, reading from his notebook. 'He immediately embarked on a project to demolish the house that was there originally and replace it with a new one, creating the Bird Hotel. He has several other businesses. These include a successful restaurant in London and one in Brighton, and he is known to be a patron of the arts. He often appears in the society papers with various stars of the stage and screen. He is engaged to Miss Marie Monbiere, the opera singer. She is considerably younger than Sir Norman.' He had clearly been doing his homework while Matt and Inspector Lewis had been busy elsewhere.

'May I ask what Mrs Bryant and Miss Miller were doing at the hotel?' Inspector Lewis asked.

'Kitty and Alice were inspecting the hotel as Sir Norman had applied to become a member of the Torbay Hoteliers' Association,' Matt explained. Inspector Lewis's tone had implied that Kitty had somehow managed to get herself involved in yet another possible murder on purpose.

'What exactly did Mrs Bryant have to say about this Sir Norman's death?' Inspector Lewis asked.

The chief inspector referred to his notebook. 'As far as I could make out over the crackling, she said, "Sir Norman has been shot and not by his own hand, but it's been made to look like suicide. We need advice and help." The line dropped then for a few seconds, but it sounded like she said they had left the scene intact and locked the door.'

'A suicide but not a suicide?' Matt frowned. He didn't like the thought of Kitty being trapped on a remote island with a murderer and one where a gun was lying about the place.

'Who else is at this hotel? Are any members of the public there?' Inspector Lewis asked.

Matt shook his head. 'Kitty said the official opening was a few weeks away at Easter. The boat captain who took them over understood that some friends of Sir Norman were testing everything out ahead of the big day. He had taken some of them over on previous occasions, I believe.'

'And you don't know exactly who these other people, these *friends* of Sir Norman's are?' Inspector Lewis asked tetchily.

'The captain said Miss Monbiere was in charge of the group

and he thought they were all thespians, something about a play,' Matt replied evenly, refusing to allow the inspector to rile him.

The black Bakelite telephone on the chief inspector's desk began to ring.

'Greville here. Yes, put him through,' the chief inspector answered, then listened intently to whoever was on the other end.

'Within the next two hours, we can make it across. Yes, thank you, we'll be there.' He replaced the receiver. 'That was the boat captain, he says that although it will be a bumpy crossing, we can go over within the next two hours if we get down there and catch the tide. I suggest you both pack bags for a stay.'

Matt checked his watch. That should have them landing on the island just after lunch. He hoped Kitty and Alice would be all right until then.

* * *

Paul Browning had taken some persuading by the others that they should occupy themselves with a rehearsal until the police could arrive. Colin Frobisher accompanied Kitty and Alice to the smaller lounge, where they took up the seats they had occupied the previous day. The others set themselves up once more in the adjoining room. Colin was not involved in the play's performance, he had come to the island on this occasion to see Sir Norman and the finished hotel.

'You were friends with Sir Norman, Mr Frobisher. Do you know if he had a will?' Kitty asked him once they were comfortably seated and the connecting door between the rooms had been closed.

'A will? Yes, of course. We spoke about it once, not too long ago. He had an old one and I urged him to get his financial affairs in order. He was, after all, some years older than Marie and I think he had been suffering from some health issues lately.

I assume he must have made some arrangements, especially since Marie had invested so heavily in this place,' Colin said.

'I realise this is a delicate question, but the police are bound to ask it, do you know what the terms of such a will would likely be?' Kitty continued. Since Colin had been Sir Norman's friend and seemed aware of his finances, she assumed he would probably know about any bequests.

'Not in any detail, but from the way he spoke the last time we talked about it, I think he intended to leave this place to Marie. At least his share of it. I assume she already has a thirty per cent stake, although financially her contribution has been much in excess of that. Norman was quite evasive when I pressed him on the matter though, and I don't think Marie took any legal advice, which concerned me. I think he also would have left his other properties to her and the restaurants. Not that the restaurants are worth much,' Colin said, pulling a face.

'Oh?' Kitty was surprised. She had often seen the establishments in the press, usually with photographs of various famous or titled people dining at them.

'He mortgaged them up to the hilt to raise the capital to buy this place. This was his dream, you see. Now look how it's ended up.' Colin gazed unhappily around the room.

'His finances were not in a good state?' Kitty asked.

Colin gave a dry, unamused laugh. 'Norman owed money all over the place, to me, to Marie, to the bank. I was very worried about it all. I knew he was keeping things from me but that was Norman for you. All I know is that everything was riding on this hotel being a success but his accounts for here were in a bad way.'

Alice looked at Kitty.

'Do you know the other members of the party here well, sir?' Alice asked.

Colin's shoulders moved upwards in a slight shrug. 'A little. Marie, obviously, I know well. Lambert, I have met several times before in company with Marie. A rather shifty sort of character, got a bit of a reputation in the theatres. Norman wasn't keen on him at all but tolerated him for Marie's sake.'

'Paul Browning seems to be a controversial figure. He consumed quite a lot of wine at lunch yesterday. Did he know Sir Norman well?' Kitty tried her best to be diplomatic when describing the older man's drinking habits.

'Paul is an alcoholic. Tragic really, as he's actually a very fine actor. The thing is, when he's drinking, he is often unpleasant and always unreliable. He's struggling to get jobs.' Colin confirmed Kitty's thoughts.

'And yet Lambert and Marie employed him for Marie's tour?' Alice raised her neatly arched eyebrows. 'I'm surprised as they would have took the risk.'

'His name still has a cachet with the public, and, of course, he is cheap. Norman wasn't too thrilled. He, as you have just suggested, Miss Miller, felt it to be a risky strategy. I know that Norman had warned him that if he made one slip up on this tour he would be out and he would see to it that he never worked in the theatre again.' Colin looked uncomfortable. 'I think he had Paul sign a contract to that effect. Lambert told me about it. I think he found it amusing in some way.'

'Golly, that seems rather harsh,' Alice said.

'This tour is a big step for Marie. She wishes to be known as more than just an opera singer. She feels she has the talent to do well as a playwright and an actress too. You must understand that financially she is on something of a knife edge. She invested virtually all her savings in this place and her standing in the operatic world is very much the second string. She hasn't quite the power or purity of note to be truly world class. Not only that but she is well past the first flush of youth.' He gave a delicate cough. 'To recoup her money and to secure her financial future she needs the tour of her play to succeed,' Colin explained.

Colin's revelations certainly seemed to indicate to Kitty that several members of the house party could have a motive for wishing Sir Norman dead. That would appear to include Colin himself, since she and Alice had heard them arguing. Also, Colin had revealed now that he was owed money by Sir Norman.

Albert entered the room bearing a tray of coffee. 'Morning refreshments. Luncheon will be served at one o'clock.' He placed the heavy tray down on the table in front of them.

'I hope Mrs Jenkins was not upset to discover the milk pan in the sink this morning. I did put it to soak, only we couldn't sleep last night, not after, well...' Alice petered out.

'Not at all, miss. Quite understandable under the circumstances,' Albert assured her.

'By the bye, did Sir Norman take tea yesterday afternoon?' Kitty asked as the servant turned to leave.

'Yes, madam. I took it to him just before I served everyone else and collected the tray about twenty minutes later,' Albert said.

'And how did he appear to you when you saw him?' Kitty asked.

Albert's face went curiously blank. 'I can't say that I took much notice, madam. He was busy at his desk as usual. He complained that the telephone line was unreliable because of the storm.'

'Thank you,' Colin said.

'Will that be all, sir, madam?' Albert asked.

'Yes, thank you. I presume that you and Mrs Jenkins will continue here with Miss Monbiere until matters are settled with Sir Norman's affairs?' Kitty asked the question casually. From her experiences employing staff, something as momentous as their employer's death would cause a great deal of unease.

'Indeed, madam. Miss Monbiere has assured my wife that we shall be provided for.' Albert gave a stiff little bow and left the room.

'Of course, one tends to forget how the staff might be affected,' Colin murmured as Alice picked up the chrome-plated cafetière to pour their drinks.

Kitty saw her friend give him a sharp glance and suspected he had just come close to having the coffee poured in his lap, rather than in his cup.

'Alec seems a pleasant young man. Is he the romantic male lead in the play?' Kitty asked once they were all settled back again with their drinks.

'Yes, a very affable fellow. American, from New York, I think, originally. He is devoted to Marie, follows her around like a love-sick puppy. He is closer to her in age I suppose than Norman was.' Colin paused to sip his drink. 'Marie adored Norman though. She lost her father when she was very young, and I suspect there was a bit of hero worship going on in their romance.'

'I thought as Alec was friendly with Miss Selina Headingly,' Alice said.

'What? Oh, not especially. I mean in the play they are the star-crossed lovers while Marie plays a kind of good fairy to get them back together. In real life I don't think they have any special connection beyond they are of a similar age. Alec is besotted with Marie and Selina tends to keep herself to herself.' Colin helped himself to one of the small home-made biscuits that had accompanied their mid-morning refreshments.

'Did Sir Norman know Alec and Selina well?' Kitty asked when Colin had swallowed his last bit of biscuit.

'I think he found Alec's admiration for Marie amusing on the occasions they had met. I believe he knew Selina rather better, but I don't know quite what their connection was. I gathered it was a little awkward as he often seemed uncomfortable around her.' Colin placed his empty cup and saucer back on the tray and brushed the biscuit crumbs from his tweed jacket.

Alice had finished her own cup of coffee and wandered over

to the windows to look at the view. Now that the mists from yesterday had cleared Kitty saw that the hotel had a glorious uninterrupted view of the gardens down to the sea.

The sea still appeared choppy, with white horses breaking onto the rocks on the far side of the shore. The few trees that stood in the grounds were bent out of shape and leaning from the effects of the stiff breeze which continued to blow in from the sea. In the distance she could make out the Devon coast with the white villas of Torquay and Paignton.

'The sea has calmed down a bit now. I wonder if they'll be able to get a boat over soon,' Alice said, peering out through the window.

Kitty set down her cup and went to join her. 'Maybe. The man that brought us across yesterday was very experienced and his boat looked as if it could deal with rough seas.'

'We should try the telephone again. It may be back up again by now,' Colin suggested.

They followed him out to the reception area. The telephone Kitty had used earlier that day was situated on the desk. The only other one Kitty had seen was the one in Sir Norman's office and she had no intention of entering that room again in a hurry. At least not until its former occupant had been removed.

Colin picked up the handset and listened. 'No dial tone, just silence.' He dialled a number experimentally with the tip of his finger and listened again. 'Nothing.' He replaced the handset down in disgust. 'One would have hoped they might have repaired it properly by now.'

'I think it must have been a fluke that I got through to Chief Inspector Greville this morning,' Kitty said.

'Well, I suppose I had better go and do some work. I have several letters I need to write, although I suspect it may be a day or so before we are in any position to post or receive mail. I'll drop by Marie's room too and see how she is.' Colin set off up the stairs.

'He sung like a canary, didn't he?' Alice said as soon as he was out of earshot. 'Blimey, what a lot. Most of them might have had a reason to murder Sir Norman if we go by what he said.'

'I agree.' Kitty glanced at the closed door of the main lounge. 'It's not going to make the task of catching his killer very easy.'

'We could try and work out who saw him last,' Alice suggested. 'I wish our Dolly was here. She's good at things like this. You know how she loves a puzzle.'

Kitty pulled a sheet of paper from the notepad beside the telephone and picked up a pencil. 'You're right, Alice. That's a good idea. We heard Colin arguing with Sir Norman when we came out of the kitchen, so that would be at what time?'

'About half past two I reckon.' Alice leaned her arms on the countertop as Kitty made a quick note.

'Then Marie went in to see him?' Kitty asked.

'No, it must have been Albert taking the tea, then Lambert, and then Albert again to collect the tray,' Alice said. 'And then Marie.'

'So, we are to assume that he was alive and well at that point. No one mentioned hearing the shot, did they?' Kitty frowned and tapped the end of the pencil against the top of the desk.

'If we was all upstairs with the storm going on, then there wouldn't be anybody down here. I doubt as it would carry through the thick doors with the wind howling about like a banshee. We wouldn't have heard Mr Frobisher arguing with him if the door hadn't been a bit ajar,' Alice said.

'True, or he could have been killed while the piano was playing and there was the noise of the rehearsal if someone slipped out for some reason. It was a fearful racket with the music and the storm,' Kitty said. 'But then it must have been after the others had all been to see him and before the end of the rehearsal.'

'So, it could be either case then? After we all went to change or during that noisy part of them rehearsing.' Alice's forehead puckered into a frown. 'If I was a killer, I should wait till they all went upstairs. Much less chance of being heard, and no one else has said as they went to see him while the music was playing.'

'That would give a window of between about five thirty and six thirty. Dinner was due to be served at seven fifteen and people had started to gather for drinks from around six thirty. Albert would have seen anyone going in or out of Sir Norman's office while he was preparing the bar if he was killed after that time.' Kitty scribbled furiously on the sheet of paper as she spoke, anxious to capture her thoughts.

'It seems to me the best time would have been right after we all went up to dress, if whoever done it came straight back down again. That's what they would do in a film,' Alice said firmly.

'That would make sense, then if by any chance they got anything on their clothes, they were changing anyway. Bravo, Alice.' Kitty beamed at her friend.

Alice turned a pretty shade of pink. 'Perhaps our Dolly is a rubbing off on me.'

The telephone on the desk suddenly rang out startling them both. Kitty grabbed the handset hoping the connection would hold.

'Hello, Bird Hotel, Kitty Bryant speaking.'

'Mrs Bryant, Chief Inspector Greville. We are going to attempt to reach you shortly. We are waiting on the tide but should be there sometime this afternoon if the sea is not too rough.' The line was remarkably clear.

'Wonderful, thank you, sir.' Kitty could have cried with relief knowing that help was on the way.

'Your husband is with me and wishes to speak to you.' There was a rustling noise at the other end of the line before Matt's voice sounded in her ear.

'Kitty, darling, are you and Alice both bearing up all right?'

'Yes, we're both fine. Are you coming over with the police?' Kitty asked as the line began to crackle once again.

'Wild horses wouldn't keep me away. Hold tight, old thing, and I'll see you soon.' The line went dead before she had chance to reply.

'The wretched line has gone again. The police are going to attempt to get here this afternoon.' Kitty replaced the handset.

'Is Captain Bryant coming with them?' Alice asked.

'Yes.' Kitty hugged her friend. 'Oh, I shall be so glad to see him.'

'A bit of news to tell the others.' Alice nodded towards the closed lounge door.

'It'll be interesting,' said Kitty, folding up her notes and placing them inside the pocket of her dark-blue serge frock, 'to see their reactions.'

CHAPTER EIGHT

Inspector Lewis was perched miserably on a wooden bench in the centre of the upper deck of the boat. A large black rubber bucket that smelt of fish had been placed between his knees. The pitching and tossing of their boat had increased since they had left the relative calm of the harbour and the inspector had looked progressively unwell since then.

Matt, Doctor Carter and Chief Inspector Greville were seated near the wheelhouse. The chief inspector was calmly munching on a large pork pie which he had produced from the depth of his overcoat pocket.

'We should be there in about twenty minutes,' the captain called down to them from the wheelhouse.

Inspector Lewis groaned and tightened his grip on the bucket.

'Kitty and Alice will be glad to see us. I wonder what exactly has gone on there?' Matt stretched his legs out in front of him as the distant mound of Bird Island drew nearer. Kitty had sounded perfectly composed when he had spoken to her which had reassured him somewhat.

'I expect Mrs Bryant and Miss Miller will have been on the

case. No doubt they will have already started asking questions.' The chief inspector folded up the sheet of waxed paper that had contained his pork pie and returned it to his coat pocket.

Matt grinned. 'Oh, I have no doubt that Kitty will have been busy poking about looking for evidence.'

Chief Inspector Greville smiled. 'I'm sure she will have lots of useful information ready for our arrival.'

'I say, Lewis, old chap, are you doing all right?' Doctor Carter called out affably to the inspector.

Inspector Lewis raised his head slightly to cast a baleful look at the doctor before another wave had him returning his head to the depth of the bucket.

'Poor chap, no sea legs,' the doctor remarked.

* * *

The group had received the news that the police were arriving during the afternoon with muted relief. Alec immediately volunteered to inform Marie of the news, sprinting off upstairs as soon as Kitty had finished speaking.

They had just sat down to lunch when Marie entered the dining room. Dressed in black, her face pale and devoid of make-up except for the vivid crimson of her lipstick, she appeared every inch the grief-stricken fiancée.

Alec leapt up to pull out a chair for her, fussing about until she dismissed him with a wave of her hand.

'I felt it my duty to come downstairs. I have no doubt that the police will wish to ask many questions about my poor, dear Norman.' Marie accepted a glass of water and Albert began to serve the soup.

An outbreak of concerned, solicitous murmurs broke out.

'It is very brave of you, Marie, my dear. We shall stand by to ensure that they do not bully you,' Lambert said before dipping his spoon into his dish.

'Chief Inspector Greville is very unlikely to bully anyone,' Kitty said. 'He is a very good policeman. I'm sure he will soon have everything resolved.' She wondered how many encounters Lambert might have had with the police to think that they were likely to bully a recently bereaved woman.

'Forgive me, Mrs Bryant. I had forgotten that you were acquainted with the officers concerned,' Lambert said.

Kitty enjoyed her pea soup and kept a sharp eye on the others around the table. Marie merely toyed with her spoon, while Selina, Alec, Lambert and Colin cleaned their bowls. Paul, however, seemed distracted and on edge.

The dishes were cleared, and the main course of shepherd's pie was placed before them.

'We decided to continue with rehearsals this morning. You know, to keep busy,' Alec said to Marie as she prodded her lunch listlessly with her fork.

'That's good. Thank you,' Marie responded with a wan smile.

'I presume we will be continuing with the tour then?' Paul asked.

Marie looked startled by the abruptness of his question and a chorus of reproofs broke out around the table.

'What? I'm only asking what you are all thinking,' Paul muttered.

Marie swallowed. 'My intentions at the moment are to try and continue. I feel that I owe it to you and to all the theatre patrons who have already purchased tickets. This is show business after all, and carry on is what one does.' She smiled bravely as she concluded her speech.

Lambert broke into applause. 'And we shall support you all the way, won't we, my loves?'

The others all nodded and murmured their assent. Kitty caught Alice rolling her eyes and nudged her with her foot under the table.

Luncheon was concluded with a dessert of tinned peaches in evaporated milk. Colin ate his own share and took Marie's when she waved them away.

They had just finished when Albert emerged once more from the kitchen and coughed discreetly next to Marie's chair. 'Begging your pardon, miss, but I believe there is a boat tying up at the jetty.'

His words caused an exodus from the table as everyone went through to the main lounge to see for themselves through the large picture windows.

'There are four of them,' Selina said.

Kitty squeezed in on the end, unable to see over Colin or Lambert who were hogging the prime places. She peered around them.

'My husband, Inspector Lewis, Chief Inspector Greville and Doctor Carter,' she said.

'The shorter one in the dark-grey overcoat looks as green as his hat,' Selina observed. 'He must have suffered on the crossing.'

'Inspector Lewis does look a bit peaky,' Alice agreed as the four men drew closer to the hotel.

Marie had requested that a tray of coffee be brought to the lounge ready for the arrival of the police. Albert had just delivered it when the hotel door opened, and the new arrivals entered the reception area.

Kitty sprang to her feet and hurried to her husband as soon as he entered the lobby. He greeted her with a tender hug and a kiss. 'Steady on, old girl. Are you all right?' he murmured.

'All the better now that you are here,' Kitty whispered back. She shook hands with the policemen and received a kiss on the cheek from her old friend Doctor Carter as the rest of the party started their introductions.

Once the introductions were complete and Albert had taken the new arrivals' coats, Kitty produced the key to the office from her pocket. She had collected it from her room in readiness before lunch. The guests all took their seats in the lounge as Alice started to serve the coffee.

'Perhaps if you could all remain in this room while we take a look at the scene?' Chief Inspector Greville's tone made it clear that this was more of a command than a suggestion.

Marie dabbed at her eyes with a handkerchief. 'Of course, Chief Inspector.'

Matt took the key from Kitty, and the lounge door was firmly closed.

Selina switched on the wireless appearing pleased to discover it working once more. 'A little music, perhaps,' she suggested, leaving it on low in the background.

Kitty appreciated the girl's thoughtfulness. She could see that otherwise everyone would be straining a sinew to hear what was going on in the room across the hallway.

Colin continued to stand by the window staring out at the sea as Paul paced to and fro beside the piano. Alec sat near Marie while Selina had chosen to sit beside Alice. Lambert lit a cigarette and seemed unconcerned as they all waited for the police to return.

It felt like an age before the door opened and Matt slipped inside the room. His expression was grim as he closed the door behind him.

'The police will be a few more minutes while the doctor attends to Sir Norman,' he explained as Kitty moved along the sofa to make room for her husband to sit beside her.

'What's happening to Norman?' Marie asked in a faint, querulous voice.

'The doctor is examining him, and he will then make arrangements for the captain to transport the body back to the mainland,' Matt said.

'My poor, poor love.' Marie burst into a fresh bout of tears, prompting Alec to offer her the use of a large, clean white cotton handkerchief from his jacket pocket.

The door opened again some minutes later and Chief Inspector Greville entered. Selina jumped up and switched off the wireless before retaking her seat.

'My apologies, ladies and gentlemen, for taking so long, but I'm sure you will agree that your friend, Sir Norman, deserves his demise to be treated in the correct manner.'

Colin had turned to face the chief inspector and Paul took a seat on the edge of the piano stool.

'My thanks to Mrs Bryant for realising that something was amiss with Sir Norman's death and for acting so promptly to seal the scene.' Chief Inspector Greville inclined his head toward Kitty before continuing. 'To all intents and purposes, at first glance it appeared that Sir Norman had taken his own life.'

There was an uneasy stir amongst the listeners.

'I don't understand.' Marie's hand was clenched tightly around the handkerchief.

'I regret to inform you, Miss Monbiere, that I am in no doubt that Sir Norman was in fact murdered, and the murderer has attempted to make his death appear like a suicide.' Chief Inspector Greville's tone was kindly but firm.

Alec and Selina gasped as Paul seemed to slump down on the piano stool. Lambert and Colin exchanged a glance, forewarned by Kitty's suspicions the previous day.

'No, that's impossible,' said Marie. 'Norman shot himself. We all saw him, and the gun was in his hand.' She raised a tear-stained, bewildered face to the chief inspector.

'Sir Norman had an old injury to that hand which meant he could not have pulled the trigger himself. He would have had to use his other hand and the gun would have fallen on the opposite side of the desk,' Chief Inspector Greville explained.

'That's true, think about it, Marie, darling,' said Colin. 'He injured his hand in the war. He was firefighting and he severed the tendon, so he retrained himself to use his left hand for most things. You know that.'

'But why? Who? I don't understand.' Marie's face was as white as her handkerchief.

'We shall, of course, check the gun for fingerprints. I assume that the gun belonged to Sir Norman?' the chief inspector asked.

Colin nodded. 'Yes, he kept it in his desk drawer. He'd had it for years although I never knew it was loaded.'

'Thank you, sir.'

Matt gave Kitty's hand a gentle squeeze.

'I shall need to talk to all of you about your whereabouts yesterday and discover who was the last person to see Sir Norman alive. I've been told that there is another lounge through there.' The policeman indicated the door to the smaller lounge. 'Mrs Bryant, Miss Miller, perhaps if you would accompany me. You too, of course, Captain Bryant.'

Kitty, Alice and Matt rose and followed the chief inspector into the smaller of the lounges, closing the door behind them.

'You did very well, Mrs Bryant. If they had moved Sir Norman it would probably have been accepted as a suicide. At least at first, by which time the evidence might have been lost.' Chief Inspector Greville took out his notebook and sat down. 'Now, I'm sure that you and Miss Miller have gathered quite a lot of information already?' He looked expectantly at Kitty and Alice.

Kitty passed him the slip of paper on which she had made the notes before lunch and, aided by Alice, they told Matt and the chief inspector everything they had discovered so far.

'Hmm, they all sound a slippery bunch if you ask me.' The chief inspector finished making his notes and tucked his notebook back in his pocket as Inspector Lewis came to join them.

Kitty was pleased to see the man looked a little better than when he had first arrived on the island.

'The doctor has finished, and he and the boat captain have wrapped Sir Norman in tarpaulin ready to transport him back to the mainland. He says shall he go with him, or do you want him to hang on here for a bit?' Inspector Lewis asked.

'He may as well go back. He can take the things we have put for testing with him, and he will need to write his report for the inquest,' the chief inspector said.

'Very good, sir. Oh, and Mr Jenkins has asked if he can clean the office up now.'

Chief Inspector Greville gave his consent and the inspector departed to relay the instructions.

'By the way, sir, we need to tell you about that Mr Browning as well.' Alice looked at Kitty.

'Oh yes,' Kitty agreed.

Alice reported what she and Kitty had seen when they had ventured to the kitchen on the night of the murder.

'He tried to get into the office, you say?' Chief Inspector Greville looked thoughtful. 'Hmm, I wonder if it has any connection to this?' He delved into his jacket pocket and took out a small silver cufflink set with an onyx stone. 'We found this on the floor near the desk.'

'Interesting,' Matt observed.

'One of the gentlemen must have misplaced it.' The chief inspector returned it to his pocket. 'Thank you, Miss Miller.'

Alice flushed with pleasure at the chief inspector's approbation.

'Now, if you and Mrs Bryant would return to the rest of the party and just remain alert to anything that may be of interest to the investigation, I should be much obliged. Captain Bryant, perhaps you could remain present while I interview the guests? I am without a constable and it would be helpful to have an extra pair of hands so to speak,' Chief Inspector Greville asked. 'Oh, and Mrs Bryant, could you ask Miss Monbiere to come through?'

Kitty and Alice rose and re-entered the large lounge. Any talking ceased as they walked in.

'Miss Monbiere, the chief inspector has requested to speak to you first,' Kitty said as she perched on one of the armchairs.

'Yes, oh yes, of course.' The singer pressed her handkerchief to her lips and hurried through into the other room, closing the door behind her.

'Poor Marie. She really is being terribly brave,' Alec said.

'A real trooper,' Lambert agreed.

* * *

Matt watched with interest as the opera singer took her seat opposite the chief inspector. He could see that she was considerably younger than her deceased fiancé, probably in her late thirties. Her eyes were red rimmed, and she appeared pale but composed.

'My deepest condolences on your loss, Miss Monbiere. I appreciate that the news that Sir Norman was murdered must have increased your distress,' Chief Inspector Greville said.

The woman bowed her head and dabbed at her eyes with her handkerchief. 'In some ways, yes, but I couldn't understand why Norman would take his own life. Shocking though this is, it makes more sense to me.' She lifted her chin to meet the policeman's gaze. 'We were very happy, you see. We had just finished this hotel and it was ready to open, something which was Norman's dream. My play is about to go on tour. It made no sense for Norman to kill himself.'

'I understand that Sir Norman had some financial pressures?' The chief inspector phrased the question delicately.

Marie shrugged. 'He was a businessman. All businessmen go through such times and Norman was unafraid to take risks. To make this place how we had both dreamed it could be did not come cheaply. I have invested a great deal of my own money too. Once the hotel opens and my play starts to tour then the financial issues will soon be resolved.'

'Had you been engaged to Sir Norman long?' the chief inspector asked.

'Three years. We intended to marry this summer.' Marie dabbed at her eyes once more. 'The church is booked. Saint Joseph's in London. We wanted to finish the hotel first.'

Matt knew the church she meant. It was a large catholic church where he had once attended the marriage of a former fellow officer some years ago. Before he had met Kitty. Three years seemed like quite a long engagement, and he wondered why they had not tied the knot sooner. The excuse about finishing the hotel sounded flimsy and he wondered which one of them had been dragging their feet.

'Did Sir Norman know the rest of the hotel guests well?' Chief Inspector Greville asked.

'Colin was an old friend and they had conducted business together too for a long time. Lambert, he met through me originally and they were acquainted but not friends, if you know what I mean. He didn't care for Lambert because he has something of a slightly unsavoury reputation in the theatre,' Marie said.

'That's the chap who is the theatrical agent?' Chief Inspector Greville scribbled in his notebook.

Marie nodded. 'Yes, he has a great deal of sway in theatrical circles as he is very good at his job. You know, finding the right actor or actress for a role.'

'And Mr Browning?' the chief inspector asked.

'He knew of Paul and his drinking. He was concerned that he might prove a liability. I know he spoke quite sternly to him a week or so ago about ensuring that he didn't let us down.' Marie sniffed and wiped her eyes once more.

Chief Inspector Greville nodded. 'And the other two? Alec

Standish and Selina Headingly? Did Sir Norman know them at all?'

'Alec is a dear. Norman called him my pet as the darling boy is always so very solicitous to me. I don't know about Selina, again he met her through me. I had the impression that they had known one another before but how I'm not quite sure. He wouldn't tell me when I asked him. Norman didn't speak to her much and I sometimes felt as if he would rather someone else had been cast in her role.' Marie frowned as she spoke.

'You don't believe they had been involved with one another in the past?' Again the chief inspector seemed to pick his words carefully.

Marie shook her head clearly catching the inference in his question. 'Oh no, nothing like that, I'm sure. A woman knows those kinds of things. No, it was something else, but he never told me what it was.' Her voice cracked as she answered.

'Hmm, and when did you last see your fiancé?' Chief Inspector Greville asked.

Marie dabbed at her eyes once more. 'Yesterday afternoon during the rehearsal. He was so annoyed at being disturbed.'

'And you didn't hear a shot, or any kind of bang at all during the latter part of the afternoon or early evening?'

'No, Chief Inspector. The storm was loud and the doors in the hotel muffle sound very effectively,' Marie explained. 'There was nothing.'

CHAPTER NINE

The chief inspector dismissed Miss Monbiere back to the other lounge with more expressions of sympathy for her loss.

'That was interesting. I wonder how Miss Headingly might have known Sir Norman?' Matt mused. He wondered if Marie might have been jealous of the younger woman.

Inspector Lewis opened the other door to the lounge and came in. 'Doctor Carter has gone off on the boat with Sir Norman all wrapped up like a Christmas parcel. Not the most dignified way to get back to the mainland.'

'No, but given the weather and the situation, there is very little choice in the matter.' Chief Inspector Greville frowned at his junior officer. 'Perhaps you would be so good as to go and ask Mr Colin Frobisher to come and join us.'

Inspector Lewis who had just seated himself down on one of the armchairs rose reluctantly and went off into the other room. He returned a moment later accompanied by the tall, distinguished figure of Colin Frobisher.

Colin shook hands with the chief inspector and with Matt, before seating himself on the chair recently vacated by Miss Monbiere.

'Mr Frobisher, I understand that you were in business with Sir Norman? Is that correct?' Chief Inspector Greville asked once the man was settled in his seat.

'Not exactly, sir, no. We were friends and I gave him financial advice from time to time. We had a small portfolio of businesses where I had loaned him some money. This includes this hotel and his restaurants. He would consult me on various business matters, I would give him advice which he would then promptly ignore.' Colin sighed and crossed his legs.

'You knew of his financial problems, I believe?' Chief Inspector Greville continued.

Colin gave a short, mirthless laugh. 'Oh yes. We argued on the afternoon of his death. I had warned him and warned him that he was overstretching. His creditors were pressing for payment, and he stood to lose his own money, some of my money and most of Miss Monbiere's savings.'

'Since you say that you argued, I take it he wasn't happy that you were bringing this to his attention?' Chief Inspector Greville continued to make notes.

'No, he hated to admit he was in the wrong. He kept insisting that his fortunes were about to change. That the hotel would be such a success that he could start to pay off some of his creditors. Typical Norman.'

'You didn't think that this would be the case, Mr Frobisher? What kind of sums are we talking about here?' Chief Inspector Greville's pen was poised above his notebook.

'For myself, the sum was around five thousand pounds. Miss Monbiere is owed around twelve thousand pounds, perhaps more.'

Inspector Lewis gave a low whistle. 'That's a pretty penny, sir.'

The chief inspector glared at Inspector Lewis. 'Not the kinds of sums one would wish to lose. Did Miss Monbiere share her fiancé's optimism that her money would be safe?'

Colin's face was grave. 'I don't believe that Marie was fully aware of the extent of Norman's financial issues. I had asked her to seek legal advice to protect herself when she started loaning Norman money. She refused, saying she trusted his judgement. She believed that he owned the restaurants. I told him to tell her that he had re-mortgaged them, but he insisted I say nothing. I told him he had to come clean with her soon or I would tell her myself.'

'And this was the afternoon he was killed?' Matt asked.

'Yes. We argued about it for some time.' Colin shook his head. 'Marie will be devastated when she learns that the money is gone. Of course, I suppose she will have this place, the hotel, I mean, and the island.'

'Sir Norman had no life insurance that you know of?' Chief Inspector Greville asked.

'I don't know if he did. One would hope so, but Norman would often say he had done things, then would forget or put them off. Marie thinks he had insurance.' Colin sighed. 'For myself, I can stand the loss, but for Marie, it will be most of her money gone.'

'Miss Monbiere said the wedding was booked for this summer. The engagement seems to have been a long one.' The chief inspector changed tack.

Colin shrugged. It was clear he hadn't given the length of the engagement much thought. 'Norman didn't mention a wedding date to me. I rather think the length of the engagement suited him. He had quite a romantic history, I believe, until he met Marie. It was Marie that was pushing for a wedding, she hoped to start a family.'

'When did you last see Sir Norman?'

'Yesterday afternoon when we quarrelled. I closed the door and went to join the others. The next time I laid eyes on him he was dead.' Colin's expression sobered at the memory.

'And you didn't hear an unexplained bang or shot at all

during the latter part of the afternoon or before dinner?' Chief Inspector Greville asked.

'No, nothing at all. I've been trying to recall if there was anything but I'm afraid there wasn't. The storm was very loud.'

'I see, sir. Thank you.' The chief inspector dismissed Colin and took a moment to study the notes he had made, comparing them to the information Kitty and Alice had supplied.

'Do you believe him, sir? About the money, I mean? Obviously he was owed less than Miss Monbiere but it was still a tidy sum,' Inspector Lewis said.

'It's certainly interesting. Once we are back at the station, or when the telephone is working again, you can follow up with the banks. Also, we'll need to verify if Sir Norman's life insurance had lapsed and what assets, if any, he had left. Oh, and check in his office for any sign of a will. Ask Miss Monbiere if she knows if there was one and if so where it might be. One more thing too, go and check the gentlemen's rooms for the pair to that cufflink we found,' Chief Inspector Greville instructed Inspector Lewis.

The inspector scurried off.

'Would you like me to fetch one of the others in, sir?' Matt asked. He wondered if Kitty and Alice had found out anything more while they were in the other room.

'I think perhaps Mr Lambert Pike next. I'd like to leave Mr Browning till last. Just to loosen him up a little,' Chief Inspector Greville said.

'Very good, sir.' Matt opened the joining door and looked around for Lambert. He spotted him beside Selina on one of the sofas.

'Mr Pike, the chief inspector would like to see you now.' Matt caught Kitty's gaze and flashed her a brief smile, before closing the door after Lambert had walked through.

'Mr Pike, please take a seat. I believe you are a theatrical agent?' The chief inspector waved away Lambert's offer of a cigarette.

Matt also declined and sat down as Lambert lit up and took a pull from his cigarette before replying to the question.

'That's correct. I'm working with Marie on this new venture of hers.' He blew out a stream of thin blue smoke.

'Have you known Miss Monbiere for long?' the chief inspector asked.

'Quite a few years now, before she even met Norman. She mentioned that she wished to branch out from the opera world, and she'd written this play. It has a few musical interludes but is more straight drama. It sounded interesting and I said I'd help her to cast it and so on.'

'I see. Did you know Sir Norman well too?' Chief Inspector Greville asked.

'Only through Marie really. He didn't seem to care for me much, truth be told. Still, he knew that I would do a good job for her.' Lambert took another pull from his cigarette.

'You had no quarrels or arguments with him at all?' Chief Inspector Greville fixed Lambert with a steady gaze.

Lambert shifted uncomfortably in his chair. 'Here, who's been saying I argued with him?' he demanded.

'When did you and Sir Norman argue?'

Matt was impressed by the chief inspector's skill at persuading the theatrical agent to admit to a quarrel.

'The afternoon he died. When Colin came out from seeing Norman, I stepped into the office. It was a big mistake. He was in a foul mood. Red-faced and cross as two sticks. He snapped at me and asked what I wanted as he was busy.'

'And what did you want, Mr Pike?' Chief Inspector Greville asked.

'There had been a couple of issues with three of the theatres booked on the tour. Norman was supposed to have paid the fees to confirm the bookings. The theatres said they hadn't received the money and were going to withdraw if it wasn't received by next week. I wanted to ask him to sort it out.' Lambert flicked the ash from the tip of his cigarette into one of the large Lalique ashtrays.

'What was Sir Norman's response to this request?' The chief inspector's pen hovered over his notebook as he waited for the reply.

'Basically, as I said, he snapped at me. Told me to mind my own business and that he had it in hand. He said they would get the fees and to stop bothering him with trivia.' Lambert finished his cigarette.

Chief Inspector Greville surveyed Lambert with a steady gaze. 'You said that Sir Norman didn't seem to like you. Do you know why?'

Lambert shifted uneasily. 'In the theatre, Chief Inspector, as an agent one can make some people very happy and many others unhappy. The unhappy one's will make no secret of their unhappiness and rumours start to swirl around like some kind of nebulous mist. I think that perhaps Norman had been paying too much attention to these rumours.'

'And what exactly do these rumours consist of, Mr Pike?' Chief Inspector Greville continued to press.

'That I extract sexual favours from actresses in return for casting them in certain productions.' A hint of plum tinged Lambert's cheeks at this admission. 'Nonsense, of course.'

'I see, sir, thank you for your frankness. Is this the case in Miss Monbiere's production? Do you have any *connection* with Mr Alec Standish or Miss Selina Headingly?' the chief inspector asked.

'No, nothing,' he snapped. 'The same is true of Marie. I have already told you, my relationships with all of them are purely professional. I saw Alec in a play in London and Selina in a production in Bath. I thought they would be perfect for

Marie's play. Selina is pretty with a pleasant singing voice and Alec has that transatlantic charm.'

Matt suspected the chief inspector had touched a nerve.

'Mr Browning's casting is rather more controversial, I gather?'

Lambert sighed. 'Yes, but the other two don't have the draw that a bigger name would have on the posters. If Marie is on there, people will come expecting her to sing. There is music in the show, of course, but the play is the thing. So long as Paul's drinking is contained then it should work. He knows he's on his last chance. If he blows this, then no other production company will touch him. He'll be finished for good.'

'Did you know Sir Norman had spoken to Mr Browning about his drinking?'

Lambert nodded. 'Yes, Paul was somewhat affronted as Norman wanted him to sign a contract guaranteeing his good behaviour, though he did sign it, of course. He can't afford to mess up this opportunity.'

Chief Inspector Greville asked the theatrical agent the same question he had asked the others about hearing a shot or bang at any point during the afternoon.

'Nothing untoward.' Lambert appeared unsurprised by the question.

The chief inspector dismissed him back to the other lounge just as Inspector Lewis returned.

'I found this in Mr Browning's room, sir.' He held out his hand to display a cufflink, matching the one the chief inspector had in his pocket.

'Splendid. I had a feeling that might be the case. It would explain why he was so anxious to get inside Sir Norman's office last night. He must have suspected that was where he had dropped it,' Chief Inspector Greville remarked with some satisfaction.

'Time is getting on, sir,' said Inspector Lewis, looking at his watch as he spoke. 'Did you wish to speak to any of the others before they all start preparing for dinner?'

The chief inspector glanced at the clock on the mantelpiece. 'Actually, would you ask that Jenkins chap to bring us in some tea and I'll have a quick chat with him. Let the others know I'll continue with the interviews after dinner. I think our Mr Browning can continue to stew for a bit longer.'

Inspector Lewis disappeared off to the kitchen.

Matt stretched his long legs out in front of him. 'I wonder why Browning wanted to see Sir Norman? That contract Mr Pike mentioned, perhaps?'

'See him, or murder him? I think once he has had a little more time to worry over his story and possibly taken a libation or two over dinner, we may get the truth from him. If he has concocted a tale, he is more likely to trip himself up,' the chief inspector said.

Albert Jenkins arrived bearing a tray set with tea things, which he placed on the low table in front of Matt.

'You wished to see me, sir?' he asked the chief inspector.

'Yes, Mr Jenkins. I appreciate that you and your wife are busy preparing for dinner so I shall try to be quick. You have both worked for Sir Norman for some time, I believe?' The chief inspector opened his notebook once more as Matt poured them both a cup of tea.

'Yes, sir. We worked for Sir Norman at his private residences before we agreed to come here.' Albert continued to stand, his hands clasped loosely together behind his back.

'Is this a temporary or permanent arrangement?' the chief inspector asked.

'From our point of view, temporary, sir. It's an isolated spot here and we were led to believe we would be able to go back to London once the hotel was up and running and new local staff was recruited and trained.' Albert's eyes flickered towards the clock and back to the chief inspector.

'You and Mrs Jenkins were on good terms with Sir Norman?'

'I would say so, sir. Although there was, of course, the matter of our wages,' Albert said.

'Wages?' Chief Inspector Greville looked at him.

'We was owed for a couple of months wages, and he promised us a bonus if we come here to help get the hotel going.' Albert spoke almost reluctantly.

'And Sir Norman has been fobbing you off about paying what he owes?' Matt said.

'Yes, sir. We spoke to Miss Marie yesterday when she came. Me and Ethel, we thought as perhaps she might persuade him to pay. We have a daughter, you see. She's been very sick and well, the doctor's fees are a lot. She's in a sanatorium.' Albert's words came out in a rush.

'I see. I'm very sorry to hear that, Mr Jenkins. Did Miss Monbiere offer to speak to Sir Norman on your behalf?' Chief Inspector Greville asked.

'Yes, sir. She said as she would see to it as we got the money. She seemed a bit upset about it all as she knows our Maud is so poorly,' Albert said.

'When did you last see Sir Norman alive?'

Albert scratched his head. 'It would be when I collected his tea tray, sir. Just before the others finished their rehearsals and went upstairs. He was busy at his desk, writing some letters, I think. He didn't even look up when I collected the tray.'

'You and Mrs Jenkins didn't hear anything untoward yesterday, in the late afternoon or early evening, which may have been the shot that killed Sir Norman?'

'No, sir, we was busy getting ready for dinner and the doors are very thick in the hotel.' Albert glanced at the clock again, clearly eager to be off.

'Very good, thank you, Jenkins.' The chief inspector

dismissed him and helped himself to the tea which was cooling rapidly in the cup.

'It sounds as if the Jenkinses did not come here willingly if they had to be promised a bonus,' Matt said.

Chief Inspector Greville sighed and gloomily helped himself to a biscuit. 'No, and I would imagine if they desperately needed that money they were owed, then things may have been a bit uncomfortable between them and Sir Norman. I suppose Jenkins might have killed his employer in a quarrel, but it seems a stretch.'

The room had grown dark while they had been conducting the interviews. Matt switched on a couple of the table lamps which were dotted about the room.

'The wind seems to have dropped completely now.' He gazed out at the rapidly darkening sky. The sun was already setting, casting fiery orange fingers along a bank of ominous black clouds.

The chief inspector picked up another biscuit. 'Hmm, let's hope these storms abate for a while. I don't fancy being stuck here for long. No matter how fancy this place is. Not as this lot will be going anywhere until I get to the bottom of this case.'

Matt bit back a smile as the chief inspector finished off the last of the biscuits. 'No, sir, although I hope for Inspector Lewis's sake that the journey back across the bay will be calmer.'

CHAPTER TEN

Kitty and Alice decided to remain in the main lounge after the rest of the group went upstairs to dress for dinner.

'I expect as Captain Bryant will be coming out soon.' Alice looked at the closed door linking the two rooms.

'I do hope so. I must say I'm longing to find out if they've learned anything new.' Kitty would have liked to have been present herself during the discussions. It wasn't quite so exciting hearing everything second-hand.

'Miss Monbiere looked upset when she come back, didn't she? Poor thing. No wonder she went right up to her room to rest,' Alice said.

'It was interesting, wasn't it? Colin seemed relieved after his interview and was quite happy to answer all of Alec's questions about what the police had said to him.' Kitty looked at her friend.

'Yes, and Lambert Pike was right cross. Proper grumpy he seemed,' Alice remarked.

'Mr Browning was very on edge all afternoon I thought, and he wasn't even called.' Kitty yawned and stretched, raising her arms above her head.

'Very uneasy, wasn't he?' replied Alice. 'Mind you, that Selina is all of a work as well. She's trying to hide it, but she seemed to jump every time anybody even looked her way. Like a cat on hot bricks.' She stood and switched on some of the lamps in the darkening room.

'Inspector Lewis has been kept on the trot. He seems to be running about all over the place,' said Kitty, rising too and crossing over to the piano, resting her fingers on the keys.

The door opened and Matt entered, followed by Chief Inspector Greville.

'Mrs Bryant, my apologies for depriving you of your husband's company. And Miss Miller, I do hope you have not been bored by remaining out here.' The chief inspector smiled at Kitty and Alice.

'Not at all, Chief Inspector. How is it going? Do you have any progress to report?' Kitty looked expectantly at both her husband and the policeman.

'It seems to be clear that Sir Norman owed several people a great deal of money,' Matt said.

'And what have you ladies discovered?' Chief Inspector Greville asked.

Kitty told him of her and Alice's impressions of the other guests during the course of the afternoon.

'Interesting,' the chief inspector replied. 'Mr Jenkins has allocated myself and Inspector Lewis a room. I'm in Eagle, I believe he said. I shall go and freshen up before dinner and we shall resume the interviews afterwards. That's one good thing about an island, there is nowhere for your suspects to go to. At least not until the boat returns.' The chief inspector headed out of the lounge towards the hall.

'Well?' Kitty pounced on Matt as soon as the policeman was out of sight and she and Alice sat down on either side of him expectantly.

Matt laughed and told them in much more detail what had

been said during the interviews. Alice was indignant when she heard the story of the missing wages.

'Poor Mr Jenkins. Him and Mrs Jenkins must be worried witless about their daughter. I bet as they've been counting on that bonus if there's medical bills to pay.'

'It sounds as if Miss Monbiere is in for a shock too when she discovers the extent of Sir Norman's debts,' Kitty said.

'I also think that Colin Frobisher is more concerned about Sir Norman's debts to him than he was letting on,' Matt said.

'Money always causes trouble. That Lambert weren't happy when he come out from seeing the chief inspector. Something as was said had definitely rubbed him up the wrong way,' Alice added.

'It all sounds as if you found more people with a reason to murder Sir Norman,' Kitty said.

She had hoped that perhaps someone at least might have been ruled out.

'I'm afraid so,' Matt agreed. 'It's all rather puzzling at the moment.'

'We had better go and get ready for dinner. Those lot'll be back down afore we've had chance to freshen up,' Alice said.

Alice headed off to her room while Matt joined Kitty in her bedroom.

'Were you all right last night after seeing Sir Norman in his office and then finding Browning prowling about?' Matt asked as he made himself comfortable on the bed while Kitty took out her evening gown once more.

'It was pretty horrid, especially with the storm and the lights flickering. Alice stayed in here with me. I think both of us wanted the company,' Kitty confessed as she removed her blue serge frock and placed it on a hanger.

'I can imagine. I've asked Mickey to take care of Bertie by the way, until we get back. Mrs Smith is happy to take care of

Rascal. Now he is no longer a kitten he is a lot less trouble,' Matt said.

Kitty slipped on her evening gown and went to the side of the bed so Matt could assist her with the fastenings. 'Poor Bertie. Or poor Mickey. When do you think we'll be allowed home?' she asked. She knew their housekeeper would take good care of her cat and Mickey, the Dolphin's handyman and security guard, was well used to naughty Bertie and his ways.

'I don't know. I suppose you and Alice could return to the mainland tomorrow if the sea is calm. The others may well have to stay longer if the chief inspector has more questions. After all, one of them must have killed Sir Norman. There is no other solution.'

Kitty didn't relish the idea of being banished from the island while the investigation continued.

'I didn't ask how the trial went by the way?' she said as she took a seat in front of the dressing table mirror.

'We got a conviction. A real feather in the chief inspector's cap.'

'Yours too, you clever thing.' Kitty smiled as she ran a comb through her blonde curls.

There was a tap on the connecting door.

'Come in, Alice, we're almost ready to go back down,' Kitty called.

Alice stepped shyly into the room. 'I didn't fancy going downstairs by myself,' she confessed.

'Of course not.' Matt swung his legs off the bed and put his shoes back on. 'It will be my pleasure to escort you lovely ladies to dinner.'

The others were all assembled around the bar in the lounge when they arrived downstairs. Albert, in his white coat, was once again mixing cocktails with aplomb. Marie looked pale in a jet-black gown with Alec attending to her every whim. Lambert and Colin both had whisky tumblers in their hands and Selina, graceful as ever, was smoking a cigarette and nursing a cocktail. In the background someone had turned on the wireless and the strains of soft jazz filled the air.

Paul Browning sat a little apart from the others. He too had what appeared to be a cut crystal glass containing whisky in front of him. Inspector Lewis was also present but didn't appear to have collected a drink. The chief inspector was missing.

'Inspector Lewis, would you care for a drink?' Matt asked once Alice and Kitty had taken seats at one of the small side tables.

'Thank you, Captain Bryant. I thought I would wait for the chief inspector. There's no beer on the island apparently.' Inspector Lewis surveyed the array of bottles behind the bar with a somewhat gloomy gaze.

'No, I suppose not.' Matt asked Albert for three White Lady cocktails.

Chief Inspector Greville arrived just as Albert had finished pouring.

'Drink, Chief Inspector?' Matt asked.

'Thank you, a small Scotch would be very welcome.' The chief inspector saw his colleague didn't have a glass in front of him. 'Lewis?'

'There's no beer, sir.' Inspector Lewis looked askance as Matt carried cocktails to Kitty and Alice before taking a sip from his own drink.

With everyone served, Albert departed back to the kitchen to assist his wife with the dinner preparations.

The chief inspector quickly made it known that no one would be able to leave the island until the case was resolved. This meant that conversation was muted in the presence of the two policemen and mostly centred around plans for the play rehearsals to continue. Kitty sipped her cocktail and hoped that dinner would not prove too awkward. She supposed that continuing with rehearsals would serve as a distraction until they could return to the mainland.

Albert reappeared after a few minutes to announce that they could go through to the dining room. Alec took a seat near Marie and Selina sat beside Colin. Alice and Kitty sat on either side of Matt, opposite the policemen. Lambert and Paul sat opposite Selina and Colin.

'Soup smells delicious,' Colin observed as a bowl of French onion soup was placed before them.

'I have no appetite.' Marie stirred her serving dispiritedly with her spoon.

'You must try and keep up your strength. Do try and have a little of it at least,' Alec suggested.

Chief Inspector Greville had applied himself with gusto to his dish, though Inspector Lewis didn't appear impressed with the course.

The table was quiet, with the odd remark on the weather and how the next day was supposed to be better.

The second course was a roast joint of pork with winter vegetables. Inspector Lewis's expression brightened considerably when the gravy jug was placed opposite him, and Kitty guessed he was a man who preferred plain fare.

Paul Browning managed to obtain several refills of his wine glass before Lambert noticed and had Albert discreetly remove the bottle. Dessert was a lemon meringue pie with clotted cream.

Once everyone had finished, the chief inspector rapped the end of his spoon on the table.

'Ladies and gentlemen. The people I have interviewed already are free to enjoy the rest of the evening as they wish. Mr Browning, Miss Headingly and Mr Standish, if you would be so good as to make yourselves available in the lounge, my inspector will call you through when I'm ready. Thank you.'

The guests exchanged nervous glances as they rose from their seats and departed from the dining room.

'Captain Bryant, would you accompany me during the interviews? Mrs Bryant, would you and Miss Miller remain in the main lounge and stay alert to anything that may be of interest to the investigation?' he asked discreetly when the others were out of earshot.

Inspector Lewis looked most unhappy as the chief inspector gave his instructions. Kitty guessed this was because she and Alice had been asked to assist, albeit in a minor way.

'Of course, sir,' Kitty answered for herself and Alice. She would have much preferred to be present at the interviews but at least Matt would be able to tell her everything that went on.

Matt and the two policemen headed for the small lounge as she and Alice rejoined the other guests. Albert had placed a tray of coffee ready, and Selina was busy serving the others as they entered.

'Coffee, Mrs Bryant? Miss Miller?' she asked.

'Thank you.' Kitty accepted a cup and wandered over to the windows. The curtains had not yet been drawn and in the distance, across the ink-black sea, she could see the faint twinkling lights of Torquay.

'So near and yet so far.' Paul Browning stood at her elbow.

'Yes, indeed,' Kitty said. 'Has the chief inspector called for you yet?' She glanced around to see if she could see if anyone had gone through.

'I think young Standish has been summoned. It's rather like waiting for the dentist, all this.'

'I suppose it is, rather,' Kitty replied sympathetically.

'I wish I knew...' His voice tailed off and he stared out at the night sky.

'Wish you knew what?' Kitty asked.

'Oh, nothing really. I've never been involved with anything

like this before. Poor old Norman. He was an annoying old stick, but murder...' Paul shook his head and moved away.

* * *

Alec Standish looked nervous as he took his place in front of the chief inspector. Matt guessed him to be in his late twenties at most. He was definitely some years younger than Marie Monbiere.

Matt had chosen to sit discreetly in a corner of the room where he could see both the policemen and the interviewees. Inspector Lewis had taken a seat beside his superior officer, clearly keen to impress that this was an official police enquiry.

'Now, Mr Standish, could you tell us how you knew Sir Norman?' the chief inspector asked.

Alec fidgeted with the cuff of his dinner jacket. 'Marie introduced me a couple of months ago. I'd been appearing in a play in London and Lambert had suggested that I might be suitable for a role in Marie's production. She and Sir Norman came to the theatre, and we had dinner afterwards. I think I've met him some seven or eight times since, before coming here.'

'And you and Sir Norman were on good terms?' the chief inspector asked.

Alec flushed. 'Well, yes, I suppose so. We never argued or anything.'

Chief Inspector Greville squiggled in his notebook. 'But you didn't like him?'

Alec started in his seat. 'Gosh, well, I... no, I suppose not.'

'Because of Miss Monbiere?' The chief inspector looked at Alec.

Matt could see the man becoming flustered. 'Now look here, there is nothing improper between myself and Marie you know.'

'Of course not, Mr Standish, but you do admire the lady, do

you not?' Chief Inspector Greville raised his eyebrows as he waited for Alec's response.

'He treated her badly, you see,' Alec said in a rush. 'Kept dangling a wedding in front of her but not doing anything about it. Then she gave him most of her money.' The flush on Alec's cheeks deepened.

'Was Sir Norman aware of your views?' Inspector Lewis chipped in.

'I tried to remonstrate with him. Not here, before we came to the island,' Alec said.

'How did he take that?' Chief Inspector Greville asked.

'He laughed. Patted me on the shoulder like I was some schoolboy and brushed me aside.'

Matt noticed that Alec's hands had curled into fists.

'Did Miss Monbiere know you had spoken to her fiancé on her behalf?' Inspector Lewis asked.

Alec shook his head. 'No, of course not.'

'Did you go to see Sir Norman again once you were here on the island?' Chief Inspector Greville's pen was poised once more over his notes.

'No. He was with Colin all afternoon, then Lambert went to see him, and Marie. I wanted to wait and see how the land lay the next day, but, of course, by then it was too late.' Alec shuddered. 'It was so awful. I thought he had taken his own life you see.' He swallowed. 'Then when you said it was murder.'

'Thank you, sir. You may return to the others.' The chief inspector dismissed him back to the lounge when it was clear that Alec had no further useful information.

'Interesting. Just Miss Headingly and Mr Browning left to go now. I think we'll have Miss Headingly next. We seem to know very little about her,' Chief Inspector Greville said, nodding at his colleague to collect the young actress.

CHAPTER ELEVEN

The brunette actress followed Inspector Lewis into the lounge and placed herself decorously on the chair recently vacated by Alec Standish.

'Miss Headingly, please could you tell us how you were connected to Sir Norman Whittier?' Chief Inspector Greville turned over the page in his notebook ready to write.

'Connected is an unusual choice of words, Chief Inspector,' Selina observed, raising her neatly arched eyebrows. 'Do you mind if I smoke, by the way?'

Chief Inspector Greville nodded his assent, and Selina inserted a small cigarette into her ebony holder. Inspector Lewis sprang forward to offer her a light.

Matt wondered if the cigarette was a ploy to give the actress more thinking time before answering the question. He suspected that despite her apparent poise, the girl was nervous.

'Lambert had suggested that I might be suitable as the romantic lead for Marie's play,' she said, having pulled on her now-lit cigarette. 'He had seen me in a number of productions. This would be a step up for me, so of course I was interested.' Selina blew out a thin plume of smoke.

'And so you met Sir Norman, when?' Chief Inspector Greville asked.

'A few months ago. October, not long after my birthday. He and Marie came to see me in a play I was in at Bath,' Selina said.

So far it was a similar story to Alec's but Matt sensed the girl was holding something back. Her eyes were wary and her hand holding her cigarette holder had a slight tremor.

'Have you met him since then, before coming to Bird Island?' the chief inspector asked, making more notes.

'Yes, socially a few times. Usually with Marie.' Selina shifted in her seat.

'What was your opinion of Sir Norman?' Chief Inspector Greville seemed to have picked up on Selina's evasiveness.

'I didn't know him very well so it's hard to make a judgement. He was, I think, very unfair to Marie. She seemed to be the one making all the effort in their relationship, and I thought he took advantage of that. I think he also had quite a reputation with women.'

Inspector Lewis's brows rose at this statement. 'You think he had affairs?'

Selina gave a slight shrug. 'It wouldn't surprise me if he did. I know he did so in the past.'

Chief Inspector Greville's brow creased in perplexity. 'Forgive me, Miss Headingly, but how do you know this to be a fact?'

Selina extinguished her cigarette in the glass ashtray. 'Because I am the product of one of his liaisons.'

There was a general movement at this statement.

'You are Sir Norman's daughter?' Inspector Lewis's tone betrayed his own astonishment at this admission.

Colour suffused the girl's face and she bowed her head gracefully. 'Yes. He met my mother when she dined at one of his restaurants. He pursued her and she became pregnant. He then dropped her like a red-hot coal and disappeared back to London. He denied all culpability.'

'Did he know you were his daughter?' Chief Inspector Greville asked.

Selina shook her head. 'No. No one knows except for myself and my mother. I accepted the role in Marie's production because I was curious. I wanted to meet him, to see what kind of man my father really was.'

Matt wondered how true this was. He sensed there was a lot more to this story than Selina was willing to admit.

'Did you intend to reveal your identity to him?' Inspector Lewis asked, his foxy gaze scanning the girl's face as if he too didn't believe she was telling the truth.

'I hadn't decided. It would have made things very awkward for me and for everyone else. He would probably have denied it, and I would have had to leave the company. It would have placed Marie in a difficult position and Lambert would probably have ensured that I would struggle to find new roles.' Selina's expressive face and the faint quiver of her lower lip showing her despair. 'Also, from my brief acquaintance with him, I must admit that I disliked Sir Norman. He was not a man that I cared to get to know better.'

'Did you visit him in his office yesterday?' Chief Inspector Greville asked.

The actress shook her head. 'No, I remained in the rehearsal room and then went straight upstairs to dress for dinner. When I came back down, I went into the lounge to join the others. After that, well, you know what happened.' She shuddered at the recollection.

'You didn't hear a shot or bang?'

'Nothing at all. The wind was howling around the hotel, and I didn't hear anything out of the ordinary,' the girl said.

'Thank you for your frankness, Miss Headingly.' Chief Inspector Greville set down his pen.

'Chief Inspector, if you wouldn't mind, I would rather that no one else knew about my relationship to Sir Norman. There seems to be little point in upsetting the apple cart now he is dead.' Selina stood ready to leave.

'Very well,' the chief inspector agreed.

Matt could see her point. They also weren't sure who had killed Sir Norman or why, and until that was known it was safer not to potentially place his daughter in a killer's sights.

'Well then,' Inspector Lewis said, rubbing his hands together once the door had closed behind Selina. 'That was a bit of a bombshell, eh?'

'Quite. Most unexpected. I wonder if there are any more illegitimate children fathered by Sir Norman?' Chief Inspector Greville mused.

'Sir Norman appears to be a man with a number of skeletons in his closet,' Matt agreed. He wondered what Kitty would make of this revelation. He also wondered what else Selina had not been telling them. There was *something*, he was sure of it.

'Well, they're all tumbling out now,' Inspector Lewis said. 'Shall I go and fetch the last of them, sir?'

'Yes please, Lewis. I think our Mr Browning should be nicely stewed by now,' said the chief inspector.

Matt wondered how much Paul would have imbibed whilst he was waiting to be called through. Alcohol might have loosened the man's tongue so much that they might well get a true explanation of why his cufflink had been discovered in the office. It was clear the chief inspector thought Browning was his main suspect, but Matt couldn't quite see his motive for killing Sir Norman. The business about a contract was possible, but was it enough? Would Sir Norman's death end the contract terms?

Paul Browning followed Inspector Lewis into the lounge. The actor appeared calm and collected, but as he took his seat Matt noticed a few beads of sweat on his temples.

'Mr Browning, my apologies for leaving you until last,' Chief Inspector Greville said, turning over a new page in his notebook.

'Not at all, Chief Inspector. Someone has to go last, and it would have been most unfair to keep the ladies waiting.' Paul's airy tone belied his now slightly anxious demeanour.

'May I ask if you had known Sir Norman long, Mr Browning?' the chief inspector asked.

'No, not really. Our paths have crossed socially from time to time, after theatre dinners, that sort of thing. He was a great supporter of the arts, as I'm sure you know. I only really got to know him a little better these last few weeks when Lambert recruited me to Marie's production.' Paul's hands shook as he spoke, and he clasped them together in his lap.

'You had no quarrels with Sir Norman?' Chief Inspector Greville said, looking keenly at Paul.

'No, none at all,' Paul replied.

Matt's brow raised at this response. Paul obviously didn't intend to mention the contract regarding his behaviour.

Chief Inspector Greville made some more notes in his book. 'Did you visit Sir Norman in his office yesterday?'

'No. The only time I went near his office was when Marie insisted the door be opened because we thought he may have been taken ill. Even then I didn't go in. I remained in the reception area with Selina and Alec.' Paul's tone was confident.

'You are quite certain of that, Mr Browning?' Inspector Lewis asked.

Matt saw the beads of sweat on Paul's temples had grown more noticeable.

'Yes.'

Chief Inspector Greville reached inside his jacket pocket and opened his hand out flat in front of the actor. In the centre of his palm was the silver and onyx cufflink that the policeman had discovered in Sir Norman's office.

'Do you recognise this at all, sir?'

Paul's mouth gaped open for a moment. 'I... yes, that's my missing cufflink. I lost it last night.'

'It may interest you to know, sir, that we found it inside Sir Norman's office. It was near his desk.' The chief inspector watched Paul intently as he relayed this piece of information.

'Then I don't know how it got there. I never entered that room. I can only suppose I must have lost it in the reception area. Someone may have kicked it in with their foot when we opened the door.' Paul took out his handkerchief and dabbed at his temples before returning the white cotton square to his pocket.

'And that is your explanation, Mr Browning?' Inspector Lewis asked with a disbelieving air.

'Well, yes. What else could it be? Unless you think someone may have placed it in that dreadful room on purpose?' Paul's voice rose slightly in his agitation.

'Do you consider that a possibility, sir?' the chief inspector asked.

Paul subsided. 'I don't know. I have no idea how it got there. I didn't realise it was missing until I went upstairs last night.'

The two policemen exchanged glances.

'Then perhaps you would care to explain why you attempted to gain access to Sir Norman's office on the night of his murder after everyone had supposedly retired for the night?' Chief Inspector Greville asked.

'What? I...' Paul gazed wildly from one man to the other. 'I went upstairs. I saw my cufflink was missing and I tried to retrace my steps. I didn't see it anywhere and I wondered if it could have ended up in Sir Norman's office by accident. I knew if it had it would look bad, so I looked for the key to try and check. I'd had a bit to drink and wasn't thinking straight.'

'Or you knew you had been in that room and that was where you had probably lost it,' Inspector Lewis suggested.

'No. I had no reason to wish harm to Sir Norman,' Paul protested, leaning forward in his seat.

'Even though he was opposed to your being cast in his fiancée's production? And he had warned both you and Mr Pike of the consequences should your drinking habits cause Miss Monbiere a problem? He even pressed you to sign a contract guaranteeing you would stay sober during the run of the play,' said Inspector Lewis, and he leaned back in his chair looking satisfied with his argument.

'No, I've told you, no.' Paul ran his hand through his hair. 'The casting decisions for the production were Marie and Lambert's. I *did* sign a contract for Sir Norman on Lambert's advice about my conduct. I had little choice in the matter if I wished to work. Sir Norman could make life awkward for Lambert I suppose, but at the end of the day, Marie was the one in charge of the company.'

'Thank you. Finally, you didn't hear a shot or bang at all yesterday afternoon?' Chief Inspector Greville asked.

'What? No, nothing.'

'Very well, sir. We shall leave things there for now. I suggest that if you do wish to add to or change your statement that you see either myself or Inspector Lewis as soon as possible.'

Matt watched Paul stumble out of the room and guessed the man would be heading straight for the bar.

'What did you think, Captain Bryant? Do you believe him?' Chief Inspector Greville tucked his notebook inside his jacket pocket and replaced the cap on his pen.

'I don't know, sir. I got the impression that something was troubling him, but he was quite vehement that he had not been inside Sir Norman's office,' Matt said.

'You surely are not giving any credence to the suggestion that someone else placed his cufflink in the office on purpose?' Inspector Lewis scoffed.

'It's a possibility. The murderer may have found it and done exactly that in order to point the finger elsewhere,' Matt replied. He didn't think it was impossible. If Paul had murdered Sir Norman, his reason for doing so appeared pretty weak compared to other members of the theatre company.

'It's getting late,' said Chief Inspector Greville. 'I think we have done all we can for today. Hopefully we can review our progress tomorrow and see where we are with it all. I checked the telephones before dinner, and they are still not functioning.' He stood up with a sigh.

'Very good, sir. Goodnight, Captain Bryant,' said Inspector Lewis, getting to his feet and heading out of the other door.

'Goodnight, sir. At least the wind has died down so we should get some sleep,' Matt said, glancing at the darkness outside the windows.

'Yes, please say goodnight to Miss Miller and Mrs Bryant for me.' The chief inspector left through the same door as Inspector Lewis.

Matt walked back into the main lounge. Paul, as he had expected was drowning his sorrows with a large glass of whisky. Marie and Selina were both absent so he assumed they must have gone upstairs. Colin, Alec and Lambert were playing cards at one of the tables, while Kitty and Alice were studying a book they must have borrowed from the shelves in the other room.

'Come and sit down, darling. Do you want a drink?' Kitty asked.

'No, that's all right, thank you.' Matt took his place beside his wife. The others in the room looked in his direction but continued with their occupations. 'The chief inspector and Inspector Lewis have retired for the night,' Matt said.

'It is getting quite late.' Kitty looked at the clock above the bar.

'I think I'll turn in as well. I'll see you both in the morning,' said Alice as she closed the book. She placed it down on the table before retiring.

'*Birds of the British Isles*,' Matt read the title aloud.

'We were wondering about the names of the rooms,' Kitty said. 'I couldn't find any detective stories and Alice has finished her *Movie* magazine.'

Paul tossed back the rest of his drink and stalked off without saying goodnight to anyone.

'Paul is in a bad mood,' Lambert observed.

'It's been a difficult day,' Colin said, folding his hand of cards and starting to tot up the scores.

'Beastly,' Alec agreed.

'Are the police any closer to deciding which of us killed Norman?' Lambert looked at Matt.

Matt shrugged. 'I'm not party to what the police may think. I believe they only asked me to be present as a courtesy and since they have no constable with them.'

'Just thought you might have some idea about which way the wind was blowing,' Lambert remarked as he picked up the pack of cards and returned them to their box.

'It seems impossible to me that any of us would have killed Norman. There has to be some other explanation,' Alec said.

'I can't see any of the people from the cottages or the light-house keeper coming all the way over here in a storm to murder him, and there's no one else on the island. I asked Jenkins this morning,' Colin said.

'I say, you don't think it could have been Jenkins, do you?' Alec asked.

'I suppose it's as likely to be him as any of us, eh, Captain Bryant?' Colin attempted a jovial tone.

'Better be careful with breakfast in the morning. Might find arsenic in the bacon,' Lambert joined in with the joke.

'Someone murdered Sir Norman and tried to make it look like suicide,' Kitty said softly. 'Whoever it was clearly hoped to quite literally get away with murder. In our experience, murderers often don't just stop at one death.' She rose from her place on the sofa.

The men at the table sobered immediately. 'Of course not, Mrs Bryant. I'm sorry, just an attempt to lighten the tone,' Colin apologised sheepishly.

'Goodnight, gentlemen.' Matt accompanied his wife out of the lounge and up the stairs to their room.

'Ugh, this place makes my skin crawl now,' Kitty said as she removed her pearls and dropped them back into their case. 'I know they didn't mean to be so crass, but murder really isn't a laughing matter.'

Matt wrapped his arms around her to hold her close. 'I agree, darling. Someone here is a cunning killer.'

CHAPTER TWELVE

The sun was out when Kitty, Matt and Alice went downstairs for breakfast the following morning. A brisk wind was blowing from the east and the waves on the sea were still capped with white as they twinkled in the morning sunlight.

'I don't know as a boat could get across to us again yet. This wind is whipping the waves up,' Alice observed as they paused in the lounge to watch the waves smack against the jetty at the bottom of the hill. The spray flew up into the air as the gulls wheeled overhead, screaming in the wind.

'No, it does look rather rough. There's a good swell on the waves,' Kitty agreed. 'It may improve this afternoon if this wind drops.'

On reaching the dining room it seemed that most of the guests had already eaten. Only Inspector Lewis and Chief Inspector Greville remained at the breakfast table.

'Good morning,' Chief Inspector Greville greeted them affably as he finished off the last of his eggs and bacon.

Inspector Lewis had clearly finished his meal and was about to leave the room.

'Have we missed everyone?' Kitty asked as they greeted the policemen and took their places at the table.

'I think most of them were in early. Miss Monbiere has taken a tray in her room.' Chief Inspector Greville helped himself to more tea as Albert brought in fresh racks of toast.

'If you'll all excuse me, I'll head over to the cottages and the lighthouse.' Inspector Lewis nodded to his superior and left the room.

'I thought it best to tie up any loose ends. Not that anyone is likely to have been roaming around the island in the middle of a storm, but you never know,' the chief inspector explained.

'It's a much pleasanter morning today, even if the sea is still quite choppy. Are the telephone lines back up yet, sir, do you know?' Matt asked as he helped himself to bacon and sausages from the silver-lidded dishes set on the sideboard.

'They are. I've already made several calls back to the police station in Torquay. If the sea calms down I'm hopeful the boat can cross back this afternoon. No doubt you and Miss Miller are anxious to return home, Mrs Bryant?' the chief inspector asked.

Kitty was in no hurry to return and leave an unsolved murder, but she recognised that the police would be anxious to make an arrest and wrap the case up as soon as possible. After all, the rest of the party would no doubt wish to leave the island soon too.

'We have enough to write our report for the hoteliers' association, but with Sir Norman's death I'm not sure now if Miss Monbiere will wish to proceed with a membership application. I assume that she is now the owner?' Kitty said.

'Sir Norman's solicitor is calling me back later this morning. I have left a message with my sergeant to establish the terms of Sir Norman's will and the amounts owed to his creditors.' The chief inspector helped himself to more toast.

'Do we know about the life insurance?' Matt said.

'That is something else we are looking into. If he had any and, if so, who the beneficiaries would be.' The chief inspector applied a thick layer of strawberry jam to his buttered toast.

'Do you think you know who may have killed him, sir?' Alice asked.

'I think there are a few outstanding questions which I need to ask.' The policeman skirted around answering Alice directly. 'I shall be going through my notes this morning and depending on the answers I receive to my telephone enquiries I'm hopeful we may discover our killer.'

They were forced to be satisfied with the chief inspector's response. He finished his toast and excused himself from the table. Kitty wondered if he thought the contents of a will or the discovery of an insurance policy might provide a motive for the murder.

'Shall we go for a walk after breakfast?' Matt suggested. 'I don't know about you ladies but I'm finding this all rather claustrophobic.'

'A bit of fresh air would be nice,' Alice agreed.

Kitty felt the same way. She was also curious to see a little more of the island.

'I expect you'll be glad to get back to the mainland, Alice. I bet Robert will be wondering where you are,' Matt said.

Kitty aimed a gentle warning kick at Matt's ankle under the table.

Alice tossed her auburn curls. 'I doubt as Robert Potter has even noticed I've gone away,' she replied with a sniff.

Matt gave Kitty a puzzled and slightly wounded look and she responded with a faint shake of her head.

Accordingly, once breakfast was finished, they wrapped up in their outdoor clothes and set off for a brisk walk to explore the grounds of the hotel and beyond. Kitty knew from the pamphlet in her room that the island was quite small, about seven miles in one direction and five in width.

There were three small stone cottages sited about three quarters of a mile away from the hotel. These belonged to smallholders who made their living by crofting, fishing and, in summer, offering a room and teas to visitors to the island. They also had recently started supplying the hotel with milk, cream and eggs.

The lighthouse was a small squat building about two storeys high. It was situated on a prominent craggy point with another stone cottage nearby which belonged to the lighthouse keeper. Alice said that she had heard that the lighthouse was to be mechanised and the keeper retired soon.

There was a stiff breeze as they left the relative shelter of the hotel gardens that were surrounded by a mix of low stone walls and thorny hedges mixed with fuchsias. A tennis court had been built on one side of the hotel. Kitty and Alice both placed a protective hand on their hats as they walked along the path leading away from the hotel and the jetty area.

They passed the donkey field and headed towards the path leading to the cliffs. There were more birds now as they drew nearer to the edge. The island had long been popular with naturalists and birdwatchers keen to see the different species that nested on the rocky crevices overlooking the sea.

They paused for breath at one of the higher points to look out over the restless sea towards the mainland. The headland at Berry Head and the curve of the harbour at Brixham were more visible from this point.

'It is quite lovely as a setting, isn't it?' Kitty shaded her eyes as she looked across the water.

'Quite remarkable. Stay clear of the edge of the path though, Kitty, the rain may well have softened the rocks,' Matt cautioned.

'Captain Bryant, what is that?' Alice's voice quavered as she pointed, not across the bay where Kitty and Matt had been looking, but down to the sea-lashed rocks at the foot of the cliff.

Kitty followed her friend's finger to see a bundle of something bobbing in the water below, bashing against the rocks. A man's body in a dark-grey overcoat. She leaned forward to get a better look and Matt immediately placed his arm to hold her back from the edge.

'Who is it?' Kitty couldn't see who it might be.

'I'm not certain.' He leaned forward a little more. 'Good grief, that looks like Paul Browning.' He peered at the corpse which was partially obscured by the spray and swirling water.

'We must get back to the hotel and find the chief inspector,' Kitty said, tugging urgently at Matt's coat sleeve.

The three of them turned and hurried back towards the hotel.

'Do you think he fell from the cliff?' Alice gasped as they scurried along the path.

'Possibly, that edge is quite unstable. Or he could have jumped,' Matt said.

'Or been pushed,' Kitty added. Had someone sent Paul Browning to his death? Perhaps there *had* been someone who had placed his cufflink at the scene of Sir Norman's murder on purpose. Had Paul discovered the murderer's identity?

They rounded the corner through the small wooden gate back into the hotel grounds.

'There's Inspector Lewis,' Alice panted, waving her arms to attract the policeman's attention.

'Miss Miller. Whatever is the matter?' The inspector hurried over to them.

'There's a body at the foot of the cliffs,' Kitty said, trying to catch her breath. She had a stitch in her side from running. The inspector's expression changed.

'It looks like Paul Browning,' Matt explained.

The inspector muttered an oath under his breath. 'I'd better get the chief inspector, then you can show us where he is.'

'Go with him,' Kitty urged as the inspector darted off.

Matt accompanied the inspector, leaving Alice and Kitty to make their way back to the hotel at a slower pace.

'My legs am all of a wobble,' Alice said as they entered the reception area.

'Mine too.' Kitty held on to her friend's arm, and they entered the main lounge to take a seat. The discovery of Paul's body and the race back to the hotel had shaken her up.

'Miss Miller, Mrs Bryant, are you all right?' Alec Standish had been seated at the piano with Selina. They broke off from playing and immediately came over.

'There seems to have been an accident,' Kitty said. Her heart was still thumping, and she tried to steady her breath.

'An accident?' Selina asked with a puzzled frown.

'Paul Browning is in the sea at the foot of the cliffs. The police have gone there now with Matt. I'm not sure how they will recover him,' Kitty said.

'Oh my goodness.' Selina sat down on the sofa opposite Kitty and Alice, her face ashen with shock. 'That's awful. What's happened? Did you find him?'

'It looks as if he has fallen. The path isn't very safe at that point,' Alice said.

'Brandy, I'll get brandy.' Alec went to the bar and returned with a bottle and some glasses. He poured them all a measure, including Selina. 'Was he drunk, do you think?'

'Not at this time of day, surely,' Selina said, sipping her drink, the liquor restoring some colour to her pale features.

'You think it was an accident? I know you just said the path was bad,' Alec asked. 'But after what happened with Sir Norman?' He didn't need to say anything more.

'You mean you think someone could have pushed him? Murdered him?' Selina's question came out as a horrified whisper.

'No, well... I don't know.' Alec tried to backtrack.

'You don't think he could have killed Sir Norman and then taken his own life, do you?' Selina asked. 'In a fit of remorse or something?'

Kitty sipped her brandy. The warmth of the spirit seemed to calm her nerves. 'We don't know. It's just too horrid. We will have to wait for the police to recover him and then I suppose we might find out more.'

Colin entered the room, a bundle of sheet music in his hand. He paused when he saw the group huddled around the table.

'I say, what's wrong? You all look like you've lost a shilling and found a farthing.'

'It's Paul. He's fallen from the cliffs,' Alec said.

Colin sank down slowly onto a nearby chair. 'Paul? You mean he's dead?'

Selina nodded. 'Mrs Bryant and Miss Miller found him. The police have gone out there now.'

'But I only saw him at breakfast an hour or two ago.' Colin looked at them all, his brow creased in bewilderment.

'What was he like at breakfast?' Kitty asked. 'Did he say anything about going outside?'

'Well, he seemed thoughtful, I suppose. I wondered if perhaps he was a bit hungover. I asked him if he was all right and he said he had to get some air as he needed to think. He didn't seem in bad spirits though. That was it, wasn't it, Lambert?' Colin appealed to the theatrical agent who had just entered the room.

'What was that?' Lambert asked, his eyes widening slightly when he noticed the brandy bottle at such an early hour.

'Paul, this morning at breakfast. He said he was going outside for some air because he needed to think,' Colin repeated.

'Yes, he did. He looked a bit off. I think he'd had a bit too

much of the sauce again last night. Why? What's wrong?'
Lambert sat down near Alec.

'Paul's dead. Miss Miller and Mrs Bryant found him at the
foot of the cliffs in the sea,' Selina said. Her teeth chattered on
the edge of the brandy glass as she took another gulp.

Lambert's brows raised and he emitted a low whistle. 'I
don't understand. Paul? Dead?'

There was a kerfuffle in the reception area as the chief
inspector followed by Matt and Inspector Lewis re-entered the
hotel. The chief inspector went straight to the telephone on the
reception desk while Inspector Lewis headed for the kitchen.

Matt came into the lounge. 'It's definitely Browning. The
chief inspector is telephoning Torquay to request Doctor Carter
and a boat as soon as possible. Inspector Lewis has gone to see
Jenkins about rope and a way to reach the foot of the cliffs
safely.'

'I don't suppose you can get a boat round there,' said Alice.
''Tis too rocky and the sea is too wild. Maybe when the tide goes
out a bit you might be able to get round on foot,' she suggested.

'The inspector has said he will also go and ask the lighthouse keeper as he knows the tides and the area well.' Matt
glanced at the brandy bottle and glasses. 'Are you and Alice
all right, Kitty, old thing? This has been the most ghastly
shock.'

'We're all right now, aren't we, Alice?' Kitty looked at her
friend.

'I was a bit wobbly, but Mr Standish has been taking good
care of us,' Alice replied with a grateful look at the American
actor.

'Marie will need to be told.' Alec rose from his seat as if
about to dash upstairs straight away to inform her.

'What will I need to be told? What's going on?' Marie stood
in the doorway of the lounge, clad in a black silk dress. She
looked around at the assembled guests.

'Marie, my dear, please come and sit down.' Lambert got up and gently steered her towards his seat.

'I am afraid there is no easy way to put this,' said Colin, 'but it seems that Paul is dead.'

CHAPTER THIRTEEN

Marie appeared frozen to the spot as she attempted to comprehend what Colin had just said.

'Paul? Dead? How? When?' She looked at Colin and then at Lambert as if expecting one of them to have an answer.

'We don't know exactly what happened yet,' explained Matt. 'But it looks as if Mr Browning may have fallen from the cliffs into the sea. The police have yet to recover him from the rocks.'

'A fall?' Marie still looked bewildered. 'Had he been drinking again?'

'We don't know. The path seems to have been damaged by the recent storm though,' Kitty said.

It was possible that his death was simply a tragic accident, but coming so soon after Sir Norman's death she had her suspicions.

From her seat she could see that Chief Inspector Greville was conferring with Inspector Lewis in the reception area. Albert Jenkins joined them carrying a large coil of rope over one shoulder.

Matt also noticed the men gathering in the hall and

excused himself to go and join them. The others watched him depart with Albert and the police. Selina wrapped her arms around herself and went to stand by the window, watching the small group as they headed down the hill towards the jetty.

Alec fetched an extra glass to pour some brandy for Marie. 'Take a sip, it's been such a terrible couple of days,' he urged.

'It's all ruined, isn't it? Everything. There is some kind of curse on me, on this place and on the play,' Marie said as Alec guided the glass towards her lips.

Lambert paced up and down. 'I know it feels that way now, Marie, but we don't know what has happened with Paul. It may be simply an awful accident.'

Kitty wondered if he believed that.

'Do you think he could have killed Sir Norman?' Selina asked. 'I mean, it's possible, isn't it? Then he might have thrown himself off the cliff.' Her voice trailed off into a gulping sob and she fumbled in the pocket of her pink velveteen frock for her handkerchief.

Kitty wondered if Selina was trying to convince herself or others of this explanation. It was the second time she had made the suggestion. Did Selina really think this was what had happened? If so, why? Paul had appeared to have the weakest motive of all for murdering Sir Norman. Surely Colin and Marie who were owed money, Lambert who had an unsavoury reputation and even the Jenkinses had stronger motives. Not to mention Selina herself.

'And he might just have easily have taken a hair of the dog after breakfast to cure his hangover and slipped near the clifftop,' Lambert reposted.

'Did anyone else see Paul this morning?' Kitty asked. 'After breakfast?'

'That was the last time I saw him,' Colin said.

'I saw him in the hall with his coat on, but I was coming in here, so we didn't speak,' Lambert said. 'That would be about nine forty-five, I think.'

'I didn't see him at all,' Alec said. 'I had breakfast early and went back to my room. I thought I should pack some of my things in case the police wished us to return to the mainland when the boat next came in.'

'I didn't bother with breakfast at all. I was tired as I didn't sleep well. By the time I came downstairs everyone had gone, except for Colin and Lambert who were in here,' Selina explained.

'I was upstairs all morning. I thought I should write to some of Norman's colleagues and friends. I wanted to have the letters ready to post when the boat next came across.' Marie swallowed the last sip of brandy from her glass.

Alice looked at the clock above the bar. 'Well, I'm going to slip along to the kitchen to see if Mrs Jenkins is all right. It'll be lunchtime before long and that poor woman is all on her own now Albert has gone off helping the police.'

'You're right,' Kitty said. 'I'll come too. It's a lot of work for one person.' She was glad of an excuse to escape from the lounge.

Mrs Jenkins looked hot and frazzled when they arrived in the kitchen. Various pots were simmering on the range cooker and a delicious scent of baking filled the air.

She looked rather dubious when Alice volunteered their services as her assistants but found them both aprons and set them to work when she realised they were serious.

Kitty was dispatched to set the dining table and Alice deputised to chop more vegetables. The quiet of the dining room and the orderly placing of cutlery and glasses was very soothing to Kitty's spirits. By the time she returned to the kitchen for her next set of instructions, she already felt much better.

'Could I trouble you to wash up, Mrs Bryant?' Ethel asked.

'Washing-up is something I am quite good at,' Kitty agreed cheerfully as she looked at the mountain of dishes in the scullery sink.

'I really am most grateful to the both of you. I don't know how I would have managed with Albert going off to help the police this morning.' Ethel shook her head, a few grey curls escaping from under her cap, as she expertly filleted fish at the kitchen table.

'It's the least we can do,' Kitty assured her as she started to fill the large, enamelled sink with water.

'I asked Miss Monbiere this morning if I could make the dishes a bit simpler as it was all too much for just me and Albert to manage.' Ethel placed the fish fillets on a metal tray and added salt.

'I trust she was amenable to your request?' Kitty asked.

'She weren't too happy, but she had to agree. I mean there's extra people now the police are here and, of course, the girl we was expecting to have come and help isn't here.' Ethel slid the tray of fish into the oven.

'I hope she is sorting out your salary and the rest of the money Sir Norman owed you,' Alice said as she added a dish of diced carrots into a saucepan.

Ethel sniffed. 'She says she will, but I don't know. I don't mind saying as I'm worried. Even if she pays us what's owed in the next few days it might be too late for our Maud.' Ethel pulled a large, slightly grubby white handkerchief from her apron pocket and blew her nose.

'Is that your daughter?' Kitty asked as she stacked plates on the wooden dish rack to drain.

Ethel nodded. 'She's in a bad way in the sanatorium and she has three little kiddies. Her husband is doing his best, God bless him. His mum helps them out but he's on short time. He was wounded in the war so them as is stronger and fitter get given more hours.' She started to scour the tabletop ready for her next task. 'You know how it is, Mrs Bryant, don't you?'

'Yes, yes, I do.' Matt was also a veteran and although he had some physical issues from his wounds, the mental scarring lay much deeper.

'Let's hope that the police can sort out Sir Norman's death quickly,' Alice said in a sympathetic tone.

'Who knows now that Mr Browning has been found dead. We saw him setting off this morning as we was having our morning cuppa,' Ethel said. 'He weren't heading towards the cliffs though. He was going towards the cottages. Still, I expect he just followed the path back around.'

'Did he seem all right when he was walking? I mean not unsteady or staggering?' Kitty asked as she dried the plates with a tea cloth.

'Did I think he was drunk you mean? Fond of the bottle that one, wasn't he? No, he seemed fine to me. He was cheery enough, striding out along the path. Who knows how he come to end up on the rocks.' Ethel gave a small shudder. 'I'll be glad to get away from this place, I will. Me and Albert. We can go and help our Maud's family for a bit while we find another situation.'

Kitty started on the pots, attacking them with wire wool where the food had been burnt on. Alice continued to work under Ethel's instructions.

'Did you see anyone else outside this morning?' Alice asked as she stirred the sauce.

'I think as they were all out at one time or another,' Ethel said. 'I just sees them go by the window like.'

Alice exchanged a glance with Kitty. None of the people in the lounge had admitted to venturing outside that morning.

'There you go, Mrs Jenkins.' Kitty drained the water from the sink and placed the wet tea cloths on the Sheila Maid to air.

'Bless you both, I can't thank you enough for giving me a

hand with all this. Lunch should be ready for just after one.'
Ethel gave them a slightly weary but thankful smile.

Kitty and Alice made their way out of the kitchen and
walked through the dining room back towards the lounge.

'I wonder why no one said they'd been outside this morning?' Kitty murmured to Alice as they opened the door into the
reception area.

'That's what I was a wondering as well,' Alice said.

* * *

Matt followed the two policemen and Albert down the hill to
the jetty. Another man was waiting there for them. Dressed in a
woollen jersey and with thick rubber waders over the top of his
trousers, Matt guessed he must be the lighthouse keeper. He
had a pipe clenched between his teeth and his longish grey hair
was mostly covered by a blue knit cap with a hole in the brim.

'Follow me,' the man said. He set off on a narrow rabbit path
that led away from the jetty and skirted the shore just above the
waterline. The tide had started to recede and more of the black
jagged rocks that lay under the cliffs were being revealed. Here
and there Matt saw signs of fresh rock falls from the cliffs, the
red lumps of stone and soil turning the water a reddish brown.

The spray from the waves settled on Matt's face and overcoat in a fine mist and he could smell the dark-brown seaweed
left by the storm that was now ensnared in the rock pools. The
path was muddy and awkward, and his feet slipped a couple of
times as they made their way around the headland.

Their guide appeared to have no such difficulties and Matt
could see he was used to the terrain. Eventually they came out
onto a slightly broader, flatter point in the path where they
paused. Ahead of them, Matt could see Paul's body bobbing up
and down wildly with each wave.

'We'll need to act fast and secure him or else he'll be swept out and into the bay yonder.' The lighthouse keeper removed his pipe from his mouth as he spoke and waved it in the general direction of Torquay.

Matt could see what he meant; the body had already begun to drift away from the foot of the cliff. The choppy, white-water whirling around the rocks.

'Can you reach him?' the chief inspector asked.

'I'll give it a go. Mind you keep clear of the overhang of the cliffs.' The man took the rope from Albert and started carefully down away from the path and into the sea. He stopped when he was in the water to throw the end of the rope back to Albert. 'Keep tight hold in case the current tries to take me.'

Albert nodded and wrapped the end of the rope around his waist as the other man started to wade out towards Paul's body. By the time he reached him, he was almost chest deep in the sea. He secured the rope around Paul's waist and started to make his way back towards them, bringing Paul with him as he did so.

Once he was closer, Inspector Lewis slithered down from the path to help him in, bringing Paul up and out of the sea. Matt and the chief inspector scrambled to assist them. Eventually Paul was out of the water and lay dripping on the path, salt-water streaming from his clothing.

Their guide panted up the path to join them, sitting down on a nearby rock to relight his pipe. The chief inspector and Inspector Lewis leaned over Paul's body.

'Large wound on the back of his head, sir,' Inspector Lewis said.

'Yes, unlikely to have been caused by the fall, don't you think? I would have thought if he had slipped then he would have fallen face first, and if he had jumped then he would again have been less likely to land on his back.' Chief Inspector Greville straightened up to study the cliff face above them. 'No protruding rocks that he might have caught on his way down, although I think more stones may have fallen recently. I daresay Doctor Carter will be able to give us a better judgement when he sees him.'

'Do you think it worthwhile to study the top of the cliff for possible weapons, sir? If he might have been hit from behind?' Matt suggested. He supposed that if Paul had been attacked, whoever did it could have thrown whatever they hit him with down after him into the sea. Still, it had to be worth checking.

The chief inspector stroked his moustache thoughtfully. 'It's best to be thorough. Yes, good call, Captain Bryant.'

'Now we needs to get him back along this path,' Albert said, eyeing the body with a concerned look.

'I have an old door in my outhouse at the lighthouse. If you and I go fetch it, Albert, we can manage him between the four of us if we goes careful,' the lighthouse keeper suggested as he heaved himself up from his rocky seat.

'Good thinking, thank you,' the chief inspector agreed, and Albert and the lighthouse keeper set off to collect the door.

Inspector Lewis had begun a delicate search of Paul's pockets. 'Silver hip flask, empty.' He had shaken the flask in an experimental fashion before unscrewing the cap to take a sniff. 'Once contained brandy.'

'Doctor Carter will no doubt check the contents of his stomach and his blood to see if he had imbibed anything in the time before you, Mrs Bryant and Miss Miller discovered him,' the chief inspector said, looking at Matt.

Inspector Lewis retrieved Paul's wallet, a worn, monogrammed, tattered brown leather thing that looked as if it had been in his possession for many years. Apart from a handkerchief the rest of his pockets were empty. He had no watch or rings or anything else of value.

The inspector straightened up and opened the sodden wallet with care. Like Paul's pockets it too was empty. Only a faded black and white picture of an older couple remained. Matt guessed they were probably his parents.

'It looks as if Mr Browning was indeed on his uppers. He must have been counting on this role in Miss Monbiere's play,' Inspector Lewis said.

Matt was inclined to agree. Of all the guests in the theatre company, Paul was clearly the one who seemed to be struggling the most financially. His clothes were shabby and shoes, although once good, were now worn. Matt wondered if he had pawned anything he had of value in order to stay afloat. This offer from Lambert must have seemed like a true lifeline.

He was roused from his thoughts by the sound of Albert and the lighthouse keeper returning along the path carrying the door. Between them they manhandled Paul's body onto the makeshift stretcher and set off back towards the jetty.

'You can place him in my outhouse for now. 'Tis cool in there and he'll not be disturbed till your doctor comes over on the boat,' the keeper offered.

The chief inspector thanked him, and they followed the man's suggestion, leaving Paul's body covered by an old sheet on a trestle table in the small stone hut at the end of the lighthouse keeper's garden.

Albert hurried off to the hotel to assist his wife with lunch, leaving Matt with the two policemen.

'I think, Inspector Lewis, if you would go and look around on the clifftop for any indication of a weapon, stone, stick et cetera, as Captain Bryant has suggested. I need to examine Mr Browning's room in case there is a note or message of any kind to indicate his frame of mind this morning,' the chief inspector said.

Inspector Lewis gave Matt a sour look. Matt guessed he was not pleased that he had not been the one who had suggested examining the clifftop.

'Can I be of any further assistance, sir?' Matt asked. He was keen to appraise Kitty and Alice of the latest information.

'Thank you, Captain Bryant. Could I ask you and your good lady wife, and, of course, Miss Miller, to continue observing your fellow guests?'

'Of course,' Matt agreed.

'Oh, and if you could ask Mrs Jenkins to keep a plate for myself and the inspector from luncheon, we would be most grateful,' Chief Inspector Greville asked with a twinkle in his eye.

CHAPTER FOURTEEN

Kitty and Alice assisted Mrs Jenkins with serving lunch and clearing the table. Albert arrived to join them just as they were finishing dessert.

'Thank you for your assistance, Mrs Bryant, Miss Miller, the missus and I are most grateful,' Albert thanked them both quietly as he collected the empty dishes from the table.

'Not at all, we were glad to help,' Kitty assured him. She hoped that Marie would sort out the money the couple were owed, and quickly so they could help their daughter.

The others around the table murmured their thanks to Kitty and Alice too, although Kitty suspected they were simply relieved that they had not been expected to assist in any menial tasks.

They had moved out of the dining room and back into the lounge by the time Matt and the chief inspector returned. Matt went through to the kitchen and Chief Inspector Greville went upstairs.

'What do you suppose is happening now?' Marie asked as she took a seat next to Alec. 'Do you think they found him?'

'I don't know. I suppose we will have to wait. I dare say they will tell us soon enough. I hope a boat is able to come across,' Alice said. 'The sea is much calmer now than it was this morning.'

Kitty looked out and saw her friend was right. The white horses on the waves had diminished and the earlier breeze seemed to have softened.

'I want to leave here as soon as possible,' Selina announced. 'I'm sorry, Marie, but this whole thing has been so awful that even if you recast Paul's role, I don't think I can continue with the play.'

'Selina, darling, I can quite understand. Obviously, all of us feel terrible about Norman and now poor Paul. Marie herself has suffered greatly. I think perhaps a break and then we can reconsider the future of the play and the tour. What say you, Marie, my dear?' Lambert said and looked at Marie for a response.

Marie nodded. 'Of course. I'm so sorry, my dears. I need to sort out the insurance aspect of everything. I hope that Norman had made some provisions. I don't know about Norman's will or even what will happen to this place. It's all so horribly mixed up right now.' A tear escaped from the corner of her eye and ran down her cheek.

'Please don't distress yourself, Marie, darling. We will all support you as best as we can,' Alec rushed to reassure her, proffering her his handkerchief.

Through the open door into the reception area Kitty saw the chief inspector come back down the stairs and head in the direction of the kitchen. She wondered where Inspector Lewis had gone.

'There is a boat coming!' Colin alerted the group and they all turned to look through the window. Sure enough they could see the familiar shape of the boat that had brought them to the island making its way across the water.

'Do you think we will be able to leave on it?' Selina asked in a hopeful voice.

'I don't suppose any of us will be allowed to go anywhere until the police have an answer to who killed Norman and what happened to Paul,' Colin replied.

'Surely the obvious explanation is that Paul must have murdered Norman and then took his own life in a fit of remorse,' Marie said.

'Perhaps,' Kitty agreed. She saw no point in opposing the singer's suggestion. One of the group was a murderer, and she wasn't convinced that Paul had been the culprit. There seemed no benefit, however, to pointing this out and perhaps placing a target on her own back.

Matt entered the lounge, and everyone turned towards him, eager for news.

'Captain Bryant, were you able to, you know, recover Paul?' Colin asked.

Matt nodded. 'Yes, although it was quite tricky. We had some assistance from the lighthouse keeper and Mr Browning's body is now awaiting the arrival of the doctor.' He looked out to where the small boat was approaching the jetty.

'Do you think it was suicide?' Lambert asked.

Matt shrugged. 'I really couldn't say what may have happened to him. None of us are medical men. I'm sure the doctor will be able to determine what is likely.'

Kitty knew her husband well enough to know that he was being quite circumspect in his reply. This led her to suspect that the police were not convinced that Paul's death was an accident or suicide.

The group watched from the lounge as the boat docked and was met by Inspector Lewis, before he and Dr Carter walked away in the direction of the lighthouse. The boat captain, however, started up the path to the hotel bearing what appeared to be a grey mail bag of post and a large wooden box of vegetables. He disappeared around the side of the hotel and Kitty guessed he must be taking the provisions and post to the kitchen. A few moments later, a wailing keening sound rent the air.

'What on earth?' Kitty jumped up and hurried down the corridor towards the kitchen, Matt and Alice hard on her heels with the others following behind her.

Inside the kitchen she saw Mrs Jenkins being supported by her husband as she leaned over the kitchen sink, alternately retching and screaming. The chief inspector and the boat captain stood near the table watching helplessly.

A telegram lay open beside the chief inspector's interrupted late luncheon. Kitty glimpsed the words I'M SORRY TO INFORM YOU THAT...

'Is it Maud?' she asked the chief inspector quietly.

He nodded. 'She passed away yesterday.'

Kitty ushered the others back toward the lounge. The chief inspector and the boat captain accompanied them. Alice collected the remains of the brandy and two glasses and slipped back to the kitchen with them.

'What's happened?' Lambert asked once they were all back in the lounge.

'The Jenkinses only daughter was seriously ill, and it seems she has now passed away,' Kitty explained.

'Oh, how awful.' Selina sank down on the sofa, her face pale with distress.

'Three deaths in such a short space of time,' Marie murmured.

The theatre company exchanged nervous glances and Kitty remembered how superstitious many actors were.

'The inspector and the doctor are coming.' Colin had returned to his watch post by the window.

'I had better go and meet them.' Chief Inspector Greville leapt up and headed outside. The boat captain followed him.

The group watched as he met the other two men on the path and a short conversation followed. Inspector Lewis produced something large and heavy wrapped in brown paper from the capacious pocket of his overcoat.

After a few more moments of discussion the men proceeded up to the hotel and entered the reception area. The boat captain went back down towards the jetty. Inspector Lewis and the doctor went off to the kitchen and the chief inspector entered the smaller lounge.

Matt placed his arm around Kitty's waist and gave her a comforting hug. Kitty exchanged a reassuring glance with Alice. It was clear that something was afoot. Whatever it was had to be connected to the doctor's visit to the lighthouse keeper's shed and whatever was contained inside Inspector Lewis's parcel.

The chief inspector came to the connecting door between the lounges some ten minutes later. 'Captain Bryant, Mrs Bryant, may I see you both for a moment, please?'

Kitty followed Matt into the other room. Dr Carter was seated on one of the armchairs, twiddling his hat between his fingers. He sprang to his feet as Kitty entered to greet her with a kiss on her cheek.

'My dear Kitty, another body, eh?'

'I'm afraid so,' Kitty replied as she took a seat next to Matt.

'Thanks to your suggestion, Captain Bryant, Inspector Lewis conducted a search on the clifftop in the area where you saw the body in the sea. He discovered this amongst a pile of rocks from a tumbled down wall.' The chief inspector unwrapped the mystery package and Kitty saw a large, jagged piece of stone. Attached to the rock she saw some hair and a dark red smear of blood.

'Oh dear.' Kitty's stomach rolled, and she hoped her recently eaten lunch was not about to make a return.

'Murder again then, sir,' Matt said as the chief inspector covered the rock back up.

'It would seem that Mr Browning was hit over the head and then either fell or was pushed over the cliff.' Chief Inspector Greville looked at Dr Carter.

'I would concur. The blow itself may have been sufficient to kill him. However, I can see that he has sustained several fractures from landing on the rocks. Even if he had been merely stunned by the first blow, the fall would have finished him off.' Dr Carter smiled cherubically at them. 'Oh, by the by, when I was on the mainland I completed my examination of Sir Norman. He definitely couldn't have fired the gun with that hand. Still, his heart was in a dreadful state, you know. If he hadn't been shot, then he could have dropped dead at any time.'

Kitty told them what the rest of the party had said about their movements earlier in the morning. She also repeated the information Mrs Jenkins had given them about seeing various people going out.

'I have just been to see Mrs Jenkins and administered a sedative. Poor lady has had a terrible shock.' Dr Carter's face grew sombre.

'We shall, of course, have to speak to her about what she saw but under the circumstances that interview can wait until tomorrow,' Chief Inspector Greville said. 'I shall also leave Mr Jenkins until tomorrow.'

'Did you discover anything in Mr Browning's room, sir?' Matt asked.

Kitty's ears perked up at this. There had to be a reason why Paul had been killed so soon after the demise of Sir Norman. Had he seen or heard something that might indicate who the killer was?

'You will recall that Mr Browning's wallet was empty when we recovered him from the rocks?' The chief inspector looked at Matt as he spoke.

Matt nodded in agreement.

'In Mr Browning's room, hidden amongst his undergarments, was a small pile of crisp five-pound notes. Forty pounds in total,' the chief inspector said.

'You think he may have been trying a spot of blackmail?' Kitty asked. That could surely be the only possible explanation. Paul had no money of his own. If he had pressed the murderer for money, they must have bought him off with whatever cash they had on them at the island. No doubt they would have promised more when they were back on the mainland.

'I think it was fairly obvious that Mr Browning was struggling for money. He must have spotted an opportunity with Sir Norman's death. Unfortunately, for him, it seems the murderer saw the chance to rid themselves of the blackmailer, probably hoping to pin the murder on him too. That would leave them free and clear,' the chief inspector said.

Kitty could see that was a pretty good hypothesis. Marie, for one, had suggested that Paul may have been the murderer and had taken his own life. However, the others had also seemed to think the same way. Selina too had been quick to assume that Paul may have jumped from the cliff.

All of them had motives for wishing Sir Norman dead and would have had the opportunity to kill him. She could see that whoever shot the hotelier would have had no compunction about killing for a second time.

There was a tap at the door from the corridor and Inspector Lewis entered the room. 'The boat captain is asking, sir, if you wish to transport Mr Browning back to the mainland, only he needs to leave soon if so.'

'Yes, I have prepared him for transportation,' said Dr Carter. 'If he would like to go along to the lighthouse keeper's cottage I'll come along and meet him there. I presume you have no further need of my services, Chief Inspector?'

'No, thank you, Doctor,' the chief inspector agreed.

The doctor collected his large leather medical bag. He bade

farewell to Matt and Kitty and accompanied Inspector Lewis out of the room.

'I presume you wish to start interviewing the others, Chief Inspector?' Matt asked.

'Yes. It will be interesting to hear if any of them admits they were outside the hotel this morning without a helpful reminder from me.' The chief inspector took out his trusty notebook once more.

Kitty would have dearly loved to remain and listen to what was said. She suspected, however, that unless she and Alice organised something in the kitchen there would be no supper that evening with the Jenkinses being out of action. Something would have to be done and she and Alice were the ones best placed to do it.

'Shall I ask someone to come through, Chief Inspector?' Kitty asked.

'Thank you, Mrs Bryant, I think I'll begin with the ladies. Perhaps Miss Monbiere?' Chief Inspector Greville suggested.

Kitty left Matt with the chief inspector and went into the main lounge. 'Miss Monbiere, the chief inspector would like to see you.'

Marie looked slightly startled by the summons but rose and left the room.

'What's afoot?' Alice murmured as Kitty came to sit beside her.

'I'll tell you in the kitchen. I'm afraid it looks as if we shall need to prepare some supper, or everyone will go hungry tonight.'

'Yes, poor Mrs Jenkins will be in no fit state to see to anything,' Alice agreed.

They made their way out of the lounge and headed to the kitchen. The dirty things from lunch were still in the sink and the kitchen table was covered in used crockery and cups.

'Right, best set to and clean this lot up,' Alice said, taking a clean white apron from the hook on the back of the pantry door and wrapping it around her slender form. 'Remind me when you suggest a nice holiday to me in future that I should take a big pinch of salt,' Alice said with a smile as Kitty took down another apron from the hook for herself.

'Busman's holiday for both of us,' Kitty agreed as she collected the used plates from the table and carried them to the sink.

'What did the doctor and Chief Inspector Greville have to say to you then?' Alice asked after glancing around the empty kitchen to make sure they could not be overheard.

Kitty told Alice everything she had learned while they washed the dishes and cleaned up the kitchen.

'Blimey, that's not good. That means as one of them out there killed Mr Browning *and* Sir Norman. I were thinking of getting the men to come and give us a hand peeling the potatoes but I don't fancy having them around sharp knives now.' Alice hung the damp tea clothes on the drying rack before inspecting the contents of the pantry.

'I know what you mean.' Kitty joined her friend at the pantry door.

'What am we going to cook, then?' Alice asked.

'The boat captain has restocked the fresh vegetables and there is plenty of milk, cheese and eggs.' Kitty looked at the contents of the cold store. 'You know too that I am not a good cook.'

Kitty's housekeeper, Mrs Smith, prepared and organised most of her and Matt's meals. Living in a hotel for most of her life she had never been permitted or encouraged to learn to cook beyond simple dishes. The hotel kitchen had been a busy working place and it had not been wise to have a young girl underfoot.

'Hmm.' Alice grinned at her. 'Well, I can only do plain cooking, nothing fancy.'

'I rather think they should be grateful for anything they get, and they can jolly well all come and wash up afterwards too,' Kitty said.

'That sounds fair to me. There's a nice big apple pie here that can do for pudding with some cream, and I reckon if we chop up some of this veg with that lamb, then we can put a big pot of stew on,' Alice suggested.

'That seems sensible,' Kitty agreed.

'That means as Mr and Mrs Jenkins can have a plate if they want one. And if the rest of them don't like it, well they can lump it,' Alice said, picking up a large knife ready to dice the meat.

CHAPTER FIFTEEN

The opera singer took a seat in front of Chief Inspector Greville. Her face was pale, and she was clearly making an effort to appear composed.

'Good afternoon, Miss Monbiere,' he began. 'I realise that this discussion will be very distressing so soon after the recent murder of your fiancé, Sir Norman Whittier. Unfortunately, as you know, the body of another member of your party, Mr Paul Browning, was discovered this morning in the sea below the cliffs outside the hotel. On closer inspection, following a medical examination and the discovery of a weapon on the clifftop, it seems that Mr Browning was also murdered.' The chief inspector regarded the singer with a level gaze.

'Paul was murdered? I don't understand. I mean, why?' Marie appeared perplexed, her brow furrowing as she tried to understand the chief inspector's statement.

'Had you, or anyone else here, quarrelled with Mr Browning?' the policeman asked.

'No, we hadn't. Paul could be very annoying when he'd had too much to drink but as far as I know he was on good terms with everyone,' Marie said.

'May I ask, when did you last see Mr Browning?'

'Well, last night, before we went upstairs. Yes, I think it must have been last night,' Marie said.

'You didn't see him at all this morning? Are you sure about that?' the chief inspector asked.

'No, I had breakfast in my room. I wasn't hungry so I just had tea and toast on a tray. I thought I should catch up with writing letters to Norman's friends and colleagues so that they could be informed of his death. If I got them ready, then they could go with the boat when it next came across,' Marie said. She smoothed the material of her dress across her knees.

Chief Inspector Greville scribbled in his notebook. 'I see. You didn't give Mr Browning any money at all, Miss Monbiere? A loan, perhaps, or repayment of a debt? An advance on his wages?'

Marie looked confused. 'No. Paul had no need of money here. Everything was paid for.'

'And Mr Browning didn't approach you for any money at all yesterday or today?' the chief inspector persisted.

'No. I mean, Paul had no money. He had asked Lambert for an advance on his salary before we came here. We refused as we suspected he would have only drunk the money away,' Marie said.

'When exactly did he ask Mr Pike for this money?' the chief inspector asked.

'Oh, about a week ago. This was when he was first offered the role. He was living freely here so until he went back to the mainland, he wouldn't require any money, would he?'

The chief inspector gave a grunt of assent to this comment. 'You remained in your room until shortly before lunch today? You didn't leave it at all at any time to step outside for any reason?'

'No, as I said I had letters to write. Norman had a cousin near Basingstoke and a very elderly aunt in Bournemouth. I wanted to write something to them so they wouldn't be shocked when they learned of his death if something got into the newspapers. They are his only family that I know of, so I thought I should tell them what had happened.' Marie fished out her handkerchief and dabbed at her eyes as she spoke.

'Very well, thank you, Miss Monbiere. Perhaps you would be so kind as to send Miss Headingly in next.' The chief inspector appeared unmoved by the singer's tears.

'Of course.' Marie gave a final sniff and walked out of the room.

'Do you believe her, sir?' Matt asked quickly before Miss Headingly arrived.

'I might have if I hadn't noticed fresh mud on the sides of her shoes,' the chief inspector murmured as he and Matt rose to greet Selina.

'Miss Headingly, thank you for agreeing to be interviewed again,' the chief inspector said as he retook his seat.

'I wasn't aware that I had a choice in the matter,' Selina remarked drily.

'I am sorry to confirm that your late colleague, Mr Browning, was murdered.'

Selina started forward in her seat, her eyes wide. 'Murdered? It wasn't an accident? Or suicide?'

'Doctor Carter is quite sure, Miss Headingly, and my inspector has already discovered the murder weapon. Mr Browning was hit over the head and then either fell or was pushed to his death,' Chief Inspector Greville said.

Selina shuddered. 'That's awful, just too awful for words. I had thought, perhaps, that Paul had murdered Norman and then couldn't live with the consequences, but if what you're saying is true...' She broke off.

'Yes, Miss Headingly?' the chief inspector asked.

'...if what you said is true, then someone here killed both of them, didn't they?' Selina finished her sentence, her face pale with shock.

'I'm afraid realistically there is no other conclusion that can be drawn. May I ask when you last saw Mr Browning?' The chief inspector was calm but firm.

'Paul? I think... well, I suppose it was yesterday. Last night, when we all went upstairs to bed.' Selina seemed distracted as she replied.

'Are you quite sure of that, Miss Headingly? You didn't see him this morning during breakfast or afterwards?' Chief Inspector Greville continued to press her.

'No, I didn't bother with breakfast this morning. I came downstairs late as I had a headache from last night. I arrived just as Mr Jenkins was clearing the dining room and he very kindly made me a pot of tea. I drank it in here. Colin and Lambert were in the other lounge, and I was not in the mood for company.' Selina glanced around as if half expecting the tea tray to still be there.

'Did you venture outside the hotel at all after you had finished your tea, Miss Headingly?' the chief inspector asked.

'I...' Selina appeared to be struggling to think. 'Yes, I saw the sun was out, so I took a short walk around the gardens. I thought it might help my headache.'

Chief Inspector Greville scribbled more notes in his book. 'Did you see any of the other guests while you were outside?'

Selina's hands trembled and she fumbled in her bag to retrieve her cigarettes. Once she had inserted one into her holder and Matt had provided her with a light, she appeared more composed.

'I only walked around the boundary and looked at some of the early bulbs that have opened. There are some snowdrops near a hazel tree. I thought I saw Colin walking towards the jetty, but he didn't see me,' Selina said.

'You saw no sign of Mr Browning?' the chief inspector asked.

'No. I saw Mrs Bryant's party leave the hotel and then I came back inside. I'd started to feel cold.' Selina glanced at Matt and tapped the ash from the end of her cigarette into one of the crystal ashtrays.

'May I ask if Mr Browning ever mentioned his financial concerns to you?' the chief inspector asked.

Selina seemed surprised by the question. 'Paul was always complaining about having no money. Whenever we met before coming here he would try to beg cigarettes, or a drink.' Selina rolled her eyes.

'And since you arrived on the island? Did he ask for money from you or any other person that you know of?' The chief inspector's pen was poised above his notebook.

Selina extinguished her cigarette. 'Not from me. He knew that I didn't have any money to spare. My stepfather gives me a small allowance for my clothes but other than that I'm pretty much on my own, and acting doesn't pay terribly well.'

'And did you or anyone else here have any quarrels or disagreements with Mr Browning?'

Selina shook her head. 'No, Chief Inspector, it sounds dreadfully boring, doesn't it? But we all get on fairly well.'

'I see, thank you, Miss Headingly.'

The actress left the room and the chief inspector stretched and rubbed his eyes. 'What do you think so far, Captain Bryant?'

'Marie was lying about not going outside. She had fresh mud on her shoes and a couple of small mud spatters on her stockings. Selina admitted being in the grounds and said she saw Colin going towards the jetty, which was interesting. She also had assumed that Paul had murdered Sir Norman before taking his own life.' Matt wondered why Marie had lied. Had she been the person who had given Paul the money? Or was that someone else?

There was a tap at the door and Alice peeped in.

'I hopes I'm not interrupting but Kitty and I thought as you might like a cup of tea.'

Matt leapt up to open the door wider for her and she carried in a tray of tea things, which she set down on the table. He noticed that her smart print dress was covered by a vast white apron.

'That's very thoughtful of you both, Miss Miller.' The chief inspector's eyes lit up when he saw that a plate of biscuits had been included with the teacups.

'Not at all, sir. We thought we would prepare dinner for tonight as well since the Jenkinses had been given such terrible news,' Alice explained.

Matt smiled. 'Don't tell me Kitty is cooking?'

Alice grinned. 'No, just assisting, although we will be expecting everybody to pitch in tonight to do the clearing up.'

The chief inspector laughed. 'That sounds very fair to me, Miss Miller. Mrs Greville would assure you that I am a dab hand with a tea cloth when required.'

'I shall bear that in mind, sir,' Alice said as she left the room.

The chief inspector poured tea for himself and Matt before taking several biscuits from the tray. 'Miss Miller and Mrs Bryant are very enterprising ladies,' he remarked before crunching a ginger biscuit.

'Indeed, and at least we are being spared Kitty's cooking. She has been attempting to learn more dishes, but I have to say that it is not her forte.' Matt picked up his cup. Much as he loved his wife, he knew that she would be the first to agree with his assessment.

'Mrs Greville does a nice steak and kidney pudding, although since I was promoted, she spends less time in the kitchen, and we have acquired a cook.' The chief inspector looked somewhat mournful, and Matt wondered if he sometimes regretted going for the chief inspector's post.

'Who did you wish to see next, sir?' Matt asked as they continued to sip their tea.

'I think we'll have young Standish in here next. According to what you and Mrs Bryant told me, he claimed he was in his room packing some of his things. Which sounds a bit of a tale as I can't see it would have taken him long to do that.' The chief inspector consulted his notebook.

Matt set his empty cup down on its saucer and the chief inspector brushed biscuit crumbs from his tie.

'Very good, sir. I'll go and fetch him,' Matt suggested.

The lounge next door was quiet. Marie was missing and Selina was occupying herself with a crossword puzzle. The three men were playing cards at a table in the window.

'Mr Standish, could you come through, please?' Matt asked.

Alec folded his hand and apologised to his fellow players, before following Matt back through into the other room.

'Please take a seat, Mr Standish.' The chief inspector motioned the actor to one of the chairs opposite his own seat.

Matt retook his chair at the side where he could observe both men.

'Mr Standish, may I ask when you last saw Mr Browning?' Chief Inspector Greville asked.

'This morning at breakfast. I was just finishing; I think I was the first one there and as I was leaving Paul came in,' Alec said.

His response came quickly, and Matt wondered if he had been rehearsing his reply based on the questions the ladies had been asked.

'Did you have any conversation with Mr Browning at breakfast?' The chief inspector was ready with his notebook.

Alec shrugged. 'The usual things, good morning, the weather. I wasn't there for very long as I'd finished eating.'

Chief Inspector Greville made his notes. 'And how did Mr Browning seem in himself?'

Alec frowned. 'You know that's the odd thing now you come to mention it. He was almost, well, pleased with himself. That's the only way I could describe it.'

'Did he mention any plans to you about going out for a walk at all?'

Matt leaned forward in his seat as he waited to see what Alec's response to the policeman's question would be.

'We agreed the weather had improved and I said I hoped a boat might come over. He didn't mention anything about his plans to me I don't think.' Alec's frown deepened. 'No, just that he was looking forward to going back to the mainland soon.'

'You didn't see him again?' Chief Inspector Greville asked. 'Outside the hotel?'

'No, that was the last time I saw him. I had my breakfast, pottered about a bit in the lounge and then thought I ought to put a few things in my case. I thought that if the boat did come across then we might all be sent packing, so I should be ready,' Alec said.

'Did you see any of the other guests after your finished breakfast?' Chief Inspector Greville stopped writing to look up at the actor.

'Well, I popped along to Marie's room, you know, to see if she was all right and if she wanted anything.' Colour crept into Alec's cheeks. 'I just tapped on her door.'

'And was Miss Monbiere in need of anything?' Chief Inspector Greville asked.

'She didn't answer so I assumed she must be asleep. Then I saw Selina on the landing, she said she had a headache and was going downstairs to get some tea,' Alec said.

It sounded to Matt as if either Marie had been absent when Alec had knocked, or had guessed it was likely to be her admirer and had decided not to respond.

'You say you were packing some of your things, Mr Standish. You didn't leave your room at all to go out for a walk yourself?' the chief inspector asked in a mild tone.

'No, well, I mean...' Alec paused, clearly uncomfortable.

'Did you or didn't you go outside?' Chief Inspector Greville asked firmly.

'All right, yes, I may have stepped outside just for a few minutes. I didn't go far, just towards the lighthouse. I've never been inside a lighthouse, and I thought if the keeper was there, he might show me,' Alec said.

Chief Inspector Greville leaned back in his chair. 'And did you see the keeper? Or see anyone else while you were out?'

'No, the cottage was empty, so I turned around and came back. I saw Lambert and Colin in the lounge and went to join them.'

'Thank you, sir. Did you, or any of the others, have any disagreements with Mr Browning since you've been here?'

'No. Paul drank, but I don't think he had upset anyone. We all got on rather well,' Alec said.

His reply appeared to support what the others had said.

'One more thing. Did Mr Browning ever ask you for money?'

Alec was clearly surprised by the policeman's question. 'Money? No, well, not since we've been here. Paul was always broke, but he knew I wasn't particularly wealthy. I don't have the kind of funds to do more than buy a chap a pint or offer a cigarette.'

The chief inspector dismissed Alec back to the other room.

'Well, what do you think now, Captain Bryant? That was quite a story.'

'Marie didn't answer his knock. He claims he saw no one outside the hotel,' Matt said with a frown. 'I can't see that placing a few things in a case would have taken him all morning. That story about the lighthouse sounded a bit fishy too.'

'I agree, he was keeping something back. It's clear that after we've spoken to these next two, we shall need to talk to Miss Monbiere again. It's a shame Mrs Jenkins is not well enough to talk to us. Her testimony may make all the difference.' A hint of frustration sounded in the chief inspector's voice.

'I agree, sir. Who shall I get next? Mr Frobisher or Mr Pike?' Matt asked.

He was very keen to hear what both men had to say for themselves.

CHAPTER SIXTEEN

Lambert Pike sauntered into the room behind Matt and took his place in front of the chief inspector. He appeared quite composed and resigned to being interviewed.

'Good afternoon, Mr Pike. I wonder if you could tell me when you last saw Mr Browning?' The chief inspector turned over a fresh page in his notebook as he waited for the response.

'Certainly, that would be at breakfast this morning. I arrived at the dining room with Colin, and Paul was already in there finishing off his cup of tea,' Lambert replied.

'Did you speak to him at all, have any conversation?' the chief inspector asked.

Lambert flicked a small piece of lint from the knee of his grey flannel trousers. 'We remarked on the weather, if there was still plenty of bacon left in the chafing dishes, that kind of thing. Nothing special.'

The chief inspector made a note in his book. 'How did he seem in himself to you, sir?'

Lambert looked slightly surprised by the question. 'Thinking about it now, I guess he seemed quite cheerful for Paul. He was a naturally morose kind of fellow normally.'

'I suppose that you are now aware that Mr Browning was murdered?' Chief Inspector Greville asked.

Lambert looked slightly abashed. 'Um, yes, Marie told us all after she returned from seeing you. It was quite a shock. I think we had all started to believe that perhaps Paul had been responsible for shooting Norman and had, well, jumped off the cliff to avoid being caught. It seemed the only possible explanation.'

'You didn't see him or speak to him again after breakfast?'

Lambert appeared to consider the chief inspector's question. 'No, I don't think so, not to speak to. He had said he intended going for a stroll for some fresh air. I must admit I thought it was probably to shake off a hangover. I saw him step out in his hat and coat later when I was in the lounge.'

'You and Mr Frobisher finished your breakfast together and went to the lounge?' Chief Inspector Greville asked.

'No, I went upstairs to collect a book I'd started reading. Colin went to the lounge I think but he wasn't there when I came downstairs. He joined me a little later. I assumed he must have been in his room,' Lambert said.

'Did Mr Browning ever ask you for money, Mr Pike?' the chief inspector asked.

Lambert gave a snort of laughter. 'Paul was constantly after money. Could someone spot him a loan for this, that, or the other? We all knew it was to buy more drink, so the answer was always no, I'm afraid. He asked me before we came here for an advance on his salary. That would have been fatal in his case.' Lambert stopped short as if suddenly aware of the implications of his words. 'Sorry, I didn't mean... Well, he would have disappeared with the old spondulicks, got roaring drunk and been useless for the play, so obviously I refused. His stay here was free anyway so he wouldn't need any money until later and Marie had organised lodgings for the company at each town.'

'He hasn't requested money again since you've been here?' Chief Inspector Greville persisted.

Lambert shook his head. 'No, why would he? Everything here is paid for. Marie arranged it that way to avoid paying wages before the tour actually began. It also helped Norman out by making sure the hotel was ready to open. You know, catching any snags.'

Chief Inspector Greville scribbled furiously in his notebook. 'You remained in the lounge all morning? You didn't step outside at all, sir?'

'No, I stayed put. Fresh air isn't really my thing and I simply abhor nature. Too many buzzy, flying, flappy things. I'm a city man. I prefer the buzz of a crowd and the convenience of omnibuses, clubs and shops,' Lambert said.

'While you were in the lounge did you see any of the others in the gardens or on the path?' the chief inspector asked.

'I was reading my book so I must admit I only glanced outside if I paused to light a cigarette or to adjust my position. I saw Selina wandering around out there looking at plants. Oh, and Alec, I think he must have been out for a stroll.' Lambert looked thoughtful.

'Had Mr Browning upset anyone lately? Or had a quarrel with any of the others in the company?' Chief Inspector Greville made a show of flicking back through his notes as he posed the question.

'No, I don't think so. We're a harmonious little group apart from someone bumping off members of our party.' Lambert raised his eyebrows as he responded.

The chief inspector dismissed Lambert back to the other room. 'Just Mr Frobisher and the Jenkinses to go. We didn't get a lot from that one.'

'No, he didn't have much to tell us. We need to see Miss Monbiere once again too,' Matt reminded the policeman.

'Quite.'

The door from the corridor opened and Inspector Lewis entered.

'The boat has gone off again, sir, with the doctor and Mr Browning.' He cast an envious glance at the tea tray.

'Thank you, Inspector. Mrs Bryant and Miss Miller are in the kitchen, perhaps you could return this tray to them and I'm sure they will be happy to point you in the direction of the tea caddy. You must be ready for some refreshments yourself by now,' the chief inspector suggested. 'We just have Mr Frobisher to interview before dinner, then we can resume later, and I'll go through my notes with you.'

The inspector didn't look terribly happy but dutifully collected the tray and disappeared in the direction of the kitchen. Matt couldn't help feeling a little bit sorry for him.

'Right ho, let's have Mr Frobisher in then.' Chief Inspector Greville rubbed his hands together as Matt went to call him through.

Matt thought that Colin appeared quite nervy as he entered the lounge to sit in front of the chief inspector.

'I'm sorry to have kept you waiting, Mr Frobisher, but I'm sure you understand that we have to be very thorough in these matters.'

'Of course, Chief Inspector,' Colin agreed.

'I believe Miss Monbiere has told you all that Mr Browning was murdered?' The chief inspector turned over a page in his notebook.

'Yes, yes she did. It's a most dreadful shock. I mean we all thought that perhaps Paul had killed Norman, and then, well, you know this morning was an accident or suicide...' Colin stammered to a halt.

Matt supposed that the idea that Paul had been the murderer and had then made away with himself would have resolved things quite nicely.

'Has anyone here quarrelled with Mr Browning recently?' the chief inspector asked.

'No, no, not at all. I'm sure everyone has said what Paul was like, but as far as I'm aware everyone rubbed along together quite well. That's what makes all of this even more terrible.' The faint frown on Colin's forehead deepened.

The chief inspector made a note. 'Did Mr Browning ever ask you for money?'

Colin looked embarrassed. 'Well, yes, I think he tried to touch everyone at some point. We all, I think, refused.'

'And since you've been here on the island? Has he asked again?'

'No, not at all.' Colin seemed surprised by the question.

'When did you last see Mr Browning?' The chief inspector continued with his questions.

'Lambert and I saw him at breakfast as I'm sure he told you. We exchanged a few pleasantries as one does. He mentioned something about a stroll and left. Lambert and I finished our breakfast together.' Colin gave a slight shrug.

'And after breakfast, sir, where did you go then?' Chief Inspector Greville asked.

'I think I went to the lounge for a while,' Colin replied.

'With Mr Pike?' The chief inspector raised his head to look at Colin.

'No, at first, I was by myself. Lambert went upstairs to get a book, I think. At least he was reading later when I came back.'

Matt's ears perked up.

'Where did you go, sir?' Chief Inspector Greville's gaze sharpened.

'I, um, well, as the weather had improved a bit I thought I'd pop out into the gardens and mosey around a little. Get some air by the tennis courts.'

Matt's brows lifted at Colin's response. The hotel grounds were not that extensive inside the boundary wall and Selina had made no mention of encountering Colin in the garden. She had said he had been walking down the hill towards the jetty.

'The gardens, sir? Are you certain that was where you

were?' Chief Inspector Greville's deceptively mild manner masked his interest in Colin's reply.

Matt could see that Colin looked very uncomfortable as he fidgeted on the chair. 'Well, I may have gone a little further, I sort of wandered about a bit.'

'Please try and recollect where this wandering took you, sir. Did it take you in the direction of the cliffs?' Chief Inspector Greville's tone altered to become quite sharp.

Colin's face flushed under the chief inspector's scrutiny. 'No, nowhere near the cliffs. I went down to the jetty to see if the sea was settling and to look for the prospect of a boat.'

Chief Inspector Greville scribbled more notes in his book. 'Did you see any of the others while you were outside?'

Colin shuffled again. 'Selina was in the garden, she had her back to me so I don't think she noticed me go past her. I thought I saw Alec on his way back.'

'Which direction was Mr Standish approaching from, sir?'

Beads of sweat were forming on Colin's brow now and Matt could see he was not keen on answering the policeman's question.

'From the cliff side of the path.'

'Not from the lighthouse side?' Chief Inspector Greville's eyes gleamed.

No. I don't know if he had come from the cliffs though. He may not have walked that far,' Colin said.

'Mr Pike was in the lounge when you returned?' the chief inspector asked.

'Yes, and then Selina joined us, followed by Alec. Marie didn't come downstairs until after Captain Bryant there and his party had entered the hotel and told us what had happened.' Colin glanced at Matt.

Chief Inspector Greville glanced at the modern clock on the mantelpiece. 'Thank you, Mr Frobisher. I think we will take a break for now while I update my inspector. I shall be speaking to you all again later today.'

Colin rose and straightened his tweed jacket before returning to the lounge.

'It would seem that Alec Standish has also not been entirely truthful with us either,' Chief Inspector Greville said as the door closed behind Colin.

'No, it's all quite confusing still, isn't it, sir? Someone gave Paul that money. He certainly didn't have it when he came here. Right up until he boarded the boat it sounds as if he had been asking various members of the company for loans.' Matt was thoughtful.

'I suspect that that money was all the cash the person that gave it to him had on them. I suspect it was a down payment to keep quiet about whatever Paul had seen, heard or discovered,' Chief Inspector Greville said.

'No one is admitting that Paul asked them for money, so he clearly *had* seen or heard something that made him realise who had shot Sir Norman. It wasn't a scattergun approach to try his luck.' Matt wished the actor had gone to the police with whatever it was he had known. He would still have been alive if he had.

'Yes, indeed. I think he saw a payday looming that would make his financial woes disappear and the temptation was too much.' The chief inspector stroked his moustache thoughtfully.

'It will be interesting to discover what Mr and Mrs Jenkins have to say tomorrow,' Matt responded.

He didn't think they could entirely eliminate the Jenkinses from the investigation either. Sir Norman's failure to pay them the money they were owed so they could procure better medical care for their daughter gave them a good motive for wishing him dead. Especially if it had become clear to them that he had never intended nor had the means to pay them.

However, the Jenkinses would not have had forty pounds lying around to pay off Paul. They were too poor to have that kind of money, unless they had stolen it from Sir Norman after they had killed him, perhaps taken from his wallet as part payment of what he owed them. Then they could have sent it to their daughter as quickly as possible once the boat was able to return.

'I agree. I had better go and find Inspector Lewis before he annoys your good lady too much.' Chief Inspector Greville's eyes twinkled as he took his leave to find his junior officer.

* * *

Kitty and Alice left the stew on a low heat and Inspector Lewis drinking his cup of tea at the table. He had tried hinting that they should prepare him a drink, but Alice had pointed him towards the kettle and taken off her apron. Kitty had followed suit and they walked off together to see if the chief inspector had completed his interviews.

A peep inside the main lounge revealed that the rest of the party were all variously occupied. Lambert was playing the piano and the gentle sounds of Chopin were surprisingly soothing.

Chief Inspector Greville emerged from the other door and walked towards the kitchen.

'He must have finished. Captain Bryant is probably still in there.' Alice nudged Kitty and nodded her head in the direction of the small lounge.

They hurried the short distance along the corridor and found Matt standing by the window looking out at the darkening sky across the sea.

'How did it go? What did you find out?' Kitty asked after ensuring the door was closed, muting the piano music.

Alice and Kitty sat and waited eagerly for Matt to share the results of the interviews.

'Phew, that's a lot to take in, isn't it?' Alice said when he had finished giving them a précis of everything he'd learned.

'It's worrying that so many of them seem to have omitted important facts or seem to have deliberately lied,' Kitty agreed.

'That money is a puzzle. I don't know as many people would have that amount on them, even posh people, especially coming here where they know as they haven't got anything to spend it on,' Alice said.

'Do you think the money may have come from Sir Norman himself?' Kitty asked, looking at Matt. 'He may have given it to Paul before he was killed. Perhaps *he* was the person Paul was blackmailing.'

'That is a very good point. If Sir Norman did give him the money, then perhaps whatever hold Paul had over him was known to his killer who may have had even more to lose and decided to eliminate both of them,' Matt said, taking a seat next to Kitty.

'I saw a film last year where a bloke was being blackmailed and then he said he weren't going to pay no more. It was one of those gangster films, a protection racket. Anyway, he said he wouldn't pay so they killed him. His girlfriend had overheard it all. They didn't know as she was there and then she killed the blackmailer. When they found out, they came after her.' Alice's eyes brightened. 'It could be something like that, couldn't it?'

Matt grinned. 'Yes, I suppose it could be a similar thing. It's one hypothesis to consider certainly. We also have to remember that the money may have been taken from Sir Norman after he died. From his wallet, or perhaps from his safe.'

'Then if there could be one or two people involved, it could be anybody here. Do you think as even Mr and Mrs Jenkins could have done it?' Alice looked appalled. 'Surely not. Those poor people.'

'Those poor people do have a very strong motive remember,' Matt said. 'Albert could have shot Sir Norman when he collected the tea tray. Perhaps they had words over the money they were owed. Then he could have taken the cash and scarpered.'

Kitty hoped Matt was wrong but she was forced to admit to herself that it was a possibility.

Alice's eyes widened in dismay. 'Oh dear.'

'And why did Marie and Alec both lie?' Kitty asked. 'Are they in it together, do you think? Did Marie discover that Sir Norman had spent all her money and was about to go bankrupt?'

'Alec is very attached to Marie,' said Alice. 'Perhaps as he found out and shot Sir Norman to try and save her. Especially as there was a bit of talk as there might be an insurance policy. She would be expecting to be in his will too,' Alice suggested.

'I wonder if that part is true? Sir Norman seemed to have a lot of secrets. I'm sure Chief Inspector Greville said he was looking into Sir Norman's will and his insurance policies,' Matt said.

'It might be as all poor Miss Monbiere inherits is a big pile of bills,' Alice remarked.

CHAPTER SEVENTEEN

Alec Standish volunteered to run the meals from the kitchen to the table while Alice plated them up. Lambert and Colin agreed to clear and assist with the washing-up afterwards. Dinner, therefore, despite the terrible events of the day, ended up being a more relaxed affair than Kitty had been anticipating.

Marie professed herself to be very grateful for everyone's help while Mrs Jenkins was indisposed. Alice's cooking also appeared to be well received as the plates that went back to the kitchen had very little left on them. The compliments she received from the others called a rosy-pink hue to her cheeks.

The telephone on the reception desk rang as the dessert dishes were being cleared and Chief Inspector Greville hurried away from the table to answer it. He was there for quite some time talking to whoever was on the other end of the line. By the time he had finished, and the group had returned to the lounge, Kitty saw that he seemed to have made quite a few notes in his book.

Much to her frustration, immediately after the call ended the chief inspector took Inspector Lewis, and they went to the smaller room. Kitty longed to know what his telephone call had been about. From the snippet she had caught on her way to the lounge it had sounded as if he was receiving answers regarding Sir Norman's financial affairs. It would be very interesting to discover details about a possible will and insurance policies.

Once everyone was settled in the lounge, Colin and Lambert wheeled in a trolley containing coffee, which they presented with a flourish.

'Shall I be mother?' Lambert had a tea cloth over his arm as he bowed to Marie.

'Thank you,' she accepted graciously.

Lambert served the drinks and Selina switched on the wireless for some background music.

Kitty, Alice and Matt took their coffees and sat a little away from the others.

'Who do you think was calling the chief inspector?' Kitty murmured to Matt. She hoped the chief inspector might have mentioned something to Matt about the information he was expecting to receive.

'He was waiting for the answers to some of his enquiries about the will. The phone lines have been going in and out all day, so perhaps the sergeant at the station was relaying some information,' Matt said.

Kitty was forced to be satisfied with her husband's response. She glanced across the room to where Selina appeared to have detached herself from the main party.

The girl was sitting alone near the wireless, a cigarette in her holder and her thoughts clearly miles away from Bird Island. Her delicate china coffee cup sat on its saucer, the liquid it contained growing cold in front of her.

A chill ran down Kitty's spine. Had the death of Sir Norman affected Selina more than she had realised? She was his daughter after all, even if the rest of the group remained oblivious to the fact. Paul's death following so swiftly was enough to distress anyone. Or was there something more sinister behind Selina's solitude?

The rest of the party were talking quietly together around the coffee table. Alec, as usual, was paying close attention to Marie, while Colin and Lambert were mostly conversing together. Everything looked so normal except that it wasn't and the air in the room held a note of tension.

'I'm afraid I really must retire to bed. Forgive me for being a bad hostess but I'm sure you all understand.' Marie set down her cup and rose to make her farewells.

'Of course, my dear, do try and get some sleep,' Colin replied gallantly.

She gave him a wan smile by way of reply and left the room to a chorus of goodnights from the rest of the party.

'If the chief inspector wanted to speak to her again, he'll have to wait till morning now,' Alice murmured in Kitty's ear.

'I suppose so. Poor woman, she has been very brave about all of this,' Kitty said.

With Marie's departure, Lambert, Colin and Alec appeared to have decided to return to their card game.

'Selina, can we tempt you?' Alec called to the actress as he drew up some chairs around the small card table they had used earlier.

His question broke her reverie. 'No, thank you. I don't think I could concentrate on cards right now.'

'Anyone else up for a game?' Alec looked in Kitty, Matt and Alice's direction.

'No, thank you,' Matt answered for all of them as Kitty and Alice shook their heads.

'I'm going to take that trolley back to the kitchen. I don't want Mrs Jenkins to find a sink full of crockery if'n she feels well enough to go in there in the morning,' Alice said, starting to gather up their empty cups.

'Shall I help you?' Kitty offered.

'No, I'll do it. You and Captain Bryant have a bit of time together.' Alice fixed her with a steely gaze which quelled the protest on Kitty's lips.

Matt took Kitty's hand in his. 'Thank you, Alice, you're very kind.'

Alice smiled and went to collect the rest of the crockery before trundling the trolley out of the lounge towards the kitchen.

'We seem to have had very little time alone since we've been here,' Matt observed. 'Which is not surprising, considering everything that's happened.'

'Very true.' Kitty rested her head lightly on his shoulder. 'To think this was supposed to be a simple job and a nice treat for Alice, and now we're up to our necks in murder again.'

'What's going on with Alice, by the way? You gave me quite the tap on my ankle earlier when I mentioned Robert Potter?' Matt asked.

'Oh dear, yes. I'm afraid that things seem to be rather sticky on that front.' Kitty explained what Alice had said about her romance.

To her surprise Matt looked quite sheepish when she had finished her story.

'Do you know something about this? Has Robert spoken to you?' Kitty asked, her suspicions now fully aroused. She knew that her husband would sometimes join Robert and his father for a pint at the Ship in Dartmouth.

'I can't say anything. I'm sworn to secrecy.' Matt turned his head to look at her directly.

Kitty was most dissatisfied. 'Very well if you have given your word but if Robert doesn't do something soon to make things right with Alice, he may find that it's too late,' Kitty told him.

'I'll warn him when we get back to Dartmouth.' Matt kissed the tip of her nose, calling a blush to her cheeks.

'I should go and see how Alice is getting on in the kitchen. With a murderer amongst us I don't like her being by herself,' Kitty said.

Matt went to watch the card game while Kitty set off for the kitchen. There had been no sign of the chief inspector or Inspector Lewis since they had gone into the other lounge. She paused outside the closed door to the smaller lounge but frustratingly couldn't hear anything. After reminding herself that eavesdropping was not a good look, she carried on to find Alice.

When she reached the kitchen, she saw her friend was seated at the kitchen table talking to Mr Jenkins. A brown teapot was placed between them, and they each had a thick white china cup and saucer. Mr Jenkins looked pale, and his eyes were red-rimmed.

'Albert has just took a tray of tea for Mrs Jenkins,' Alice said as Kitty slipped into one of the empty chairs.

'How is Mrs Jenkins now?' Kitty asked. She couldn't imagine how the woman must be feeling. The news of her daughter's death in the telegram must have destroyed her.

Mr Jenkins moved his shoulders in a despairing motion. 'Not good, Mrs Bryant, as you might expect. The sedative the doctor gave her has worn off now. She has another she can take tonight to help her sleep but...' His voice tailed off.

'I'm so terribly sorry for your loss. I expect you both wish to leave here as soon as possible to go to your son-in-law and grandchildren,' Kitty said.

'I dread to think how they'm coping. If only we could leave here, but we've no money unless Miss Monbiere makes good on the wages Sir Norman owed us. We'd be two extra people for them to house and feed.' Albert's body sagged as if he had the weight of the world upon him.

'That money would make all the difference I suppose,' Alice said sympathetically.

'We could at least pay for a funeral and get the children some new clothes and shoes. Spend a bit of time with them while we looked for a new situation near them.' Albert's hand trembled as he placed it around the handle of his cup. 'It seems hopeless at the minute. There's the medical bills at the sanatorium to pay too.'

'All we can do for now is hope the police make an arrest soon and let us all go. Then perhaps your financial situation can be resolved.' Kitty exchanged a glance with Alice while Albert took a somewhat shaky slurp of his tea.

'I hope they do and do it quick. Worst thing we ever did was to come here.' Albert set down his empty cup.

'Who do you think could have killed Sir Norman?' Kitty asked.

Albert gave another shrug. 'I don't know, to be honest, Mrs Bryant. Him and Mr Frobisher had words that afternoon and I think as he argued with Mr Pike as well. Arguing with somebody is different from shooting them dead though. Sir Norman often had fallings out with people. He could be charm itself one minute and red faced with temper the next.'

'The gun was Sir Norman's, wasn't it?' Kitty asked.

'Yes, he kept it in his desk drawer. It wasn't locked or anything. I never thought as it were loaded. You would see it when he opened the drawer to get papers out so anyone could have known as it were there,' Albert said.

'The murderer would have had to have took it out earlier though, wouldn't they?' Alice said suddenly. 'I mean, Sir Norman wouldn't have just sat there while someone come in his office and opened his own desk to use his gun to shoot him.'

Albert looked startled. 'I hadn't thought of that, Miss Miller. Unless as Sir Norman had it on top of his desk already. He would often lift it out of the drawer to get to his chequebook and papers, then leave it out on the top of his desk. I've dropped it back in the drawer myself a time or two.'

'So, he could have argued with someone and had the gun out already and left it out on top of his desk. Then whoever entered the office later could have simply picked it up and shot him with it.' Kitty's mind raced as she worked through the different scenarios.

'I suppose so, Mrs Bryant. I hadn't thought about it really, but yes, I suspect as that's what happened,' Albert agreed. 'If you'll excuse me, I had best get back to the missus. I don't like to leave her alone for too long. Thank you, Miss Miller, Mrs Bryant, for everything as you've done to help us. I'm more grateful than I can say.'

Alice waited until the manservant had left the kitchen. 'The poor man. I really feel for him and his wife.'

Kitty gathered up the cups and took them to the sink.

'Any chance of tea?' Inspector Lewis wandered into the room and looked hopefully at the teapot.

'That one's finished now but the kettle should still be pretty hot. It won't take you long to make a fresh pot,' Alice said.

The inspector crossed to the kitchen range and picked up the kettle to check there was enough water before placing it on the hob to heat.

'Was that Mr Jenkins who was just in here?' he asked as he looked around the kitchen for the tea caddy.

'Yes, poor man. He came in for a drink and to take something up for his wife,' Alice said as she placed the tea caddy and the sugar in front of the policeman.

'I don't suppose he said anything useful?' Inspector Lewis started to hunt in the cupboards for the teacups.

Alice rolled her eyes as she fished out two clean cups and saucers, placing them on a tray ready for the inspector. 'That all depends on what you mean by useful,' she said.

The kettle began to whistle, and the inspector lifted it from the hob to pour boiling water onto the tea leaves in the teapot.

'Well, anything connected with either of the deaths. Anything he saw or heard.'

'I expect you'll have the chance to ask him yourself tomorrow,' Kitty remarked as she finished drying up the crockery Albert and Alice had used. 'We were just talking about the gun.'

Inspector Lewis's foxy face perked up. 'Oh yes, what about the gun?'

Kitty told the inspector what had just been said as Alice finished off preparing the tea tray.

'Right, hmm. Sounds as if anyone could have got hold of it then,' Inspector Lewis said dismissively, collecting the tray ready to take it through to the smaller lounge.

Alice poked her tongue out at the inspector's retreating back. 'That man is so irritating,' she said.

Kitty laughed. 'I know. I sometimes wonder who annoys me more, Mrs Craven or Inspector Lewis.'

Alice grinned. 'That is a close call, especially after how he behaved a few months back when that poor girl was killed at the beauty pageant. Your grandmother's friend is definitely still in the running for top spot though.'

With the kitchen put to rights Kitty decided an early night wouldn't go amiss. It was clear the police were still reviewing all of their notes and it didn't look as if they would be calling anyone back for more questioning until morning.

Alice said she also intended to turn in early so accordingly they said goodnight to the others, collected Matt and went upstairs.

While she was undressing, Kitty told Matt what Mr Jenkins had said.

'That would explain how the murderer got hold of the gun,' Matt agreed.

Kitty thought he seemed unusually quiet as they finished preparing for bed.

'Is everything all right?' she asked as she slid under the covers and snuggled down beneath the blankets.

'I was thinking about the Jenkinses and how they must feel losing their daughter,' Matt said.

Kitty's heart ached for her husband, knowing that he too had lost a child. His first wife and baby had been killed during the raids on London during the war. Matt had been in the trenches then, near Ypres, and it had taken a long time for the news of their deaths to reach him.

'I'm so sorry, Matt.' Kitty placed her hand on his chest. She could feel his heart beating steady and strong beneath her fingers. Her own grief at discovering the body of her missing mother was still fairly recent, so she could empathise with how her husband felt. It had taken him a long time to recover from the loss of his family.

'I was thinking recently, before we came here, about us,' Matt said, tilting his head on the pillow to look at her.

His comment took her by surprise.

'Oh, what about us?' Kitty asked. She could see the outline of his face in the moonlight coming through the partly opened curtains.

'If we should perhaps have a baby,' Matt said.

Kitty stirred in the bed. She wasn't sure how to respond. It wasn't as if they hadn't discussed having a family before they were married. Nothing had happened on that front since, and she wasn't quite sure how she felt about it. Having a baby of her own wasn't something that was often on her mind.

She knew Matt would make a wonderful father, but she wasn't sure if she was ready for motherhood, or indeed even if she would be any good at it. There had been various gentle hints from her grandmother, stronger hints from Matt's mother and pointed hints from Mrs Craven about when a baby would come along.

'Would you like us to have a baby?' Kitty asked. Her heart rate speeded, not sure of what she wanted him to say.

A gentle snore came in response to her question, leaving Kitty to lie awake for a long time while Matt slept peacefully beside her.

CHAPTER EIGHTEEN

Kitty woke the next morning to discover that Matt had already risen and presumably gone downstairs. A moment later, there was a tap on the door.

'Morning.' Alice entered the room carrying a tray of tea and toast. She deposited the tray on the bedside cabinet before opening the curtains to reveal a fresh and sparkling day.

'Matt said as you were still asleep so I thought as I would bring us up a tray. Like old times this is,' Alice said chirpily as she poured them both a cup of tea.

Kitty rubbed the sleep from her eyes and propped herself up on the pillows. 'What time is it?'

'Half past nine.' Alice added milk to the cups.

'Goodness!' Kitty couldn't believe she was so late waking up. Memories of last night's unfinished conversation flooded back into her head and she wondered if Matt had left her to sleep deliberately. Then they wouldn't have to continue the thorny issue of whether they should have a baby, or even in fact if they could have a baby.

'Albert has cooked some breakfast for everybody. Toast, eggs and bacon. The chief inspector give him a hand and got Inspector Lewis to do the washing-up.' Alice chuckled to herself.

'Did he mention anything about resuming the interviews?' Kitty asked as she spread butter onto her toast.

'He told everybody to stay in and around the hotel as him and the inspector would need to speak to them all again,' Alice confirmed.

'And how is Mrs Jenkins today?' Kitty added marmalade from the tiny glass dish to her toast.

'Albert says as she's better than yesterday but still not right. He's going to do sandwiches for lunch. I said as I didn't mind helping and Miss Headingly has volunteered as well,' Alice said, before taking a sip of her tea. 'I think as the chief inspector is talking to Mrs Jenkins first this morning.'

'Poor woman, at least it would get one ordeal out of the way for her,' Kitty said.

'Are you feeling all right this morning? You look a bit peaky.' Alice scrutinised Kitty's face with a concerned gaze.

'It took me a long time to get to sleep last night. I've a lot on my mind at the moment,' Kitty said, putting her toast down on her plate with a sigh.

'I don't want to pry or nothing but is everything all right with you and Captain Bryant?' Alice asked. 'You seem a bit... well, not yourself.'

Kitty gave a wan smile; her friend knew her far too well. 'Yes, we're all right. It's just, I don't know, Alice. We've been married for a while now and I suppose everyone expects us to start a family and it simply hasn't happened. Though we haven't really tried not to have one and...' She paused, blushing deeply to gather her thoughts while Alice continued to gaze sympathetically at her. 'We haven't been desperately trying to have a baby either so I don't know if we actually do want a baby yet and if we did, then could we?' She stopped, aware that she sounded muddled.

'You mean you think as how you might not be able to have a baby as you haven't fallen for one yet?' Alice asked.

'I suppose so but also do we want one in the first place? Or rather, do I want one? You know Lucy had a miscarriage just before Christmas?' Kitty asked.

Her cousin had confided about her loss in a letter. She knew that Lucy and her husband both very much wanted a child to continue his family line.

Alice patted her hand. 'I know, poor love. If it's meant to be then it'll happen and if not, well, that's all right too. 'Tis not the end of the world. So long as the two of you am happy together then you'll work it out.'

Kitty smiled at her friend. 'You're always so sensible.'

'I have got seven younger brothers and sisters,' Alice reminded her with a wry smile. 'Now then, best shake your feathers. I dare say as you'll want to know everything as the chief inspector finds out today.'

* * *

Matt was invited to join Chief Inspector Greville and Inspector Lewis when they asked Mrs Jenkins to join them in the smaller lounge. Albert had made breakfast for everyone while his wife had dressed ready to meet with the two policemen.

She sat before them in a shabby black dress, her grey hair scraped back in a bun at the nape of her neck and her eyes red and puffy from crying.

'Thank you for seeing us, Mrs Jenkins. We appreciate it very much after the terrible news you and your husband received yesterday.' Chief Inspector Greville's tone was kind.

The woman inclined her head in response and pressed her hands together on her lap to stop them from trembling.

'We have already spoken to you about events on the day Sir Norman died. You said you were in the kitchen all day preparing food for the guests and only saw Sir Norman when you came out to serve drinks and to issue room keys. Is that correct?'

'Yes, sir. Albert had taken the donkey cart to collect the luggage and meet the guests off the boat. Sir Norman asked me to have champagne ready to greet everyone. He was keen to impress Mrs Bryant and Miss Miller since they were going to inspect the hotel. He wanted to join the hoteliers' association. After that, I was to give out the keys afore I went back to seeing to the lunch.' Mrs Jenkins sounded tired.

'Your husband took afternoon tea to Sir Norman and then collected the finished tray later that afternoon?' Chief Inspector Greville continued.

'Yes, sir.'

Matt wondered why the chief inspector was going over old ground when he could see the woman was struggling to focus on his questions.

'Mr Jenkins didn't say anything about Sir Norman when he returned the tray to the kitchen?' the chief inspector persisted.

Mrs Jenkins frowned. 'No, I don't think he did. He said something like Sir Norman was in a bad mood, that's all.'

'You assumed this was because of Sir Norman's disagreement with Mr Frobisher?' Inspector Lewis chipped in.

'Well, yes. Albert had said earlier as he'd heard them rowing, the door wasn't quite shut to.'

The chief inspector continued his questions. 'Now yesterday morning you looked out of the kitchen window and saw Mr Browning set off for a walk?'

'Yes, sir. The kitchen is at the back of the hotel, as you know, and the window there has a view of the path leading to the cliffs. I was at the sink when I saw Mr Browning go by. He was whistling to himself, and I had the window open a crack, so I heard him.'

'He seemed in a good mood?'

'Yes, I think so,' Mrs Jenkins replied.

'Would anyone heading towards the cliffs have to pass near the kitchen window?' Inspector Lewis asked.

The crease on Mrs Jenkins's forehead deepened. 'No, sir. There is another path that branches off from near the lighthouse that cuts across but it's a longer route. You have to go out by the tennis courts.'

Matt was interested in this piece of information.

'Did you notice anyone else yesterday morning venture out along the path, either before or after Mr Browning?' Inspector Lewis leaned forward in his seat when the chief inspector posed this particular question.

'Yes, sir, I saw Mr Frobisher go out after Mr Browning but he weren't away for long. I also saw Miss Headingly pottering about in the garden. I couldn't say though if she went up the path or not as I was busy with my chores. Then I saw Mrs Bryant and her party setting off.' Mrs Jenkins looked troubled as she gave her response and glanced at Matt as if for reassurance. Matt wondered if she was concerned that she might be somehow speaking out of turn.

'That's very helpful, Mrs Jenkins. Where was Mr Jenkins yesterday morning while you were in the kitchen?' Chief Inspector Greville asked.

'He cleared the breakfast things and did some of the rooms. You know, made the beds and such. Then he came back and went out with the cart to fetch more milk and cream from the cottages on the other side. He came back just before lunch and went to finish the last of the rooms and then you arrived and said as Mr Browning had fallen off the cliff.' She looked at Inspector Lewis.

'And until Inspector Lewis came to request assistance from your husband everything seemed as normal?' Chief Inspector Greville asked.

Mrs Jenkins looked puzzled by his question. 'Well as normal as a place could be when your employer has been shot dead.' This time there was a touch of asperity in her response and Matt wondered if the questions about her husband had concerned her.

'One more thing, Mrs Jenkins, I don't suppose you would know if Sir Norman usually kept any money on his person, or in the small safe in his office?' Chief Inspector Greville asked.

'He usually had a bit of money on him as I had to give him my accounts every week for what I'd spent on groceries and such. He would reimburse me after he'd checked them all over. There is a tin in the kitchen, hid in the pantry. I had to top it up so as I could pay the smallholders for the milk, and the boat captain for the vegetables and meat, that sort of thing. I used to do it before when we worked at his house in Suffolk. It carried on since we came here a month or so ago when the place was being all set up,' Mrs Jenkins said.

'He would give you the money from his wallet?' Chief Inspector Greville asked.

'Usually, sir, yes. And a right palaver he would make about it too. I had to account for every penny as I spent.' A faint flush of indignation crept into Mrs Jenkins's cheeks. 'Like as if I would swindle him for tuppence ha'penny.'

'When were you next due to present your accounts?' Chief Inspector Greville asked.

'Thursday evening. He always wanted to see them on a Thursday,' the woman confirmed.

'And when did Sir Norman arrive here?' Inspector Lewis asked.

'He came over on the Saturday before everybody else got

here. He'd arranged for a delivery from the wine merchant and brought it with him,' Mrs Jenkins said.

Matt found the interview quite enlightening. Since the party had arrived, and Sir Norman had been murdered on the Monday, then the odds were that he would have had sufficient notes in his wallet to reimburse Mrs Jenkins on the following Thursday evening.

Chief Inspector Greville had clearly decided to try and determine where the money that had been discovered in Paul Browning's drawer had originated from. He presumed that the police must have checked Sir Norman's wallet and found it empty. So had Paul shot Sir Norman and stolen the money after all? But if that were the case, then who had murdered Paul and why?

Inspector Lewis escorted Mrs Jenkins back to her room and returned to the lounge.

'That was very enlightening, don't you think?' Inspector Lewis rubbed his hands together as he retook his seat.

Chief Inspector Greville was engaged in rereading his notes. 'It certainly gives us a clearer picture of the arrangements within the hotel between Sir Norman and the Jenkinses.'

'What do you think, Captain Bryant?' The chief inspector looked at Matt.

'It provided us with a possible source for the notes found in Mr Browning's drawer. But if Browning murdered Sir Norman and took the money, then who murdered Browning and why? It doesn't fit really, unless of course it was for revenge. I'm more inclined to think someone else killed Sir Norman and took the cash. Then when Browning blackmailed them, they paid him off, arranged a meeting away from the hotel to discuss future arrangements and Browning ended up dead at the foot of the cliffs,' Matt said.

'That's how I'm reading matters too,' the chief inspector

agreed. 'I think we should talk to Mr Jenkins next and see if his account of affairs marries up to that of his wife.'

Inspector Lewis was dispatched to locate Albert Jenkins and returned with him a few moments later.

Albert, like his wife, looked tired and drawn, the signs of grief still visible on his face. He took his place before the policemen and waited patiently for their questions.

'Mr Jenkins, I am very sorry that we are compelled to ask you these questions at such a difficult time, but since two people have died in the space of a few days I'm sure you can see the necessity.' Chief Inspector Greville regarded the man with a level gaze.

Albert bowed his head. 'I do, sir. I'll try my best to assist you. We just want to get away from here as soon as possible.'

'If I may, I'd first like to revisit the day Sir Norman was killed. You went to greet the party at the jetty?' the chief inspector asked.

'Yes, sir. I'd taken the donkey cart to transport the luggage and so as any person not fit enough to come up the steep path and the steps could ride on the cart,' Albert explained.

'Then what did you do?' Chief Inspector Greville asked.

'I took the luggage around the back of the hotel and unhitched the cart. I turned old Meg out into her field and fastened her to her chain before I carried the luggage in and placed it all in the rooms. I had a list from Sir Norman of who was to go where,' Albert said. 'Then I took over from Ethel so as she could get back to preparing lunch.'

'After luncheon was served, Sir Norman retired to the office behind the front desk to work?' Chief Inspector Greville added to his notes.

'That's correct, sir. He asked me to bring him his tea as usual,' Albert confirmed.

'You didn't see anything of Sir Norman between lunch and

when you delivered his afternoon refreshments?' Inspector Lewis asked.

Albert shook his head. 'No, sir, I helped the missus clear away from lunch and we had a bite ourselves. Then I made up the afternoon tea things. Mrs Bryant and Miss Miller come for a look around the kitchen while we were working. After that I took refreshments out and went to drop a tray into Sir Norman. I heard him arguing with Mr Frobisher, so I hung on for a minute till Mr Frobisher came out before taking the tray in.'

'Then what did you do?' Chief Inspector Greville asked.

'I went back to the dining room and set it up for dinner before I went back to collect the tea things,' Albert said.

'How was Sir Norman when you returned?' the chief inspector asked.

'Bad tempered and out of sorts. Muttered how he was sick of interruptions. I took his tray and got out. When he was in a mood like that then you was best keeping well clear of him,' Albert said.

'Please can you think back, Mr Jenkins, and this is very important. Do you recall seeing Sir Norman's gun at this point?' Chief Inspector Greville waited, his pen poised, for the man to reply.

Matt too was very interested in the answer to this.

Albert frowned, the skin on his forehead puckering into deep creases as he tried to remember. 'Yes, sir, I do believe it was on the desk. I've been thinking about this after what Mrs Bryant and Miss Miller said yesterday. He'd moved the tray off the desk onto a little side table as he's got in there, but the cup was missing. I looked about and it was on his desk beside the gun.' Albert looked around triumphantly, clearly pleased that he had finally managed to recall the events.

Matt saw a gleam of satisfaction in the chief inspector's eyes. 'You are certain of this, Mr Jenkins?'

Albert nodded vigorously. 'Cross my heart and hope to die,

sir. I picked up the cup and saucer from the far side of the desk, near his left hand. Sir Norman was a bit crippled in his right hand and the gun was on the opposite side, nearest to the door.'

That would have meant that anyone entering the room would have seen it and could have snatched it up and fired the fatal shot. Had the murderer made a joke of it in case the gun had not been loaded? A shiver ran along Matt's spine.

CHAPTER NINETEEN

When Kitty and Alice arrived downstairs, they discovered the main lounge empty except for Selina. She was seated by the window, smoking a cigarette as she gazed out at the sea.

'Where is everyone this morning?' Kitty asked after they had greeted her.

'The police and your husband are talking to Mr and Mrs Jenkins in the other lounge. The men are strolling around the hotel gardens and Marie, I think, is still in her room,' Selina said as Kitty and Alice sat down nearby.

Kitty thought the girl looked tired and unhappy. Which was no surprise in the circumstances.

'How are you coping with all of this?' Kitty asked.

Selina responded with a slight shrug of her slim shoulders. 'I want to get away from here as soon as they will let us leave. It's so frightening now. One of the people I am friends with, and was working with, has killed two people. All the time we carry on talking, eating dinner, exchanging pleasantries as if nothing had happened. It's as if I'm trapped in a nightmare.' The girl shuddered.

'What will you do when you leave here? Do you have somewhere to go?' Alice asked.

Selina stubbed out her cigarette and removed it from the holder. 'I'll go home for a while, see my mother and stepfather. Then I guess I'll look for more acting work in the *Stage* magazine. Marie's production is unlikely to go ahead. She's putting on a brave front but she's in no state to launch her first play. At least I don't think so, and, truthfully, I don't think I would want to be in it any more.'

'I'm so sorry, I suppose getting this role was a big step up for you, wasn't it?' Kitty asked.

'Yes. I've been an understudy and played quite a few minor parts, but this would have seen my name in big letters on the posters. Beneath Marie and Paul, but still...' Selina smiled wryly. 'I suppose I shall have to wait and hope something else comes along.'

'Would Mr Pike not be able to find you a role in something?' Alice asked.

A flicker of some undefinable emotion crossed the actress's expressive face. 'I don't know. He may not be happy when I say I'm pulling out of this production.'

Kitty wondered how the interviews were progressing in the other room. She was still deeply frustrated that she couldn't be in there, but at least the chief inspector was permitting Matt to take part. She would have to be content with continuing to hear the progress in the case second-hand.

'We shall have to go and start preparing lunch soon,' Alice said, glancing at the clock above the bar.

'Mr Jenkins has been in there for a while, they must have plenty to talk about.' Selina looked at the closed interconnecting door between the lounges.

'Let's hope they finish with him soon then and we can make a start, else everyone is going to be very hungry,' Alice said.

* * *

Chief Inspector Greville progressed to asking about Albert's movements on the day Paul Browning died.

'I did the dining room, served breakfast, and cleared. Got the cart to collect the milk and cream from the cottages and cleaned some of the rooms. Made the beds and so on. I'd not long got back to the kitchen when your inspector came to find me asking if I had a coil of rope.' Albert looked at Inspector Lewis.

'Did you see Mr Browning at all, or speak to him during the morning?' the chief inspector asked.

'I saw him at the breakfast table when I went in to check the burners under the chafing dishes and he requested a pot of tea,' Albert said.

'And how did he seem to you?' Inspector Lewis asked.

'A bit hungover but in a pleasant mood,' Albert replied. 'Nothing out of the ordinary.'

'Did you see him again later?' Chief Inspector Greville asked as he made notes in his book.

'I saw him go out of the hotel when I was hitching Meg up to the cart. Only briefly in the distance, going towards the cliffs,' Albert said. 'The next time I saw him was when we fetched him out of the sea.' He gave a faint shudder.

'Did you see anyone else outside the hotel?' the chief inspector asked.

'Miss Headingly was in the garden, and I saw Mr Standish in the distance when I was coming back with the cart,' Albert said. 'He was on the path cutting across from the lighthouse to the cliffs.'

Inspector Lewis exchanged a glance with the chief inspector. It sounded to Matt as if Alec would have a few more questions to answer.

'Mrs Jenkins said that she presented the housekeeping

accounts for the week to Sir Norman on Thursday evenings. He would then recompense her with money from his wallet, which you would then use for the coming week. Is that correct?' the chief inspector asked.

Albert looked a little surprised by the change of topic. 'Yes, sir. He would usually pay for the wine merchant on account but the butcher and greengrocer, fish and such, well, they would rather have money paid on delivery. They have small businesses and can't afford to wait to be paid,' Albert explained.

'Your wife said this housekeeping money is kept in a tin in the kitchen?'

Albert looked at the chief inspector. 'Yes, sir, we keep it hidden in the pantry. Did you want to see it?'

The chief inspector confirmed that he would like to check the tin. Albert hurried off to the kitchen returning a few minutes later with a battered tin tea caddy that was locked with a small key. He also bought a small notebook filled with tidy columns of figures, all carefully annotated with where the money had been spent. He placed them in front of the chief inspector.

'I'll unlock it for you, sir.' Albert took a large bunch of keys from his trouser pocket and selected a tiny one to fit the lock on the caddy.

Matt leaned forward so he could see the contents of the tin. There were a few receipts, some coins and some notes. The chief inspector picked up the notes and examined them. He took some other notes from his pocket and Matt could see he was comparing the serial numbers.

'Thank you, Mr Jenkins, you may return your tin to its hiding place.'

Albert scuttled back to the kitchen to stow the tin safely away once more.

'The serial numbers run in line. Those notes from Mr Browning's drawer are from the same batch as the money Sir

Norman gave the Jenkinses.' The chief inspector looked at Matt and Inspector Lewis.

Albert re-entered the room, his face slightly flushed from his exertions. 'Begging your pardon, sir, but will there be anything more? Only I shall need to commence preparing lunch soon.'

The chief inspector glanced at the clock. 'Thank you, Mr Jenkins, we shall leave it there for now. You have been most obliging.'

Once Albert had gone, Matt rose and stretched. He wanted to go and find Kitty to bring her up to speed. There was also the small matter of their unfinished discussion from last night. Although that particular subject might be best left until the murderer was behind bars and they were all safely off the island.

'Shall we pause for a few moments? Perhaps, Inspector Lewis, you might pop along to the kitchen and get us some tea. Then you could find our young American friend, Mr Standish, and tell him we shall see him in about fifteen minutes time.' Chief Inspector Greville looked at his junior officer.

'Of course, sir.' The inspector disappeared to do the chief inspector's bidding.

'He is getting very good at making tea,' the chief inspector mused.

Matt bit back a smile. 'I'm just going to make sure Kitty is all right, sir.'

'Oh, of course, Captain Bryant. I'm sure she will wish to be kept abreast of events,' the chief inspector responded with a twinkle in his eye.

Matt discovered Kitty sitting by herself in the lounge gazing out of the window.

'Where is Alice?'

'She and Selina have gone to the kitchen to help Albert

prepare lunch. I thought I would wait here to see if there was any progress in the case,' Kitty explained.

'We're on a short break for tea, then it's Alec Standish's turn again.' Matt quickly told her everything the Jenkinses had said.

'And Albert was certain about the gun being on the desk?' Kitty asked.

'Yes. He said it had been troubling him since you and Alice had asked about it.' Matt smiled at her.

'Well, I'm glad I can be a little bit useful even if I can't sit in at the interviews,' Kitty said, sounding slightly annoyed.

'I wish you could be there, but with Inspector Lewis being there as well it might seem rather intimidating. Also, you know Inspector Lewis's views on private investigators,' Matt sympathised. 'You are doing a marvellous job even without being involved in the questions. You and Alice have found so much out already.'

From the expression on Kitty's face, he had a horrible suspicion that he had sounded patronising. 'If it helps at all, Inspector Lewis seems to have been promoted to tea boy.'

Kitty broke into a smile. 'That really shouldn't cheer me up, but it does.'

Matt kissed her briefly on the lips before jumping up ready to return to the other room. 'I can see Alec Standish and the inspector coming this way. I had better go back.'

* * *

Kitty watched him go and sighed disconsolately. This case was so frustrating. She felt as if all she was doing was twiddling her thumbs. Even her offer to assist in the kitchen preparing lunch had been dismissed.

Lambert and Colin were still outside in the garden wrapped up against the wind blowing in from the sea and enjoying the bright winter sunshine. At least she assumed

Colin was enjoying it, Lambert looked as if he was there under duress. The purple and yellow aconites had started to open now in the lee of the stone boundary wall. As she watched, a seagull landed gracefully nearby and peered in at her, its head tilted on one side as if questioning why she wasn't outdoors.

Her mind made up, Kitty went to collect her coat, gloves and hat. The atmosphere inside the hotel was claustrophobic and she needed to burn off some of the restless energy that was consuming her. A short stroll, perhaps to the jetty and back, might give her an appetite for lunch.

The sea air was cool against her cheeks but not as cold as she had expected. The men, talking together in the garden didn't appear to notice her walking away down the path that led out through the gap in the low wall down to the sea.

The birds that gave the island its name wheeled and cried overhead. She and Alice had been studying one of the books they had discovered in the hotel library hoping they might learn more about them. Some of them she knew already from a life always lived on the coast, though others were less familiar.

Kitty walked out onto the wooden jetty and looked out across the sea towards Torquay. What had Paul Browning said? So near and yet so far. A shiver ran along her spine. Had he been aware then of the danger he was in?

She strolled along the platform to the far end and perched herself on one of the nearby rocks. The fresh salt laden air was definitely helping to clear her head. She couldn't help feeling there was something she had missed about Sir Norman's death. And, after the unfinished conversation with Matt last night, she was unsettled and no nearer to deciding how she felt on that subject either.

A shadow fell across her and one of the planks of the jetty creaked. Kitty looked up in surprise to find Marie had joined her.

'Please forgive me if I startled you, Mrs Bryant,' Marie said, staring out at the view.

'No, it's quite all right, and please call me Kitty.' She waited as the older woman eased herself down onto another nearby rock.

'This is one of my favourite places too,' Marie confided as she adjusted the fur shawl collar of her coat. 'At least it was.'

'I'm so very sorry about Sir Norman,' Kitty said.

Marie sighed. 'We came here shortly after we first met. The previous owner had a house party, and we were invited. It was when he was thinking of selling – the house was a big gothic mansion then. I don't know if you recall it at all?'

'Yes, you could see it from the pleasure boats that come out in the summer. This is my first time on the island though.' Kitty gazed out at the waves lapping against the wooden posts supporting the jetty.

'We fell in love with the island and each other, and Norman said if he could afford it, he would buy it for me.' Marie appeared lost in a world of her own. 'Then the colonel said he intended to sell so we got it.'

'That's very romantic.' Kitty thought it was also very impractical, but she kept those thoughts to herself.

'To build a hotel as lovely as its surroundings was our dream, and now Norman has gone.' Marie's face crumpled and she hunted in her coat pocket for a handkerchief.

'Do you think you will keep the island and the hotel?' Kitty asked.

'I don't know. I presume Norman will have left it to me. I've invested most of my savings in this place and he only has a couple of living relatives, both of them elderly.' Marie sniffed and looked around her.

'Did you have any kind of contract with Sir Norman, you know, to protect yourself financially?' Kitty thought it a little strange that Marie seemed to have no clear idea about her fiancé's intentions considering she had obviously given him a large sum of money.

Marie dabbed at her eyes. 'No, we were getting married in June. The church is booked, and I've already had fittings for my dress.'

'But surely your name is on the deeds for the island and the hotel?' Kitty asked.

Marie blinked. 'Oh dear, you will think me very foolish, Mrs Bryant, but I really don't know.'

'I'm sure the chief inspector will have spoken to Sir Norman's solicitor so he may know about a will and any bequests. He may tell you when you speak to him. You should have a better idea about it all then,' Kitty suggested. She did think it foolish that Marie appeared to have done so little to protect herself after giving her fiancé so much money.

Kitty also was keen to know the contents of Sir Norman's will. In her experience money was very often a motive for murder.

'Do you think so?' Marie's face brightened. 'It's just that I promised the Jenkinses that I'd pay the money they are owed in wages and the bonus Norman said he would give them. After what's happened to their daughter, I'm sure they are desperate to go to their grandchildren. Until I can speak to my bank I'm not certain if I can draw enough to pay them what they are owed in full.'

'Do you know what will happen with your play?' Kitty asked.

Marie returned her handkerchief to her pocket. 'I think it will have to be postponed. Lambert thinks he can reschedule it for an autumn run instead but we shall have to recast I suppose.'

'At least you shouldn't lose as much money from cancelling the venues if you can reschedule things,' Kitty said.

Marie glanced at her. 'No, that's very true. My finances are quite straitened at present. There will be Norman's affairs and his funeral to sort out too I expect.'

Kitty stood and brushed some particles of sand from the back of her coat. 'We had better return to the hotel. Alice, Selina and Mr Jenkins were preparing lunch for everyone.'

'You and your friend have been very kind. This trip was not at all what Norman and I had intended. We had both hoped you would love the hotel as much as we did. He really wanted to join the association. He felt it would add a seal of approval to our enterprise,' Marie said as she rose, falling into step beside Kitty.

'It is a beautiful hotel and a unique setting, but the season for guests must be short since the weather is not reliable for much of the year to be sure of a passage across from the mainland,' Kitty said.

'We intended it to be let for house parties and events and to maximise the summer income with teas and concerts.' Marie paused as they approached the gap in the wall surrounding the hotel.

'That would be most delightful,' Kitty agreed.

'Do carry on up, Kitty. I'll be in shortly.' Marie gazed up at the hotel.

Kitty carried on along the path to the front door. When she glanced back there was no sign of Marie.

CHAPTER TWENTY

Alec Standish took his seat in front of the two policemen. His stance was almost combative and belligerent, his arms folded and his chin up. Matt wondered if it was because he knew he had been caught out in a lie yesterday.

'Now, Mr Standish, I wonder if we might just go over a few points from your interview yesterday? I'm sure you'll realise that in a case such as this that accuracy is of the utmost importance.' Chief Inspector Greville fixed the actor with a steely gaze. 'I think you said, sir, you had walked out to the lighthouse cottage?'

'Yes, that's right. There was no one around. I'd hoped to see inside the lighthouse itself,' Alec responded easily.

The chief inspector made a show of flicking back through the pages of his notebook. 'You only walked to the lighthouse, found no one there, and then returned to the hotel?'

Alec shifted slightly in his seat and Matt noticed Inspector Lewis's gaze sharpen. 'Well, I got to the cottage and couldn't see anyone around. The lighthouse itself was locked. I tried the door in case the keeper was inside. Then I don't know, I guess I wandered about a bit to see if I could see him, and then came back.'

'Did this "wandering about" that you did take you in the direction of the cliff path at all, sir? You are aware that there is a path running across the island behind the donkey field that goes from the lighthouse in that direction?' the chief inspector asked.

'I don't know, I was preoccupied so didn't pay much attention.' A trace of colour crept into the actor's cheeks.

A thought suddenly struck Matt. There was something about the man's demeanour and the way he seemed to be holding back that made him wonder if he was protecting someone. 'Forgive me for interrupting, Chief Inspector, but may I ask Mr Standish, were you hoping to meet someone during this walk? A lady, perhaps?'

Colour flared more brightly on Alec's face. 'I really can't say.'

The chief inspector exchanged a glance with Matt. 'We know, sir, that Miss Monbiere was out that morning. You had tried her room earlier and obtained no reply. Did you see her while you were walking?'

Alec's expression had taken on a hunted look. 'All right, yes, I went out like I said to the lighthouse cottage. There was no one around so I was about to head back, but in the distance towards the cliffs I thought I saw Marie. She has quite a distinctive dark-brown coat with a fur shawl collar. I walked across on the other path behind the field, I thought I might try and meet her. You know, in case she wanted company.'

'And *did* you meet her?' Inspector Lewis asked.

'No, I lost sight of her near the donkey field. There is a small stand of hawthorn trees there, and when I got around them, she had disappeared. So, I just came back to the hotel.' Alec sounded almost sulky now the truth had been prised out of him.

'Did you see anyone else walking in that direction?' the chief inspector asked.

Alec shook his head. 'No, but anyone could have gone that way without my noticing them. Like I said, the trees blocked my view.'

'Thank you, Mr Standish, that will be all for now,' the chief inspector said. Alec rose quickly, clearly eager to escape. 'I would advise you, sir, that this is a double murder enquiry, and you would be advised to pass on *all* information to us.'

Alec gave a curt nod and scuttled out of the room.

'He didn't want to betray his lady friend, did he? Good work, Captain Bryant,' Inspector Lewis said, sounding positively jubilant.

Matt was slightly discomfited by receiving praise from the inspector. Usually, Inspector Lewis was less than happy with Matt and Kitty being involved with any investigations.

'We now have a witness to Miss Monbiere being outside the hotel,' the chief inspector said, looking satisfied as he stowed his pen and notebook away. 'We will resume this after lunch and see what Miss Monbiere has to say for herself.'

Lunch was an informal affair of soup and sandwiches, followed by tinned peaches and cream. Matt updated Kitty in a low voice away from the rest of the party on what Alec had told them.

'I met Marie this morning too,' Kitty said. 'She was talking about the island and the hotel. I got the impression that she is only just starting to realise that her money may be gone and she doesn't know if there is a will or any insurance.' Kitty explained about Marie's apparent lack of certainty about Sir Norman's bequests.

'Hmm, the chief inspector hasn't shared anything yet about Sir Norman's will, but I know he received some information last night,' Matt said.

'Do you think he is any nearer to making an arrest?' Kitty asked.

Matt looked around to ensure no one could hear him before

replying. 'I'm not sure. He's keeping some information close to his chest, in my opinion.'

He could see Kitty was slightly disappointed by his reply. 'Chin up, darling, I'm sure this will be resolved soon, and we'll all be able to go home.'

* * *

Kitty hoped her husband was right. From everything they had discovered so far it sounded as if there were a few people who could have had the motive and the opportunity to murder both Sir Norman and Paul Browning. Everything seemed circumstantial, however, one person's word against another with no actual evidence.

In the meantime, she was inclined to agree with Selina. At least one person in their midst was a cold-blooded killer. She assisted the others to clear away the lunch things, her mind busy going over everything they had discovered so far.

Marie accompanied Matt and the police into the other lounge while Lambert stationed himself at the reception desk beside the telephone. He said he intended to try and contact the theatres to rearrange dates for the tour of Marie's play.

Kitty could understand why he had no desire to utilise the office behind the front desk. Despite Albert having cleaned it thoroughly, the image of what had occurred in there was too recent and distressing. She suspected this was also why the police had continued to conduct their interviews in the smaller lounge.

Colin and Alec resumed their card game and Selina produced a novel. Kitty returned to the kitchen to see if Alice and Albert needed any help.

'I know as you've already been out once today, but do you fancy another walk?' Alice asked Kitty as they finished the last of the tidying up.

Kitty was quick to agree. 'Of course, you've had no break at all and some air would be good for both of us.' She felt guilty that her friend appeared to have taken on so many of the duties that would normally have been carried out by the staff of the hotel. Alice was supposed to have been having a couple of days being waited on herself, not looking after others.

Kitty's earlier outing to the jetty was nothing like the walks she usually did at home when she would take Bertie out over the common or down to the beach at Broadsands. She hoped her dog was behaving and not pining while she and Matt were away. She didn't like leaving him for this long even if he was with Mickey. Her cat was quite self-sufficient and their house-keeper was very fond of Rascal. As, indeed, was Kitty's grandmother.

The sky had clouded over slightly since morning and the wind was a tad brisker.

'Let's go up the path behind the hotel. It might be a bit more sheltered there than by the sea. I reckon as I might lose my hat if we go down by the jetty,' Alice suggested, holding on to the crown of her neat navy felt hat.

Kitty happily agreed, wary of losing her own headwear to the wind. She linked arms with her friend and, laughing, they made their way around the corner of the hotel to where there was more shelter.

The path took them past the kitchen window and up through a small shrubbery that surrounded a raised stone plat-form with a bench. Kitty guessed it would probably be a lovely suntrap in the summer months.

They walked up a small flight of stone steps to a wicket gate set in the boundary wall. The wind was still blowing but it was considerably more sheltered than at the front of the hotel. The path continued beyond the gate and ahead of them Kitty could see Meg, the donkey, grazing peacefully in her field.

Alice stopped suddenly. 'Hold up a minute. I've got a stone in my shoe.'

Kitty stopped and steadied her friend while she slipped her shoe off to shake out the errant stone. Looking back at the hotel she wondered who had the rooms at the back. She and Alice had clearly been given sea facing rooms in the hope of persuading them to make a positive report to the association. She assumed Mr and Mrs Jenkins were probably housed on this side of the building.

At the corner of the hotel, Kitty noticed a wrought iron set of steps painted white that she assumed must be a fire escape since they went up to the first floor. Alice replaced her shoe and turned her head to see what Kitty was looking at.

'Funny, I never noticed a door near our rooms,' Kitty said.

'Let's have a closer look at it then,' Alice suggested.

They left the path and made their way across the small lawn around the shrubbery and to the foot of the steps.

'Wait here.' Kitty let go of Alice's arm and ran lightly up the wrought-iron steps to try the door at the top. 'Locked,' she reported when she came back down.

'I suppose it would be if it's an emergency door. You don't want any old Tom, Dick, or Harry getting up to the rooms, even if this is an island. I don't expect as it's always going to be this quiet, not if they intend to have day trippers over,' Alice said.

'True.' Kitty looked at the ground at the foot of the steps. The grass and mud was still soft from all of the recent rain and she spotted the imprints of a pair of women's shoes.

Alice had clearly noticed them too and seemed to pick up on her thoughts. 'Those could be from Miss Headingly the other day. She was in the garden most of the morning. Perhaps she also wondered about the steps and where they went.'

'You're probably right. When we go upstairs later though I want to see where the door is. I can't believe we never noticed it.' Kitty linked her arm back through Alice's again and they set off back towards the path.

'Let's walk to the lighthouse,' Alice suggested. 'We haven't seen it close up.'

The path continued to a crossroads. The way ahead was wider and there were wheel ruts, presumably caused by Albert taking Meg and the donkey cart to collect the milk from the cottages on the far side of the island. The path to the right led towards a stand of wind bent and scrubby hawthorn trees, while the left fork led to the lighthouse, clearly visible in the distance.

The lighthouse was relatively small and stubby, built on top of a rocky promontory. The lighthouse, like the hotel, was painted white. Unlike the hotel, however, it was rain marked and dirty, lashed by the storms that swept in regularly from the sea. A sun-faded blue door was at the bottom. A stone built single storey cottage stood nearby and both the cottage and the lighthouse appeared deserted.

Kitty looked around her with interest. A garden planted with what appeared to be potatoes, carrots and winter cabbage was at the front of the low stone cottage. A few forlorn sticks of sprouts wavered in the stiff breeze next to a couple of clumps of daffodils. At the rear of the house, closer to the lighthouse, was another stone outbuilding. Kitty assumed this must have been where they had taken Paul Browning after they had fetched him from the sea.

A grey cloud passed over the sun and Kitty shivered.

'Looks like we'm going to have a spot more rain. We'd best get back inside the hotel,' Alice advised, looking up at the collection of dark clouds that had appeared while they had been walking.

As her friend spoke, Kitty felt a spot of rain on her cheek. 'Yes, you're right, let's go.'

They hurried back along the path, this time taking the shorter route back around the front of the hotel. By the time they made it inside the reception area a steady drizzle had set in.

* * *

Marie Monbiere looked pale as she took her place before the policemen in the smaller lounge. The rich black silk of her mourning dress accentuated the pallor of her cheeks and the dark circles beneath her eyes. Even with the skilful use of cosmetics her grief was written large on her face.

Matt tucked himself discreetly in his corner and wondered what this interview would reveal. So far the chief inspector had not discussed any of the information he had received during his telephone call the previous evening. At least, he may have discussed it with the inspector, but he and Kitty were none the wiser.

'Thank you for bearing with us, Miss Monbiere. I do appreciate that this must all be very difficult under the circumstances.' Chief Inspector Greville had taken out his notebook once more.

'I just want whoever murdered Norman caught. Paul's killer too. I still can't believe what has happened. Here, of all places.' The woman gave her head a gentle shake.

'Quite so. May I perhaps revisit events on the day your fiancé was killed?' The chief inspector flicked back through the pages in his notes.

Marie nodded her consent.

'When did you last see Sir Norman alive?' the chief inspector asked.

The singer frowned. 'Teatime. I popped over to his office and knocked on the door. He didn't answer me, so I opened it and looked in. He was on the telephone, and he had his grumpy face on. He waved his hand at me to shoo me away, so I never had the chance to talk properly to him. I have already told you all of this.'

'Why did you wish to speak to him, Miss Monbiere?' the chief inspector asked in a calm voice, seemingly ignoring the woman's frustration at covering old ground.

'Oh, I wanted to know about the evening, you know drinks before dinner. He was a workaholic and would often not notice the time. I also wanted to ask him if he had sorted out the payments for a couple of the theatres. Lambert said there had been a hiccup.'

'Do you recall if his gun was on top of his desk at this point?'

Marie frowned. 'Yes, yes, thinking about it, it was there. He would often take his gun out of the drawer if he needed to get to something underneath it.'

Chief Inspector Greville made a series of squiggles in his book. 'Miss Monbiere, you said before that you were a major investor in the purchase of this island and in the building of the hotel?'

Marie nodded. 'Yes, we fell in love with the island a few years ago, not long after we first met. Buying it and building the hotel was a dream come true for both of us.'

'May I ask if you took any financial or legal advice before committing to the venture?' Chief Inspector Greville asked.

A hint of colour crept into the woman's pale cheeks. 'Not really. Norman did though. He saw to the purchase and organised the architect. I was in charge of the finishes, soft furnishings and things. Mr Frobisher, Colin, suggested I see a solicitor and get paperwork drawn up, but Norman and I were engaged to be married. Norman was a successful man and he reassured me, so I didn't see the need.'

The chief inspector's forehead crinkled. 'Did you and your fiancé discuss his financial affairs at all?'

Marie looked surprised. 'Not really. He has a large country estate in Suffolk and several successful restaurants, plus an apartment in Mayfair. I never saw the need to worry about the safety of my investments with him.' She gazed at the large diamond ring on her engagement finger. 'Our wedding was booked, and everything was going well for us.'

'May I be permitted to look at your engagement ring, Miss Monbiere?' Inspector Lewis asked.

'Well, I suppose so, why? What's wrong?' Marie slid the ring from her finger and passed it across to him with a perplexed expression on her face.

Inspector Lewis drew a magnifying glass from his pocket and studied the ring, holding it towards the stronger light coming in from the window so he had a clearer view.

'Captain Bryant, do you know much about gemstones?' the inspector asked.

'I have learned a great deal the last few years. Jewel thefts are common in my line of work,' Matt replied as the inspector passed both the ring and the magnifying glass across.

Marie watched in bewilderment. 'Is something wrong?'

Matt studied the ring carefully looking at the mounts and markings. He then breathed on the surface of the stone.

'What are your thoughts?' the inspector asked.

'A jeweller would confirm this but I'm afraid I believe this stone to be fake.' Matt gave the magnifying glass back to the inspector and held the ring back out towards Marie.

'Fake?' Marie made no move to take it from him. 'Why would Norman give me a fake ring?'

Matt set the ring down on the table. Marie continued to gaze at it with a stunned expression.

'The mount is gold, but the stone is paste,' Matt said.

'I took a telephone call yesterday evening from my sergeant in Torquay. I had asked him to make a number of enquiries on my behalf. It would appear that your fiancé, Sir Norman Whittier, had serious financial problems. In fact, Miss Monbiere, he was about to declare bankruptcy.' Chief Inspector Greville's tone was grave.

'No, that's not possible. He was a man of property and good standing. Our wedding was booked.' Marie's voice rose, a hint of hysteria evident in her tone.

'The restaurants are heavily mortgaged, and the payments have been defaulted. The estate you referred to in Suffolk is rented and the apartment in Mayfair has already been sold,' Chief Inspector Greville continued calmly.

Marie shook her head in disbelief. 'No. How? I don't understand? What about this place? The island and the hotel?'

'The solicitor my sergeant spoke to said that Bird Island and the hotel were both solely in Sir Norman's name. You are not listed on the deeds as a co-owner. He advised that the property would therefore be listed as one of Sir Norman's assets and when probate was made the island and hotel would be used to pay off Sir Norman's debts.' Marie stared at the chief inspector while he spoke as if unable to take in the enormity of what he was saying. 'You could, of course, apply as a creditor to say the money you provided to him was a loan. This would put you in the same position as Mr Frobisher, who I believe is also owed money by your fiancé.'

'I don't understand. It's not true. There must be something...' Marie's voice was an anguished whisper.

'I asked my sergeant to check if there were any insurance policies that Sir Norman may have held,' Chief Inspector Greville said, looking troubled. 'A policy against his life would pay out to a named beneficiary if it were either up to date or already paid in full.'

'And?' Marie asked eagerly, a hopeful glint appearing in her eyes.

'There was one, an old one taken out some twenty-five years ago. It will pay a small sum of money, a few thousand pounds which compared to the magnitude of his debts is not great,' the chief inspector said.

'Twenty-five years ago? Who is the beneficiary?' Marie asked. 'Norman only had a cousin and an elderly aunt.'

Chief Inspector Greville glanced at Matt and then at Inspector Lewis before responding. 'I'm afraid that isn't true. Sir Norman has a daughter. The money in the policy is left to her.'

Matt's brow rose at this revelation. Sir Norman had left money to Selina if he died. Had he known she was his child? Was she aware that such a policy existed?

It was evident from Marie's stunned expression that she seemed to know nothing about her fiancé having fathered a child all those years ago.

'A daughter?' Marie slumped forwards, her head in her hands. 'Who is she? Where is she? Who is her mother?'

CHAPTER TWENTY-ONE

'The child was born out of wedlock. Her mother has since gone on and married. The daughter is a respectable young woman.' Chief Inspector Greville continued to pick his words carefully.

It was clear to Matt that he did not wish to identify Selina as Sir Norman's daughter just yet. He thought this was probably a sensible decision. Who knows how Marie, or indeed how any of the others, would take such an announcement, especially after everything that had happened.

'And this girl, this unknown young woman, is the only person to inherit anything other than debt from Norman?' Marie asked.

The singer still appeared shaken by everything the chief inspector was telling her. Matt was not surprised; it was a lot to take in and none of it was good.

'Now we come to the issue of Sir Norman's will. This was made some time ago and has not been updated so far as your fiancé's solicitor was aware. Are you aware of a recent will at all, Miss Monbiere?' Chief Inspector Greville asked.

'No, not for certain. I mean Norman had said he would provide for me. I believed him. He *promised* me. Is there nothing here in the safe in his office or at the Suffolk house?' Marie cast a desperate glance in the direction of the reception area.

Chief Inspector Greville shook his head. 'Inspector Lewis has searched the office here from top to bottom and the staff in his other residences have also looked. The will held by his solicitor seems to be the only legal document recording his last wishes.'

'Then there is nothing? My money, all my savings are gone and even this place is not mine? This old will? Who was listed in that? His daughter?' Marie asked.

'I think you should seek legal advice, Miss Monbiere, when you return to the mainland, but I fear that the news is not good. There is a person who is listed in Sir Norman's will and we made extensive enquiries when his solicitor informed us about this person.' The chief inspector looked sympathetic.

Matt wondered why the chief inspector was so reluctant to tell Marie who it was.

'Who? His aunt? Or his cousin? This daughter?' Marie asked.

Chief Inspector Greville drew in a deep breath before replying. 'His wife.'

Marie looked as if someone had slapped her. A bright pink circle had appeared on each cheek.

'Wife?'

Matt felt as stunned as Marie. This was a turn up for the books. He couldn't wait to tell Kitty of this latest revelation.

'Sir Norman married his wife, Lady Anne Whittier, during the war. She was Ann Danks then, a publican in London's East End. From what we've learned, they were never divorced. I believe that Lady Anne is catholic, as indeed was Sir Norman. They parted many years ago just after the end of the war and the marriage is not common knowledge.'

Matt thought that Marie was likely to faint. The colour in

her cheeks had retreated as quickly as it had arrived. Her eyes were wide with distress.

'No, you're lying to me. Norman was marrying *me*. The church was booked, he had proposed. It just isn't possible.' She leaned forward and snatched up the ring from the table examining it as if seeing it for the first time.

Tears ran down her face and dripped unchecked onto the satin of her skirt, marring the shiny silk with dull, dark watermarks.

'I'm very sorry to be the bearer of such bad news, Miss Monbiere. It seems Sir Norman was not the man everyone thought he was,' Chief Inspector Greville said. 'You seem to have been deceived as to his character.'

Marie fumbled for her handkerchief and scrubbed at her eyes, smearing her mascara onto her cheeks. 'I had no idea about any of this. None at all. I knew he had liaisons with lots of women before we met but he swore that he was faithful to me. How could he deceive me like this?' She stared at the ring once more as if unable to comprehend her fiancé's duplicity.

'Inspector Lewis, perhaps you could get Miss Monbiere some refreshment. This has been a tremendous shock,' Chief Inspector Greville said, looking over at his junior officer who jumped up at once.

'I knew that he often delayed paying bills, but he said it was good business practice to keep the money in his pocket for longer. He owed the Jenkinses money. I asked him and he said they wouldn't have come here otherwise, and we needed to get the hotel up and running as quickly as possible. He promised my money was safe. We were going to honeymoon in Paris.' She sniffed and wiped her nose.

Inspector Lewis returned holding a crystal tumbler which appeared to contain brandy. He offered it to Marie, who accepted it gratefully and took a sip. She dropped the ring along with her handkerchief inside the small black leather handbag she had brought into the room with her.

'Thank you, Inspector.' Marie's hands trembled as she held on to the glass.

'Are you able to continue, Miss Monbiere, or do you need to take a short break?' Chief Inspector Greville asked.

Marie took another sip of brandy before replying. 'I think I would rather get this over with, Chief Inspector. I don't think there can be many more shocks to come, can there?'

'Very well, if you are sure. If we move on to yesterday, and Mr Browning's death, can I ask where you were during the morning?' The chief inspector flicked back through his notes as if looking for her previous statement.

Marie looked confused. 'I was in my room. I took breakfast there and wrote some letters. I came downstairs just before lunch and that was when I heard the news about Paul.'

Chief Inspector Greville nodded. 'Are you certain that you didn't leave your room at all for any reason during the course of the morning?'

'No, I don't think so.' The singer's tone was belligerent.

The chief inspector's eyes narrowed. 'Please cast your mind back, Miss Monbiere. This is most important.'

Marie licked her lips in a nervous gesture. 'I can't recall. I don't think I did.'

'Did you hear anyone knock at your door during the course of the morning?' the chief inspector asked.

Matt saw Marie's expression change slightly as if she had begun to realise that the police knew she was not telling the truth.

'I don't recall. I don't always answer if someone knocks, especially at the moment. It's just too distressing.' She made a helpless, fluttering gesture with her hand.

'I see. I don't suppose you would have heard someone knock if you were not in your room. If, in fact, as a witness has told us, you were outside the hotel grounds not far from the cliff path.' Chief Inspector Greville fixed her with a steely gaze.

Marie's mouth opened and closed silently before she burst into tears once more and reached back inside her bag for her handkerchief.

'I have been trying not to think about it. To forget. I saw him. Paul. He was dead, at the bottom of the cliff. The tide was washing him in and out on the rocks. I panicked and didn't know what to do. I thought he must have killed himself. That he must have been the one who killed Norman and then had thrown himself from the cliffs.' Her speech was barely coherent as she sobbed into her handkerchief.

'You say you found Mr Browning's body on the rocks below the cliff but didn't raise the alarm? This was before Captain Bryant here found him?' Inspector Lewis was incredulous.

'Yes. I was so upset and confused. I'd slipped out of my room for some fresh air. I didn't want to see any of the others. I just wanted some time alone. When I saw him, I didn't know what to do. Like I said, I thought he must have jumped off, but then I thought, what if he hadn't? You might have thought *I* had killed him. It was too much, especially after Norman. I couldn't face answering more questions and having to tell the others. I went back to my room and pretended I hadn't been outside.'

'Did you see anyone else while you were outside taking the air?' Chief Inspector Greville asked.

'No, not really. Oh, Selina was out in the garden when I got back. She looked as if she had just come up from the jetty.' Marie sniffed.

Matt's ears pricked up. This was the first time that anyone had suggested that Selina had been anywhere other than in the garden. If she had known of her father's insurance policy, it certainly gave her more of a motive for Sir Norman's death, and potentially Paul's, if he had been blackmailing her.

'Were you aware of Sir Norman's arrangements with Mrs

Jenkins about the payment of the accounts for the hotel?' the chief inspector asked.

The change in questioning appeared to take Marie by surprise. 'Yes, you mean the bills for groceries and meat? That sort of thing? He would see the books and her receipts each week and give her money to keep for that purpose. A lot of the suppliers were reluctant to run an account. He always kept a generous number of notes in his wallet.' She gave a bitter laugh. 'It seems that was all the money he probably had from what you've told me this morning.'

'Thank you, Miss Monbiere. If you recollect anything else which may be useful to us, please let us know immediately.' Chief Inspector Greville dismissed the singer and Inspector Lewis escorted her back into the other lounge.

'That was... a lot,' Matt said, leaning back in his chair.

'Indeed. My sergeant was very industrious in his enquiries. It seems Sir Norman was not the person everyone believed him to be. His debts are extensive and there was no other way out of the financial mire he was embroiled in except by declaring bankruptcy. Something that Mr Frobisher suspected. It seems that his estranged wife had not heard from him for many years. When they parted, she put a notice in the newspapers stating she would not be responsible for any of his debts, past, present or future,' Chief Inspector Greville said.

Matt raised his eyebrows. 'A somewhat unusual move, sir.'

'Yes, but from what we've learned, even back then Sir Norman was fond of taking financial risks.' Chief Inspector Greville tucked his notebook back in his pocket.

'Do you think Miss Monbiere was as oblivious to his financial issues as she claimed to be?' Matt asked.

'An interesting question, Captain Bryant. She did seem genuinely shocked that his will had not been updated to include her and that the deeds to the island and this hotel did not have her name attached to them.' The chief inspector sighed and rubbed his face.

'You noticed that Miss Monbiere thought Selina had been out of the garden?' Matt said as Inspector Lewis re-entered the room.

'Yes, everyone else has said they saw Selina in the hotel grounds. No one else has mentioned seeing her anywhere beyond the boundary wall,' Inspector Lewis said.

'Is there any chance that Miss Monbiere knows of Miss Headingly's connection to Sir Norman?' Matt asked.

'Selina said she had not told Sir Norman of the relationship,' the chief inspector said, sounding thoughtful.

'Yet Sir Norman himself,' said Matt, 'had kept up the insurance policy on his life with Selina as the beneficiary. Presumably that paperwork would have her name on it? Is Selina Headingly her real name or her stage name?' He was curious, Sir Norman must have known who she was, unless she had changed her name. If he had known he could easily have told Marie. Or Marie could have found out.

'I believe her first name is unchanged, but Headingly is her stepfather's name,' Chief Inspector Greville said. 'I also think we should speak to her again.'

* * *

Once Kitty and Alice had taken off their outdoor things, Kitty was keen to venture back upstairs to look for a door that led out onto the fire escape. She hadn't really taken much notice of the landing before. Her door and Alice's were the first ones on the side of the corridor facing towards the sea. The doors to the other rooms were a little further along the landing on the opposite wall. Those rooms would afford the guests a garden view with presumably distant glimpses of the sea on the opposite side of the island.

Kitty waited for Alice to catch her up at the top of the stairs.

'The door to that set of stairs must be along here,' Kitty said, looking along the wall.

'That first door, the one marked Osprey, I think that was Sir Norman's room,' Alice said. 'Next to Miss Monbiere's room.'

The two doors mirrored Kitty and Alice's doors on the opposite side and Kitty presumed that they too were interconnected. A blank white door was next to Miss Monbiere's room. There was no name plate attached to it and it had been cleverly designed to blend into its surroundings.

Kitty tried the discreet metal handle. 'Locked.'

'The next door along is Artic Tern, I think as that is Miss Headingly's room,' Alice said.

'Hmm. Let's go back down to the reception desk.' Kitty wondered if there might be a key to the door kept in the desk drawer where they had discovered the spare key to Sir Norman's office.

They made their way back downstairs and Kitty opened the drawer to examine the keys. Although most of the keys had two copies in the drawer, there was one ring with only one key. That one was labelled landing exit.

'It looks as if there is a key missing for that door,' Kitty said, looking at Alice.

'You think as someone might have took it?' Alice asked.

'I think someone might have thought it expedient to be able to slip in and out of the hotel via those stairs rather than using the front door. They would be shielded from whoever was in the kitchen by the shrubbery so they could sneak out unobserved if they picked a moment when Mr and Mrs Jenkins's attention was elsewhere.' Kitty closed the drawer.

'You mean Mr Browning's murderer might have gone out that way?' Alice asked.

'It's a possibility,' Kitty said. 'When we arrived, and Sir Norman and Miss Monbiere showed us around the hotel, can you recall who apart from Miss Monbiere had been here before?'

Alice frowned. 'I think as Mr Pike and Mr Frobisher definitely had. They said something about how it looked much nicer now Miss Monbiere had added some finishing touches.'

'Hmm, I wonder if the others had been here before too,' Kitty said.

'What am you thinking?' Alice asked.

Kitty sighed. 'I'm not sure, but it strikes me that whoever killed Sir Norman and Paul only had a very short time to work things out if they were unfamiliar with the hotel. Now if they had been here before they may well have known the layout of the rooms.'

'What do you think about the gun then? I mean, unless as they knew he had a gun and a bad habit of plonking it on top of his desk when he was rootling around in that drawer of his, then it couldn't have been a planned murder, could it?' Alice said.

'No, you're right. If it was someone who knew his habits, it would be, but it could equally have been a chance opportunity,' Kitty said.

'And either they didn't know about that problem with his hand, or they had to get out the office quick and hope as nobody would notice,' Alice agreed.

The door of the lounge opened, and Alec Standish appeared. 'What are you ladies doing out here?'

'We have not long come back inside. We made it just before the rain started up again and we were deciding if we should go and make a pot of tea for everyone,' Kitty said with a smile.

She was keen not to arouse any suspicion that they might have been looking in the desk drawer at the keys.

'Tea sounds a capital idea. Would you like a hand?' Alec offered, so Kitty and Alice found themselves accompanied to the kitchen.

Mr and Mrs Jenkins were both back at work. Mrs Jenkins

was preparing several meat pies for dinner and Mr Jenkins was assisting with the vegetables. They seemed surprised to see Kitty's party entering the kitchen.

'We came in search of tea, but please don't let us get in your way,' Kitty explained.

'Not at all, Mrs Bryant, leave it to me and I'll bring up a trolley along in a few minutes,' Albert assured her.

'Are you sure it won't be any bother?' Alice asked.

'Not at all, Miss Miller.' Albert started to fill the kettle at the tap.

'You're very kind. By the by, Alice and I wondered if this was the first visit anyone had made to the hotel?' Kitty asked.

'Miss Monbiere bought several people over on the boat in January,' said Albert. 'We had that pleasant spell of a couple of days. You came too I think, didn't you, Mr Standish? And Mr Pike and Mr Frobisher. Sir Norman needed some assistance with the furniture. Miss Headingly came over as well, I believe, but on a different day. Marie wasn't here that time, Miss Headingly came with another lady and Sir Norman. They only stayed a couple of hours then went right back.' Albert stood the kettle on the hob and started to set up the trolley.

Kitty wondered if Marie had known about Selina's visit.

CHAPTER TWENTY-TWO

Alec laughed. 'Yes, we stayed overnight. A bit like camping. Norman and Marie were basically after some free labour to help haul some of the stuff around in the hotel. Lambert was not amused when he discovered that was the reason for the invitation.'

Kitty wondered what the purpose of Selina's visit had been and who her mysterious companion was. Had Marie known that Sir Norman had brought them across to the island in her absence? The Jenkinses could quite easily have informed her of the visit. It certainly seemed as if there was more to Selina's connections with Sir Norman than the actress had disclosed so far.

They left Albert to continue preparing a tea trolley and returned to the lounge. Kitty had hoped to find Selina still there, but instead Marie was seated on the sofa with Lambert and Colin both gathered around her.

'What's wrong?' Kitty asked on seeing the singer's distraught expression and the telltale glass of brandy in her hand.

'Marie has just been given the most frightfully bad news,' Colin said. 'I can't quite believe what I've heard so far.'

Alec immediately rushed to the singer's side. 'What's happened? Is this something the police have told you?'

Alice and Kitty took a seat nearby and waited to find out what had occurred to make Marie so distressed.

'Oh, Alec, it's awful. How could Norman do this to me?' Marie broke into a despairing wail.

'Darling, what had Norman done?' Alec's pleasant face creased in confusion.

'It turns out that Norman was not the person we all thought him to be,' said Colin. 'Even I, as one of his oldest friends, didn't know what Marie has just been told.' He gave a heavy groan and rubbed his forehead.

'It seems that Norman was about to go bankrupt. Colin had been warning him for ages about his finances.' Lambert looked at Colin. 'He told me this morning when we were outside. Norman owed Colin quite a tidy packet.'

'When we argued on the afternoon he was killed I had begged him to tell Marie, but he insisted that he could recover. The hotel and the island would turn things around. Everyone had to be patient. I didn't realise he was about to declare bankruptcy. I knew the restaurants were mortgaged and that he'd sold the place in Mayfair.' Colin shook his head.

'I'm not on the deeds for the hotel or the island. All my savings are gone,' Marie said with a sniffle.

'But surely he had insurance? And he must have a will? Other assets? The estate in Suffolk?' Alec looked around at the group in bewilderment.

'That's the kicker, dear boy,' said Lambert. 'The Suffolk place is only rented, he didn't own it, and apparently the only insurance that the police have uncovered names some unknown woman who they say is Norman's daughter.'

'A daughter?' Alec's frown deepened. 'But he never mentioned a daughter before, did he?'

'From some liaison of his years ago,' Marie explained. 'And then, as if that wasn't bad enough, it seems dearest Norman was already *married* to someone else, called Anne, who runs a public house in London's East End!'

Colin's face paled. 'That was true then? I heard rumours years ago, but Norman always denied it. I thought it was just idle gossip. Marie, my poor girl.'

Alec looked at Marie. 'So is this Anne the mother of the daughter?'

'No, apparently not. The police said they were married in the war. Norman would have committed bigamy if he had turned up at that church to marry me.' Marie broke into a fresh bout of sobs.

Albert entered the room with the tea trolley and paused just inside the door clearly discomfited by the unexpected scene in front of him.

Alice leapt to her feet and went to take over the trolley. 'It's all right, Albert, you go on back to the kitchen.'

The man took her at her word and left the room. Alice wheeled the cart further into the lounge and started to pour and dispense tea. 'Now then, a nice cup of tea will do us all the power of good.'

'Thank you, Miss Miller.' Lambert accepted his cup and ladled a couple of spoons of sugar into the hot liquid. 'This woman, this Anne, she is named in the will then? Is that what you're saying, Marie?' he continued.

'Yes. That's what the chief inspector said. Not that she will inherit anything except debts. There is literally nothing left. The island and this hotel are the only assets Norman had. The restaurants, his estate, his apartment, all of them are gone.' Marie accepted her tea from Alice and poured what remained of her brandy into the cup.

'Then the unknown daughter, she's the only one likely to benefit in all of this? Is that right?' Colin asked.

'I think so, but not by much. A few thousand the chief inspector said.' Marie sipped her tea, the brew bringing a little colour back to her pale cheeks.

'Goodness me, what a mess,' Alice observed as she retook her place next to Kitty.

'You can always sell your ring.' Alec's expression brightened.

'If someone wants a piece of glass,' Marie said, setting down her cup on the low table in front of her and digging around inside her handbag.

She pulled out her ring and dropped it down on the table-top. 'As worthless as Norman's promises were to me. I might just as well go and throw it in the sea.'

The group stared at the ring.

Marie gave a bitter laugh. 'I'm willing to bet that the other things he gave me are just paste too. No, everything has gone. All my savings, everything I've worked for all these years. There won't even be anything to bury him with. Not that it will be my concern I don't suppose. His estranged wife can have that dubious pleasure. Or perhaps his daughter.'

* * *

Selena Headingly looked surprisingly calm and composed as she opened the door of her room to find the chief inspector standing in the corridor in front of her.

'Do come in, how may I help you this time?' she asked as she stood aside to allow the chief inspector, Matt and Inspector Lewis to enter her room. They had gone to find her when they had realised she was not with the others downstairs. From the disarray in the room it was clear she had started to pack her things.

The chief inspector took his seat on one of the two pink velvet fireside chairs. Matt and Inspector Lewis perched on the window seat. Selina took out one of her cigarettes and inserted it into its holder before seating herself opposite the chief inspector. Inspector Lewis furnished her with a light and resumed his seat.

Chief Inspector Greville took out his notebook turned back the pages. 'I'm sorry to interrupt your packing but I would like to clarify some points on your statements, Miss Headingly, just to be certain my notes are accurate.'

Selina blew out a thin stream of smoke. 'Certainly, Chief Inspector.'

'Now if I could just return to the day that Sir Norman was killed. You said you remained in the main lounge rehearsing the play with the others and didn't go to the study to see Sir Norman for any reason.' Chief Inspector Greville read back what he'd written down.

'Yes, that's correct.' Selina tapped some ash from the end of her cigarette into the crystal ashtray on the table in front of her.

'You only left the room when you went upstairs to change for dinner?' the chief inspector continued.

A flicker of impatience crossed the girl's face. 'Yes.'

'When did you next come downstairs?' Chief Inspector Greville asked.

'I came down with Alec, he came out of his room at the same time, and we went into the lounge to get a pre-dinner drink together. That must have been around ten to seven, I think.'

Chief Inspector Greville looked at his notes and made an adjustment. 'You hadn't come downstairs before then at all? To perhaps confront Sir Norman regarding your parentage?'

Selina's eyes widened slightly. 'No, why would I? It wouldn't serve any useful purpose.'

'So, you are adamant that Sir Norman was unaware of your

identity?' Chief Inspector Greville asked. 'Yet your Christian name is unchanged.'

'My name is not uncommon,' Selina said, taking another pull on her cigarette.

'Would you be surprised to discover that you are a beneficiary of a life insurance policy taken out by Sir Norman shortly after your birth? That this policy is paid up and you will receive a sum of three thousand pounds now he is dead?' Chief Inspector Greville's eyes narrowed as he asked his questions.

'A life insurance? Forgive me, Chief Inspector, but are you certain?' Selina appeared surprised by the news.

She extinguished her cigarette and detached it from the holder, dropping the stub into the ashtray.

'I am quite sure, Miss Headingly. Did Sir Norman ever visit you when you were a child, or have any contact with your mother after your birth?'

Selina frowned. 'I don't recall a visit. My mother may have received some letters when I was young. I... well, I also received a package when I was twenty-one, on my birthday.' Colour crept into her cheeks.

'May I ask what was in the package?' Chief Inspector Greville asked.

'A gold locket, along with a note that said it had been Sir Norman's mother's and he wished me to have it. That was the first time I ever really thought about him. I had a happy life, Chief Inspector. My stepfather is a good and kind man and has been a wonderful father to me. I had no reason to even think about Sir Norman,' Selina said.

'Until you received the locket, and you became curious?' Inspector Lewis said.

Selina nodded. 'Yes, I asked my mother about him and, well, she showed me some clippings from when he had been in some of the newspapers with his restaurants. There was a picture of him taken at a society party. I'd never seen what he looked like before. My mother never cared to talk about him much and she warned me that he wasn't a very nice man.'

'You said that he and Marie saw you on stage in Bath and Miss Monbiere asked you to play the lead in her play. How did this meeting come about?' Chief Inspector Greville referred back to his notes.

Matt thought Selina looked a little less comfortable now the questions were becoming deeper. She toyed with her empty cigarette holder as if she were trying to distract herself.

'I think Lambert had suggested me for the part. I was surprised to see them. Marie was lovely, very complimentary about my role.' She placed the holder down.

'And your father?' There was a gleam in the chief inspector's eye.

'I was wearing the locket. He must have recognised it, but he didn't say anything to me about it at the time.' Selina pressed her hands to the sides of her face as if hoping to cool the heat in her cheeks.

'So, Sir Norman did know who you were?' Chief Inspector Greville leaned back slightly, a satisfied look on his face. 'Was Miss Monbiere aware of your connection to him?'

'No, Marie knew nothing about it. Sir Norman didn't want her to know. He got in touch with me privately the following day and suggested meeting me without Marie finding out. He said he wanted to get to know me better. We corresponded a couple of times and he invited me here on a day when Marie was in London. I came with a friend, and he showed me around. The hotel wasn't quite finished, he was telling me all about his plans. It was almost like showing off. You know, bragging. I think he thought I would be impressed.' Selina's voice quivered.

'And were you impressed? Did you think that perhaps he was a wealthy man who could open doors for you? Or provide you with things?' Chief Inspector Greville asked.

The colour which had started to recede in Selina's

complexion deepened once more. 'No, none of those things. He asked me to refrain from telling Marie that I was his daughter. He said she could be very jealous, and he hoped this role in her play would be the start of several lead roles for me. I told him I had no intention of telling her and, while I was glad that we had met, I already had a father and was well provided for. We agreed that we should remain casual acquaintances.' The girl bit her lip as she finished speaking, her composure deserting her.

'And when you arrived here to start rehearsals you both pretended that you were virtual strangers?' Inspector Lewis looked as if he didn't believe what she had said.

'We *were* strangers.' Selina glared at him. 'I didn't want anything from him, and he had asked nothing from me. We had met a couple of times and that was it. I didn't know anything about this insurance policy, or anything other than what I'd read about him in the papers. That was enough.'

'Thank you, Miss Headingly.' Chief Inspector Greville's voice held a faint note of reproof. 'If I may, I'd like to move on to your movements on the morning of Mr Browning's death.'

Selina blew out a sigh. 'Very well.'

The chief inspector consulted his notes once more. 'You said you didn't see Mr Browning that morning because you came downstairs late?'

'Yes, I had a headache. I came downstairs, drank some tea and went into the garden to potter about in the sunshine. I came back inside before lunch and that was when the alarm was raised.'

'You had no quarrel with Mr Browning? He hadn't asked you for money?' Chief Inspector Greville asked.

Selina looked bored now, Matt thought, as the policeman went over her previous answers.

'No, I had no quarrel with Paul. It was annoying if he drank too much and put in a poor performance, and he was always trying to beg a cigarette or a drink, but he knew I didn't have lots of money, so he didn't bother me much. Look, I've told you all this before,' Selina replied.

'On the morning of his murder did you try to speak to him about anything? Did you arrange to meet him anywhere?' the chief inspector asked.

The actress's eyes widened. 'Meet Paul? No, why would I arrange an assignation with Paul? I *told* you I didn't see him.'

'He had not discovered your relationship with Sir Norman?' Chief Inspector Greville asked.

Matt thought the look of astonishment on Selina's face was genuine. 'No, no one knew. Just Sir Norman and myself.'

'And you remained inside the hotel garden the entire time you were outside?' Chief Inspector Greville continued.

Selina licked her lips nervously. 'I may have stepped through the opening to the jetty path for a few minutes, but I didn't go very far before coming back.'

'And why was that, Miss Headingly?'

Selina stared at the chief inspector. 'I saw Colin go out and head towards the jetty. I thought perhaps he'd seen a boat. He watches all the time to see if one is coming. I hoped I might get a passage off the island.' She sagged back in her seat. 'When I saw there wasn't one, I turned back and left him to his own devices. I thought he must have just decided to take a walk.'

Chief Inspector Greville made more notes in his book. 'Did you meet anyone else while you were outside?'

'I already told you who I saw,' Selina snapped.

'Did you see Miss Monbiere at all?' the chief inspector persisted.

'*No*. I saw Colin and then, later, I saw Captain Bryant's party setting off. I didn't notice anyone else.' Selina fidgeted in her seat.

'Very well, Miss Headingly, thank you.' The chief inspector

signalled to Matt and the inspector, and they returned down-stairs to the smaller lounge.

Alice and Kitty arrived with a tea trolley just as they sat down.

'That was good timing,' Kitty observed as Selina passed them in the doorway. 'We thought you might like a cup of tea now.'

Alice switched on some of the silk-shaded side lamps. 'It's getting dark already. The clouds have come over again with this rain.'

'Thank you, Mrs Bryant, Miss Miller.' Chief Inspector Greville pounced on the plate containing slices of Victoria sandwich cake while Kitty poured the drinks.

Matt could see by her bright-eyed gaze that she was keen to discover everything that had been discussed in the interviews.

'Miss Monbiere has been telling us all about Sir Norman's antics,' Alice said, taking a seat next to Kitty on one of the sofas. 'What a thing, the old rogue.'

Alice and Kitty looked at the chief inspector while Inspector Lewis frowned disapprovingly. Matt bit back a smile.

'It seems you are aware of the terms of Sir Norman's will and of his insurance arrangements?' Chief Inspector Greville's eyes twinkled as he polished off the last slice of cake.

'Miss Monbiere was very upset,' Alice said demurely.

'I bet she was,' Inspector Lewis muttered.

'Was Miss Headingly happy about her inheritance? I presume she is the named beneficiary of the insurance policy?' Kitty asked.

Matt looked at the chief inspector for permission, before telling Kitty and Alice what had been said during the interview with Selina.

'We discovered a few things ourselves. Whether they are relevant I'm not certain yet.' Kitty told them of their explo-rations outside the hotel and of the footprints at the foot of the fire escape. She also told them of the party's previous visits to the island.

Inspector Lewis rolled his eyes. 'I expect that could have been Miss Headingly when she was in the garden. And as for the key, well, they go astray all the time. Still, I suppose it confirms Miss Headingly's story of her visit here with Sir Norman.' He set his cup down on the trolley.

Matt could see Kitty and Alice were not impressed by his remarks but neither of them replied. They were used to him dismissing their contributions. It was already clear that he disagreed with their involvement in the case at all.

'Do you think as you'm any nearer to finding out who done it?' Alice asked the chief inspector.

'I think there are several people with very strong motives for killing Sir Norman and Mr Browning. The most difficult aspect is determining who could *not* have done it,' the chief inspector said.

'I'm sure you will work it out.' Kitty collected the rest of the cups. 'We had better assist Albert and take this trolley back to the kitchen. Time is getting on and dinner will be served soon.'

Matt glanced at the clock and saw she was right. The interviews had filled most of the afternoon.

'Thank you, Mrs Bryant, Miss Miller.' The chief inspector watched the two women depart with the tea trolley.

'Your good lady is correct, Captain Bryant. I think we should take a break for now and reconvene after dinner. Perhaps it will give us time to decide who is the culprit. I fear we shall have to reach a conclusion soon.'

CHAPTER TWENTY-THREE

Dinner that evening was a quiet affair. Mrs Jenkins had clearly done her best to provide a pleasant meal. Kitty wondered if Albert and Ethel knew they were unlikely to receive their salaries since Miss Monbiere seemed to be in no position now to pay them the money they were owed.

In fact, it would seem she was not obligated at all since Sir Norman had not put her name on either the hotel or the island's deeds. Conversation between courses was muted and mainly consisted of the turn taken by the weather and wondering if it would lift in time for the boat to make a return in the morning.

Selina picked at her food, her thoughts seemingly else-where. Alec was as attentive to Marie as usual, offering to fill her water glass or pass her the salt. Lambert also appeared preoccupied and spoke only occasionally to Colin.

The two policemen only joined in the discourse when invited and the atmosphere at the table was uneasy and tense. Kitty felt quite relieved when dinner was finally over, and everyone drifted off to the lounge.

Selina switched on the wireless and soon the soothing strains of classical music filled the air. The chief inspector and

Inspector Lewis seated themselves away from the rest of the group while Lambert served everyone drinks from the bar.

'Mrs Bryant? Miss Miller? A cocktail?' He rattled some ice into the silver shaker.

'Thank you.' Kitty thought a cocktail wouldn't go amiss. Alice looked less certain but consented. Selina also accepted the offer and Marie took a glass of brandy. Matt poured a whisky for himself and the two policemen.

All through dinner Kitty's mind had been working overtime thinking about the murders. It was as if the solution was there but just out of reach, and she was missing some vital piece of evidence that she had overlooked. There was something someone had said before all the revelations of today. If only she could recall what it was.

From her seat she could see the chief inspector reviewing his notes once more as he sipped his whisky. She guessed he must be having the same thoughts, trying to solve the puzzle.

'This weather is frightfully murky again tonight. You would think it would be improving the closer we get to March.' Colin turned back from where he had been standing once again at the window looking at the faint, rain blurred lights of Torbay across the night dark sea.

'Yes, it was so lovely when we came here the first time to help you shift that furniture, eh, Marie?' Alec said. 'We were talking about it earlier.'

'Yes, it was, wasn't it?' Marie managed a wan smile.

'Norman hanging out of that window while we hauled up that blessed bureau on a rope because the decorators had finished the stairs and he was worried the walls would be marked,' Colin added.

'I thought he would fall out he leaned so far over the sill,' Lambert said, looking over at Marie. 'We said he had better have good insurance if he landed on his head.'

His words fell into an awkward silence.

Marie's mouth twisted into a bitter smile. 'Well, it seems his insurance policy was destined for someone else. Perhaps he should have toppled out that day after all.'

Kitty automatically glanced in Selina's direction wondering how the girl would take this comment. The actress appeared to be unconcerned as she listened to the music from the radio while she drank her cocktail.

'Such a ghastly business,' Colin murmured. 'I did try to talk to him that last afternoon, Marie, my dear. I warned him that he needed to be frank with you about his financial affairs.'

'I know, Colin, and I do appreciate it. You have lost a great deal of money in this whole mess too,' Marie said.

Colin shrugged. 'I can withstand it. It's not ideal obviously, but I was fortunate to realise in time that he was overstretching himself. I didn't know that things were as bad as they were though.'

Kitty knew the police were listening in to the conversation even though they both appeared to be engaged in a private discussion of their own.

'That was dashed bad form about the will too,' Lambert said. 'Why on earth had he not updated it?'

Marie shrugged. 'I don't know the answers to anything any more. I really thought he had done so. He told me he had seen his solicitor about it when we were purchasing the island.' A tear rolled down her cheek and she dashed it away with the back of her hand.

'Sir Norman really was quite an extraordinary man, wasn't he?' Kitty said. 'He must have been quite brave during the war to sustain that injury to his hand when he was firefighting during the bombing raids.'

An idea which had been bubbling away in her subconscious started to become clearer.

'I suppose so.' Colin looked surprised. 'I met him in about 1925 and his hand was still functional then, but of course over time the scar tissue became worse, and it affected his grip. He had taught himself to use his left hand for most things, writing, holding a glass, that sort of thing.'

'That was why we were worried when he was handling that rope on our last visit,' Alec said. 'I thought Lambert might have ended up being squashed flat by that great solid walnut bureau. He was puffing and straining holding the rope. I thought he was going to have a heart attack.'

'It was bad enough that I had to stand on the patio supervising, dear boy. The sun may have been shining but it was still rather chilly,' Lambert remarked. 'You know fresh air is not really my thing. I much prefer a good fire and a nice glass of wine. It was fairly ghastly when Colin dragged me outside this morning.'

'I suppose this bureau wouldn't have fit up the fire escape?' Kitty became aware of Inspector Lewis looking in her direction.

'Fire escape? Oh, the wrought-iron stairs near the back of the hotel?' Alec said. 'Golly no, there's that awkward turn in the middle. I think Marie suggested that, but it wasn't possible. Pity really, it would have saved us a lot of work.'

Kitty took a fortifying sip of her cocktail, that was it, that was the only explanation that would fit. She had a pretty good idea now of what must have happened the day Sir Norman had died and who had killed Paul Browning. The difficulty was she couldn't see how it could be proved unless she could somehow force the person responsible out into the open.

'It still seems so awful, doesn't it, despite everything that we've discovered since Sir Norman was murdered,' Kitty said.

Matt gave her a sideways look and she knew he had guessed that she was up to something.

'Absolutely dreadful, and then there's poor Paul,' Lambert agreed.

'I suppose if Sir Norman had killed himself then the insurance policy would have been invalid. Isn't there a clause or

something that most of those policies have?' Kitty looked at
Colin. She remembered reading something in the newspaper a
while ago. A woman had been forced out of her home because
an insurance company had refused to pay after her husband
had killed himself leaving a load of debt behind.

'I believe that's the case, yes. I don't know, obviously, if
Norman's policy had a similar clause.' Colin looked slightly
surprised by her question.

'Indeed, it did, Mrs Bryant,' Chief Inspector Greville joined
the conversation.

'Then I suppose,' said Kitty, 'that is why his death was made
to look like a murder.'

She felt, rather than heard the sharp intake of breath from
the others in the room.

'I'm afraid I don't follow you, Mrs Bryant. Sir Norman was
murdered. The gun was in the wrong hand, he couldn't have
shot himself. We all saw him for ourselves,' Lambert said.

'Did it strike you, Mr Pike, that when we found Sir Norman
there was something... well, staged about his whole appearance?' Kitty asked.

Lambert frowned. 'I... well, yes, I guess so now that I think
back. That's why we all decided it was murder because it
couldn't have been suicide since his gun was in the wrong
hand.'

'Mrs Bryant are you suggesting that Norman managed to
shoot himself with his crippled hand after all?' Colin sounded
incredulous.

'Oh no, someone else shot him, obviously, but I think he was
already dead,' Kitty said.

Inspector Lewis snorted.

Matt looked at her, a gleam in his eye. 'Do go on, darling.'

Encouraged by his support, Kitty plunged on. 'The day
when Sir Norman died, he was in his office, and we know he

had a number of visitors all wishing to speak to him about various matters.'

'Mrs Bryant, do get to the point if there is one,' Inspector Lewis remarked, and both Matt and the chief inspector glared at him.

'Mr Frobisher had an argument with Sir Norman. He knew that Sir Norman's financial affairs were in disarray, and he urged him to confess to Marie. She was, he believed, unaware of the extent of his problems,' Kitty said. She sat up straight in her seat intent on forcing the killer into the open.

'Well yes, I've made no secret of our row. I think half the hotel heard us at the time,' Colin said, staring at Kitty.

'Doctor Carter said that when he examined Sir Norman's body he discovered that Sir Norman had a severe heart condition that could have killed him at any moment. That afternoon we know Sir Norman was stressed. He had argued with Colin and been interrupted by Lambert, Miss Monbiere and Mr Jenkins. He shouted at everyone and was grumpy and cross. He was described as looking flushed and angry,' Kitty explained.

'But he didn't have a heart attack, he was shot,' Selina said.

'No one heard the shot that allegedly killed Sir Norman. There were only two reasons why that would be the case. It would be either while everyone was upstairs dressing for dinner or while the musical part of the rehearsal was in progress.' Kitty turned to Alice. 'That was what we thought, wasn't it?'

Alice nodded in agreement. 'It had to be one of those two times.'

'Forgive me, Mrs Bryant, but if as you propose Sir Norman did indeed die of a heart attack, then why was he then shot?' Chief Inspector Greville asked.

'I think it was because the person who found him saw the notes he had been writing and panicked.' Kitty looked at the chief inspector.

'But there were no notes. If you recall we looked for a suicide letter after we found him,' Colin protested.

'The cap was off his fountain pen and there was a small pile of blank stationery on the desk. I think he had begun to write some letters, either to his creditors or to his loved ones. The person that found him took the letters and probably destroyed them,' Kitty explained.

Inspector Lewis cleared his throat. 'This is all very well, Mrs Bryant, but it's supposition. What is your point? Why was Sir Norman shot?'

'I think the person who found him wanted us to think he had been murdered. They would know that someone would realise it was impossible for him to have shot himself on that side. If not when the body was found, then the post-mortem would reveal the problem with his hand.'

'And you think it had to look like murder because then the insurance company would pay up? They would pay for death by natural causes but not for suicide?' Matt asked.

Kitty looked at Marie. 'That's so, isn't it, Miss Monbiere? That's why you shot him even though he was already dead. You knew about his finances; Colin had hinted to you several times that all was not well. You thought he had killed himself, perhaps by poison, and panicked. You believed you were a beneficiary in his will and in an insurance policy.'

Marie laughed. 'I have absolutely no idea what you are talking about, Mrs Bryant. Chief Inspector, surely you are not going to permit her to carry on with this nonsense?'

'A moment please, Miss Monbiere, I wish to hear this. Do continue, Mrs Bryant.' The chief inspector ignored the indignant look given him by Inspector Lewis.

'I think Sir Norman, after arguing with Mr Frobisher about the state of his finances and his threat to tell Marie, had started to worry. He knew that Marie's money was gone, and he was about to lose everything. I believe he knew that there was no way out of his predicament and took his gun out intending to use it. That's why it was loaded. He started to write notes and collapsed with a heart attack before he could finish the task. Miss Monbiere went to his office as she said while the rehearsal was in full swing. She found him dead and saw the notes. Naturally she assumed he must have taken something to kill himself. After all tea had not long been served. Mr Jenkins had only just collected the tray. No one was aware of his heart problem, not even Sir Norman.'

Kitty paused for breath.

'He was always complaining of indigestion,' Colin said.

Chief Inspector Greville nodded to Kitty to continue.

'She knew if it was suicide then any insurances he held would be invalid. There have been plenty of stories in the past, especially after the problems a few years ago with the stock market crash in America. She knew there was at least one which benefitted his daughter. I think she had found this when she snooped through his papers, but she believed there was another one which would name *her* as a beneficiary. She saw the gun on the desk and shot him, placing the gun in his damaged hand. That was why there was no struggle. She picked up the notes and removed them, before locking the door and taking away the key. This was a natural death during a planned suicide, staged to look like a murder itself disguised as a suicide. There was a complex and clever web surrounding Sir Norman's death.'

'But he didn't have another insurance, only the one naming his daughter. Which I knew nothing about,' Marie snapped.

'You didn't know that there was only one insurance. You knew about his daughter though. You found out that two women had visited the island in your absence. That Sir Norman had shown them around and given them lunch. Suspicious, you read his correspondence and while you were hunting through his papers you found the policy naming her. You were eaten up with jealousy. You were also furious when you discovered the extent of your financial losses. I think it was when you were trying to discover who had visited the island that you stumbled across some of the financial documents,' Kitty said.

'Rubbish. If that was true, why would I then continue to keep her in my company?' Marie's voice tailed off as she realised a moment too late that she had betrayed herself.

'What do you mean, keep her in your company? You mean that...' Alec looked around in bewilderment until his gaze fell on Selina. '*You* are Sir Norman's daughter?'

The actress was as still as a statue, her face pale and composed, although Kitty could see her hands were trembling.

'Yes, Sir Norman was my father. He was never involved in my life. The first contact I had was when he sent me this necklace.' Selina lifted up a fine gold chain around her neck to reveal a small gold locket. 'It came in the post with a note saying it had been his mother's, my grandmother's, and he wished me to have it.'

'You never said anything?' Lambert stared at her.

'He wrote to me a couple of times and we met for lunch after he and Marie came to see my show at Bath. He didn't wish Marie to know about our relationship. He thought she would be jealous.' Selina dipped her head.

Marie's cheeks were crimson with anger and where her stocking-clad legs were elegantly crossed, her free foot was waggling with indignation.

'Sir Norman and I decided we would simply be as casual acquaintances. I had no need of a father figure, and he did not wish to assume that role. It was enough that we had met and knew one another,' Selina explained.

'Did you know about the life insurance policy?' Colin asked.

Selina shook her head. 'No, it wasn't a topic we discussed. Why would I know? Or care?'

'You could have cared enough to make his death look like murder if you had known about it,' Inspector Lewis's eyes narrowed.

'But I didn't, and I didn't go to his office at all that day. I had no reason to see him.' Selina's voice was calm.

'That's true. She didn't leave the rehearsal at all,' Alec said.

'Mrs Bryant, do please continue.' The chief inspector's voice cut across the murmur of agreement that arose after Alec's statement.

'Of course, the only problem with making Sir Norman's death look like murder was that there had to be a murderer. The police would be called and there would be an investigation. I think that when Marie went upstairs to dress for dinner the implications of her actions started to dawn on her. The storm was raging, the island was cut off. That at least would buy her some time to think of something.' Kitty's heart thumped as she faced the fury in the singer's eyes. 'She had to muddy the waters, but how?'

CHAPTER TWENTY-FOUR

'I don't have to stay here and listen to this nonsense. It's ridiculous. I loved Norman!' Marie rose as if about to leave the room.

'Please remain seated, Miss Monbiere.' Chief Inspector Greville's icy glare appeared to be sufficient to compel the singer to retake her seat. 'Mrs Bryant?'

Matt placed his hand over Kitty's to give her support as she continued. She was more certain now than ever that she had worked everything out. 'Marie knew that when the office door was opened, and Sir Norman was discovered, there would be an outcry. While we were having pre-dinner drinks I think she was trying to work out how to divert attention from herself and her own possible motives. That was when she found Paul Browning's cufflink.'

'The one we discovered in the office near Sir Norman's body?' Inspector Lewis asked.

Kitty nodded. 'Yes. I think Marie carried it in with her and planted it hoping that Paul might be suspected. I think Paul may have seen her pick something up and when the police asked him about his cufflink, he recalled Marie acting in a suspicious way. He suggested to the police that someone may have planted it to cast suspicion on him. Also, we already know that he tried to get into the office on the night of the murder in case it was in there.'

Colin stared at her. 'How on earth do you know that?'

'We saw him,' Alice said. 'We came downstairs to make some warm milk as we couldn't sleep and he was trying the office door and looking for the key in the desk drawer.'

'Well, there you are then. It's obvious Paul killed Norman!' Marie burst out.

'I think he realised he had lost his cufflink when he returned to his room. He came down to look for it and recalled that you had picked something up from the floor. With Sir Norman's death already appearing suspicious, he probably guessed that it might turn up in the office even though he didn't enter that room after Sir Norman was killed, and he wouldn't have been wearing his cufflinks until he dressed for dinner,' Kitty said.

Alec looked at Marie with an expression of incredulous horror. 'Then you killed Paul?'

There was a moment's silence broken only by the sound of the rain beating against the lounge windows.

'She had no choice after Paul guessed what she had done and came to her for money,' Kitty continued. 'He, like many others, was unaware of the extent of Sir Norman's financial problems. He knew Marie had killed Sir Norman, or so it seemed, and was in line to inherit a substantial sum from his insurance and his properties. He must have thought that all his problems were over.'

'The money in Mr Browning's room came from Sir Norman's wallet. It was taken by Miss Monbiere and used as an interim payment to buy his silence,' Chief Inspector Greville said with a nod of understanding.

'I think she took the money when she shot Sir Norman. It wasn't a huge amount, but it would have enabled her to cover a few expenses until she could find out if she was in line to inherit,' Kitty said, looking at the policeman.

'That would make sense. From Mr Browning's point of view, Miss Monbiere was the proverbial golden goose,' Chief Inspector Greville said.

'Marie knew Mr Browning's requests for money wouldn't stop. Even more worryingly, because of Paul's drinking, she would never know when he might spill her secret. She had to silence him. The police were also looking for Sir Norman's murderer. If she could convince everyone that Paul had killed Sir Norman and then taken his own life, then it would solve both of her problems.'

Matt squeezed Kitty's fingers in a gesture of approval.

'So, she arranged to meet him away from the hotel, on the clifftop. Probably to discuss future payments in return for his discretion. That would account for his good mood that morning,' Chief Inspector Greville continued.

'Paul left the hotel saying he was going out for a breath of fresh air. Everyone saw him leave by the front entrance. Marie needed an alibi, so she announced she would be in her room that morning. If she had gone out through the front of the hotel, she would have been seen either by Mr Frobisher or Mr Pike, who were in the lounge, or by the Jenkinses in the kitchen.' Kitty's heart was bumping loudly now as Marie scowled at her.

'Instead,' Alice said, 'she used the key to the fire escape next to her room. She knew as the shrubbery would hide her from view until she was away along the path. We saw her footprints in the mud at the bottom of the steps.'

'This is nonsense, complete nonsense, you have to believe me,' Marie said, turning beseeching eyes towards Alec, but he gave a small shake of his head.

'She met Paul on the path at the top of the cliffs and hit him hard on the head with a large stone. The one Inspector Lewis discovered tossed aside. The blow took him by surprise, and he fell to his death onto the rocks below.'

Kitty saw Selina flinch at her words.

'Before she had time to think she spotted someone in the distance, so fled from the scene, dropping the rock instead of throwing it into the sea. She didn't realise it had some of Paul's hair and blood on it.'

Alec turned to Kitty. 'That must have been when I glimpsed her. She was on the cliff path.'

'She came back to the hotel and returned to her room using the fire escape. She thought that Paul's death would be taken as an admission of his guilt. Before the rock was found by Inspector Lewis.' Kitty nodded at the inspector.

'That's correct, Mrs Bryant,' the inspector said. 'And, of course, we realised that things weren't adding up. Mr Standish had seen her on the path, and she had mud on her shoes and on her stockings when we spoke to her.'

'That would be why, Miss Monbiere,' Chief Inspector Greville said, his tone severe, 'after Mr Standish said you hadn't answered him when he knocked on your door, you were forced to admit that you had gone out of the hotel. Then you tried to implicate Miss Headingly.'

'What? Why?' Selina looked bewildered.

'Jealousy and the need to find someone else to take the blame,' Chief Inspector Greville said.

'No, I didn't... I... it wasn't me!' Marie's protestations had a hollow ring, and the rest of the party stared at her in horror.

Chief Inspector Greville turned to Inspector Lewis. 'Please secure Miss Monbiere, and I'll arrange for the boat to return first thing tomorrow. Hopefully the weather will have settled again by dawn.'

Marie was on her feet before the inspector could produce a set of handcuffs from his jacket pocket.

'No, no!' She started towards the door leading to the reception area.

'Lewis! Stop her!' Chief Inspector Greville's instruction came too late as Marie threw over one of the glass topped side tables and fled through the door. A second later the noise of the wind and rain outside grew louder as she dashed out into the darkness.

'Get after her!' The chief inspector crunched his way over the broken pieces of glass into the lobby. 'Jenkins! Jenkins! Get lanterns and torches, hurry, man.' He bellowed his instructions down the corridor.

Kitty jumped up behind Matt with Alice at her heels. 'Where will she go? It's as black as pitch out there and there is no way off the island,' Kitty said.

Matt and the chief inspector were already pulling on their coats. Colin, Lambert and Alec followed suit while Inspector Lewis had rushed to the kitchen to collect the lights from Albert.

'I'm coming too.' Kitty pulled on her own coat as did Alice.

'Selina, stay with Mrs Jenkins in case Marie returns. You monitor the upstairs and Mrs Jenkins the downstairs. Marie may have the key to the fire escape door with her,' Kitty said, ignoring Inspector Lewis's reproving look when he approached with the lanterns.

'Pair up and stay together,' ordered Chief Inspector Greville. 'Be careful, I don't want anyone else getting hurt or killed out there. Do we know where she may head?' he asked as torches and lanterns were dispensed.

'There are some row boats kept for fishing near the cottages,' Albert suggested as he too prepared to join the search party.

'Very well.' The chief inspector paired Albert with Alec, Lambert with Colin, and himself with Inspector Lewis. Kitty, Matt and Alice made the final group. 'Jenkins, you and Standish go towards the lighthouse. The inspector and I will go towards the cottages, Mr Pike and Mr Frobisher go down towards the jetty. Captain Bryant take your party towards the cliff path, but be very careful, the ground is unstable. Report back here in an hour at the latest. If you find Miss Monbiere do not put yourselves at risk.'

His instructions given, they set off into the night. The cold wind and biting rain stung against their faces as they started along the path towards the cliff.

'Alice, you should have stayed with Ethel and Selina.' Kitty held on to her friend's arm as they stumbled across the tussocky grass together. The light from the lantern making little impression on the darkness that surrounded them.

'And leave you to try and get yourself killed? No, I'm coming with you and Captain Bryant. Though Lord knows what Miss Monbiere is thinking a taking off in this. There is nowhere for her to go,' Alice said.

'I'm afraid she is not in her right mind, Alice,' Matt said.

A dark shape loomed out of the night and Alice's grip tightened on Kitty's arm. 'Oh bless my soul, 'tis only the donkey.'

They passed Meg who had come out of her shelter to presumably see who was going past her field on such a night.

'Where could she be?' Kitty couldn't help but feel guilty. She had forced Marie into taking desperate action by exposing the truth behind Sir Norman and Paul Browning's deaths.

'I can't see that she would hope to get off the island in the dark. It's much too risky. If she wants to escape then her best hope is to lie low until daybreak and then try one of the row boats, but it's a long way to the mainland and the tide would probably be running against her.' Matt's hair was plastered against his head, and he raised the lantern higher to try to see further along the path.

'Over there!' Kitty pointed to where she thought she had seen a dark figure. It was near the spot where they had been standing when Paul's body had been discovered.

'Marie!' Matt called into the dark. 'Come back to the hotel!' His words were snatched away by the wind and Kitty wondered if the woman on the cliff path had heard them.

They quickened their pace, anxious to catch up with the fugitive.

'Stay away from me,' Marie shouted as they grew closer. She was shivering and rain drenched, her hair sticking to her cheeks and dripping onto her ruined satin evening gown. She held a huge stick in her hands, and stood perilously close to the edge of the cliff.

'Come back to the hotel,' Matt said. 'This is madness.'

Marie waved the stick at them. 'I said stay back!'

They were forced to halt on the path. The yellow lamplight casting flickering shadows that reflected in the muddy puddles on the path.

'Marie, please, this is futile. You can't get off the island,' Kitty shouted her plea into the wind. The waves pounded the cliffs below adding to the noise.

'You! This is all your doing. I loved Norman and he betrayed me. I have nothing left now, nothing at all. Everything has gone. My future, my money, my career. Why should I return with you just to face the noose?' Marie's face was contorted with a mix of fury and grief.

'The judge may take pity on you. You didn't kill Sir Norman.' Matt edged a little closer to the distraught woman.

'I said stay back!' Marie waved the branch at him once more, forcing him to stop where he was. 'I killed Paul. I didn't mean to, he kept talking about Norman and how he could help me if I helped him. I just wanted him to shut up.' Marie wiped her face with her arm. 'He turned away from me, and I saw red. The next thing I knew he had fallen over this edge and I was holding a rock.' Marie stared at her hands as if reliving the moment.

Kitty held her breath as Matt edged forward once more. 'That makes it manslaughter, unpremeditated. A good barrister could help you,' he tried again.

The singer was ominously close to the edge of the cliff and the movement of her foot sent a shower of rocks tumbling over the edge.

Marie shook her head. 'It's no use. There's no point. I've lost everything, don't you see?'

Kitty thought she heard the faint sound of voices carried on the wind and she took her gaze from Marie for a split second to see a faint bobbing light approaching in the distance. The next thing she heard was a scream and a scuffling sound as if gravel had been kicked up into the air.

She turned back and Marie was gone, the stick she had been wielding lay abandoned on what remained of the cliff path. Her first instinct was to rush forward to try to see if the singer had fallen, but Matt held her back.

'No, this rain has weakened the cliff, the path has gone.'

Alice held on tight to Kitty's arm. 'Stay back, she was just standing there one second then the ground went from under her, poor soul. Reckon she'll be on them rocks where we found Mr Browning.'

'Alice is right, this is too dangerous to attempt anything in the dark. You can hear the waves pounding away at the bottom of the cliffs. There is nothing we can do for Marie now.' Matt placed his arm around Kitty, and she turned her face into his overcoat and leaned into him. Her legs were trembling, and she felt frozen to the marrow.

'We need to go back to the hotel to dry off, and tell the chief inspector what's happened,' Alice said.

The light Kitty had seen approaching was upon them now, and Colin and Lambert joined them.

'Any sign?' Colin asked, rainwater dripping from his chin.

'Keep away from the cliff edge. The storms have eroded it and it's just collapsed, taking Marie with it. There was nothing we could do,' Matt said.

The light from the lanterns revealed the horror on Colin and Lambert's faces. Lambert muttered an oath under his breath.

There was another crash and more of the path fell away into the sea below.

'We need to get out of here, let's go and tell the others. It must be almost an hour by now,' Matt said.

They made their way back towards the welcoming lights of the hotel. Kitty clung on tight to Matt, and Alice was supported by Lambert and Colin. When they reached the lobby, Albert and Alec were already there. Mrs Jenkins had towels and hot toddy's waiting for them.

Lambert told the two men what had happened on the cliff edge as Kitty and the others took off their sodden coats and shoes. Chief Inspector Greville and Inspector Lewis arrived a moment later. They too were soaked through.

The chief inspector's expression was sombre when he learned of Marie's fate. 'There is nothing we can do for her now. The weather and the darkness are against us.'

Kitty shivered as she relived the singer's fall over again in her mind.

'Darling, come and get warm.' Matt wrapped a blanket over the towel around her shoulders and steered her into the lounge, closer to the fireplace where a comforting blaze now burned.

Her teeth chattered on the rim of the glass as she sipped the drink she was given. Alice and Selina, both looking pale and shocked, sat opposite her.

'It's so ghastly. I never thought something like that would happen,' Kitty said, leaning into Matt for support.

'None of us could have anticipated that, Mrs Bryant. You did a wonderful job piecing all the elements together and you must not think of blaming yourself in any way for what has happened to Miss Monbiere,' Chief Inspector Greville informed her in a stern tone.

'I just knew that there was so little actual evidence, but I thought if I spoke out then she might betray herself,' Kitty said.

'And she did. She may not have killed Sir Norman, but she did murder Paul Browning,' Matt reminded her.

'And she would not have hesitated to try and put the blame on me it seems,' Selina added.

'What made you suspect Sir Norman was already dead when he was killed?' Lambert asked.

Kitty shrugged. 'There was no sign of a struggle, no argument or altercation and Doctor Carter said his heart was in such a bad state. If he was shot very soon after his heart attack, then it would be very difficult to determine which way round the events had happened, or if they had been virtually simultaneous. I realised later that he had to have been writing something as the cap was off the pen and the stationery was there but no suicide note.'

Chief Inspector Greville nodded. 'He was seated at his desk and had slumped forward so even the amount of blood loss would not have told us that he was already dead when the shot was fired. A smaller amount would have been put down to the rest having pooled in his lower body on death.'

'Marie had the most to lose all along. I wonder how much detail she did know about his finances. She must have believed she was on the deed to the island and the hotel? If, as Kitty said, she had been snooping amongst his papers she would have realised something was very wrong,' Matt mused.

'That reminds me, I must try the telephone and see if I can

reach the police station. I fear Doctor Carter's services will be required once more.' Chief Inspector Greville set down his empty glass and went back out into the lobby.

Matt hugged Kitty closer to him. 'Let's hope a boat can come across in the morning. I think we shall all be glad to finally get off this island.'

CHAPTER TWENTY-FIVE

Matt rose early the following morning, leaving Kitty to continue sleeping. She had slept badly during the night, tossing and turning. The events of the previous evening no doubt had been playing on her mind. He dressed quietly and quickly before going downstairs where he found the chief inspector and Inspector Lewis at breakfast.

'Morning, Captain Bryant. The weather has improved remarkably today, looks like the tail end of the storm has finally gone. I've arranged for the boat to come over, two boats, in fact. One to take everyone off the island that wishes to leave, and one with more manpower so that we can search for Miss Monbiere's body.' Chief Inspector Greville took a slurp of his tea as he finished speaking and helped himself to more toast.

Matt hoped the tide hadn't carried Marie out to sea during the night or the search might end up becoming much more extensive.

Lambert, Colin and Alec arrived and took their places at the table.

'The wind has died down, but the sea is still rather choppy,'

Colin said, pouring himself a cup of tea as Albert refreshed the toast racks.

Matt noticed Inspector Lewis push away his untouched drink. 'Kitty is still asleep. The business last night has greatly distressed her.'

'I can imagine. The outcome was not what we would have wished, and I fear we may be partly responsible for that. I hope she will feel better after a rest,' Chief Inspector Greville responded gravely.

Matt hoped so too. Their cases lately had been increasingly difficult and dangerous, and he was concerned that it was taking a toll on Kitty. Several times now she had been put in danger. If they *were* to start a family, then something would have to change. That was not a conversation he particularly wished to have with her. She had always insisted that she be treated as an equal in their line of work. But could that continue?

Kitty, Alice and Selina came downstairs together sometime later. He was relieved to see that Kitty appeared more refreshed after sleeping for longer.

'We'm all of us packed ready for the off. I suppose as the police have gone looking for Miss Monbiere?' Alice asked.

'Yes, they have gone to talk to the lighthouse keeper to ascertain the best places to look. The cliff path is out of bounds as it seems there has been another rock fall during the night.' Matt saw Kitty shudder. 'There are two boats coming across so we can get back to the mainland while the police finish off here.'

'That's good news at least. I really want to go home now,' Selina said, and Alice squeezed her hand in silent support.

'What will happen to Mr and Mrs Jenkins?' Kitty asked.

'They will pack up and return later on another boat.' Matt had checked with Inspector Lewis about the arrangements for the hotel staff.

'What will happen to them financially? They were owed all their wages and the bonus from Sir Norman,' Kitty continued.

'When I receive Sir Norman's life insurance, I shall see that they are paid what they are owed. In fact, I shall probably give them all of the money. It's the least I can do and truthfully, I don't want it. It feels tainted somehow.' Selina shivered as she spoke.

Matt could see what she meant. He wondered what would become of Bird Island now and this beautiful building.

'I think there is some money in the housekeeping tin and Chief Inspector Greville has said they may take that on his authority to set against the money they are owed. It is not much but it should help,' Matt said.

The rest of the party came downstairs and into the lounge. 'Packing is all done. I just saw the boats approaching the jetty,' Colin said.

'Then I expect we shall be able to leave soon. Bertie will be happy to have us home again.' Kitty smiled at Matt.

'Indeed, and I expect Mickey will be happy to see us too.' The Dolphin's handyman and security guard had been caring for their dog while they had been away. However, knowing how naughty the spaniel could be, Matt suspected he would be quite pleased to return him home.

Matt hoped that Alice would be happy to see Robert Potter again when she got back. He almost said as much but, he remembered the sharp kick he had received from Kitty the last time he had mentioned Robert's name to Alice.

Once the boats were safely docked at the quayside, the hotel bustled with unaccustomed activity. Permission was given by the chief inspector, and the guests boarded the boat. Once all the bags were stowed and farewells had been made to Mr and Mrs Jenkins, they cast off towards Torquay.

Matt watched as Bird Island receded into the distance, the craggy outline muted by the sea spray as they bounced over the waves back towards the calmer waters of Torquay Harbour.

Once safely ashore they said goodbye to the others and

Matt organised a taxi to take himself, Kitty and Alice back to Churston. The others organised transport to the station.

'I am that glad to be a going home. I can't tell you,' Alice said to Kitty.

'I must say I agree. So much for a pleasant couple of days in the lap of luxury.'

The taxi dropped Kitty off at their home near the golf club, before continuing down the hill to Kingswear to take Alice and Matt over the river to Dartmouth.

'I can collect Bertie and bring him home, as I know how much Kitty has missed him,' Matt said as they waited for the river ferry to dock.

'I know as it's none of my business,' Alice said giving him a sideways glance, 'but you and Kitty are all right?'

Matt looked curiously at her. He knew Kitty confided in Alice. 'Has Kitty said something to you?'

Alice blushed and looked uncomfortable. 'I think she's been worrying about something you said to her about having a family.'

They filed on board the ferry, following the short line of fellow foot passengers.

Matt sighed. 'It's a discussion we need to have, I think.'

Alice nodded. 'Sooner the better, perhaps.'

The ferry started on its short journey across the Dart.

Matt had a feeling she was right. 'And you and Robert?' he asked.

Alice's colour deepened as she gazed at the rapidly approaching shoreline. 'I don't know what to think any more.' Her voice sounded sad.

'Talk to him,' Matt urged. He wished he could have told her what Robert had in mind, but he had given his word that he would say nothing.

'I suppose that will be two of us then needing to speak up,'

Alice remarked as the boat bumped to a halt on the opposite side of the river.

* * *

Back at Churston, Kitty lit the fire in the sitting room and went through to the kitchen to put the kettle on the hob. The house was, as always, neat as a new pin thanks to Mrs Smith, her housekeeper. Rascal greeted her by twining between her legs and purring a loud welcome.

She wandered back into the hall and picked up the small pile of post from the table. She leafed through the letters, dividing them into Matt's correspondence and letters addressed personally to her.

She paused when she came to the last one in the bunch. An official-looking envelope, typewritten and addressed to Matt with a London postmark. A sense of foreboding filled her as she placed it on top of her husband's pile for him to open when he returned. She had an uneasy feeling that this was likely to be yet another job from Matt's former employer, Brigadier Remmington-Blythe.

These jobs for the government were always difficult and often had an element of danger. She returned to the kitchen as the kettle began to whistle and hoped she was wrong. What they both really needed right now was a nice restful break while they decided what they wanted to do next. Somehow, she had a feeling the anonymous looking envelope in the hall was about to derail any such plans.

A LETTER FROM HELENA

Dear reader,

I want to say a huge thank you for choosing to read *Murder at the Island Hotel*. If you enjoyed it and would like to keep up to date with all my latest releases, just sign up at the following link. Your email address will never be shared, and you can unsubscribe at any time. There is also a free story – *The Mysterious Guest*, starring Kitty's friend, Alice.

www.bookouture.com/helena-dixon

Bird Island and the Bird Hotel are obviously fictional. The island is based on Thatchers Rock which can be seen from Torquay and the hotel is an amalgamation of places that I've visited over the years. Of course, there is the famous Burgh Island not too far away if you ever fancied staying in a place like the Bird Hotel. Hopefully minus any murders however!

I do hope you loved *Murder at the Island Hotel* and if you did, I would be very grateful if you could write a review. I'd love to hear what you think, and it makes such a difference helping new readers to discover one of my books for the first time. You can get in touch on social media or through my website.

Thanks,

Helena

KEEP IN TOUCH WITH HELENA

www.nelldixon.com

 facebook.com/nelldixonauthor
x.com/NellDixon

ACKNOWLEDGEMENTS

My thanks to my Torbay friends for all their help, support and knowledge. Special love to my Tuesday Zoomers and the Coffee Crew who help support me in so many ways. Thank you to my hard-working agent, Kate Nash, who always knows just what to say when I'm having a moment! My fabulous family too who are always there for me. Finally, much love and thanks to Maisie, my lovely editor at Bookouture, and all the people at Bookouture who work incredibly hard to make the books the best they can be. I appreciate each and every one of you.

PUBLISHING TEAM

Turning a manuscript into a book requires the efforts of many people. The publishing team at Bookouture would like to acknowledge everyone who contributed to this publication.

Audio
Alba Proko
Sinead O'Connor
Melissa Tran

Commercial
Lauren Morrissette
Jil Thielen
Imogen Allport

Cover design
Debbie Clement

Data and analysis
Mark Alder
Mohamed Bussuri

Editorial
Maisie Lawrence
Ria Clare

.

Made in United States
North Haven, CT
03 March 2024

49378170R00155